BOROUGH FEATURES

by Erica Ciccarone

To request permission, visit www.wanderinginthewordspress.com.

All characters in this book are fictitious, and any resemblance to real persons, living or dead, is coincidental.

Cover design by Elizabeth Orr Jones: www.elizabethorrjones.com

PUBLISHED BY WANDERING IN THE WORDS PRESS

ISBN
Print: 979-8-9893285-3-6
Digital: 979-8-9893285-4-3
First Edition

For Tama, who loved first novels

ONE

Nothing about the assignment sounded credible, but here she was on the F train, at six-forty-five in the morning, en route to find out something she already knew—that Darlene Dabrowski was just another New York weirdo hoping to get her photo on the bulletin board outside the restroom of a Greek diner.

Bleary-eyed, with hair still wet from the shower, Gretchen Sparks swayed with the subway car. The cup of bodega coffee she had slurped on the platform twisted in the toxic waste pit of her stomach. She belched and tasted bile.

Gretchen once found the charms of October irresistible. But that autumn, when a new girl went missing every week in New York City, Gretchen felt vexed. Nettled. She was stuck reporting for the Boroughs blog—human interest stories from outside the Nexus. On today's docket: Dabrowski, 58, of Coney Island.

At the subway station, she transferred to the city bus and rode it several blocks down Mermaid Avenue to West 28th Street. She peered out the window at houses and apartments, big empty lots, and burned-out buildings. Gretchen's family went to Riis Park instead, preferring the cleaner beaches and the bigger waves. And of course, preferring Queens to Brooklyn any day.

She stepped off the bus and trudged up the block beneath the brightening sky. She cast a glance at a middle-aged man in a long bathrobe who was hosing down his driveway, some Greek or Italian dad who performed the unnecessary chore before and after work and all day Saturday. She made her way to the address of a little duplex and let herself in the gate. Under the red awning, she put on her *Metro* ID and rang the bell.

The door swung open, forcing Gretchen to hop backward off the stoop. "What took you so long?" Darlene Dabrowski said.

She was a vision—of what, Gretchen was not sure. A pile of little pink foam curlers sat atop her small head. The turquoise eye shadow dusting her lids only served to punctuate her skin tags. A spot of what looked to be eyeliner sat above her lip in an attempt at glamour. A length of rope held in place her voluminous brown robe. "Come in!" she said, turning on her heels so quickly the screen door closed with a thwack.

The house smelled like ashtrays and air freshener. A bit of sunlight filtered through the flamingo-print curtains. End tables flanked the couch and crowded the door and the hallway. Fake palm fronds shot up from plastic vases. Stacks of magazines rose from the carpeted steps. A wiry old man sat at the edge of a big sectional couch, staring at small flat-screen TV, the volume obscenely loud.

"Jerry!" Mrs. Dabrowski waved her arms at the man. "Jerry! The reporter's here!"

"Reporta?" he yelled back. Gretchen could barely hear his voice over the sound of the morning news reporting another missing college girl, this time a junior at Cooper Union.

"It's Miss—what's your name?"

"Gretchen Sparks?" Gretchen cringed at the rising inflection in her own voice.

"Gretchen Sparks! From *The Metropolitan*! She's here about Leonard!"

The man shook his head and pointed to his ears.

Mrs. Dabrowski waved a hand at him and shuffled to the kitchen. "Sometimes I wonder"—she shook her head, her curlers bobbing—"if he isn't pretending." She opened the back door, her fingers pudgy with too-small rings. "But come on outside. This is where it all started."

A small, near-death patch of grass clumped itself in the center of a concrete lawn, and a chain-link fence laced with wild vines made for the back and side walls.

"I thought there'd be a photographer," Mrs. Dabrowski said. "It's probably just as well. He's already gone."

"Gone? The bird?"

"I know." She reached into her robe and shook a cigarette loose from a pack. "He was in a rush. He's got things to do."

"Things?"

"Yeah, things. Probably perched in the precinct parking lot right now." She lit the cigarette and sat down on a creaky folding chair. "Watchin' 'em kick people outta the drunk tank."

A tall wooden fence divided her yard from the other side of the duplex. A door opened and slammed on the other side.

"Mexicans," Mrs. Dabrowski whispered.

"Excuse me?"

"The neighbors. Mexicans." She tilted her head toward the fence, raised her eyebrows, and twisted her lips into a smirk.

Gretchen turned on her recorder. "Why don't we start from the beginning?"

"Sure." She squinted up at Gretchen and crossed her arms.

Six months before, Dabrowski had come home from a stay in the hospital. "Asthma!" she said, ashing her cigarette on the ground. "Two nights. And I got the bills to prove it!" The next morning, she'd gone out back for a smoke. A seagull roosted on her folding chair. When she came out, he stretched his neck and looked at her. "The little bastard's beady eyes just melted my heart!"

The seagull, whom she named Leonard, started bringing things to Dabrowski: a flattened beer can, an empty Fritos bag, a paper plate. Then he brought a pocketknife with what she thought looked like dried blood on the blade. "It's all here!" She whipped out a coffee can from behind her chair. A week after the pocketknife, a man snatched a woman's purse on the boardwalk, and a group of seagulls—led by none other than Leonard—attacked him, pecking his body until he dropped the purse and

3

fled. Then in August, a cop was eating funnel cake on the beach when a seagull swooped down and grabbed it. He chased the bird under the volleyball bleachers, where he caught a guy "diddling himself" and ogling some teenage girls. "That's Leonard for you!"

"What makes you think it was the same bird?"

"Because"—Mrs. Dabrowski leaned forward—"I just know. And when you know, you *know*."

Gretchen sighed.

"And he's got one yellow eye and one green. The cop and the purse snatcher reported this feature. It's very distinct."

"Oh?" Gretchen said, thinking already of the subway ride back to Union Square.

Dabrowski, undeterred, rose from her seat. "That's his house!" She pointed to a wilted cardboard box nailed to the post.

Gretchen got closer. Orange rinds and Chex mix littered the floor. "I don't think he liked his breakfast."

"He ate twice as much! He'll be back for his midmorning snack."

She turned off her recorder. "Mrs. Dabrowski, I want to thank you for your time. We'll let you know if there's a story here."

"What do you mean *if?*"

"As always, I have to run it upstairs to my editors," she conceded. "But I will let you know." The goodbye was more than generous.

"Well, you better act fast!" She turned back to the house. "WSNY is very interested!"

Gretchen saw herself out. It was eight o'clock. She could dismiss the whole thing, get some breakfast, and be back in the city by nine-thirty. Or she could head over to the police precinct to humiliate herself by asking the cops if the people of Coney Island were being kept a little safer by a delusional woman's imaginary friend. Where did Marty get this story? It was even wackier than usual. Worthy of the *Daily Schlep*, that free subway newspaper best used to line litter boxes. Gretchen shuddered.

Like every newspaper, *Metro* had taken a hit in subscribers in the early aughts and continued downhill ever since. Efforts to revive the borough markets had come "all the way from the top," Marty had said a year before as they passed containers of lo mein and General Tso's chicken over the stacks of papers, books, and mail on his desk. "It's a way for me to get you some bylines, even if the subjects are . . . less than stimulating." He had stopped eating to look up at her. His devilishly peaked eyebrows rose. "I know it's been hard to get back in the swing of things. It's a way to ease in."

So she wrote about the mom who threw out the first pitch in a Klingon costume at a Staten Island Yankees game, a self-help guru who burned his feet walking across hot coals at City Island, a group of grannies who play competitive mah-jongg in Sunnyside, and a star peacock who escaped the Prospect Park Zoo only to return thirty minutes later to his roost. And now she would write about Darlene Dabrowski and her crime-fighting seagull. "If you can turn that shit into gold," Marty had said, "you can write anything. Find the human element."

She knew he was right, but the work was a far cry from what she had done in the past when they worked together at the *Village Crier*, the little alt-weekly that could.

Her phone rang. For the first time since Marty had collapsed in the office stairway on Monday morning, Gretchen answered it.

"Hi Roberta," she said to Marty's wife.

"Gretchen! You're up! I start to dial and then I say to myself, 'What are you doing? It's way too early to call Gretchen!' But then I think, 'Maybe I'll catch her unawares and she'll answer her damn phone.'"

Gretchen headed for the bus stop. "I'm out in Coney Island."

"Coney Island? What are you reporting out there?"

"You don't wanna know. I'm heading back to the office." She turned her face toward the sun. "How are you?"

"Hanging in there. Gretchen, it doesn't look good."

"What do you mean?"

"Technically, he died. These cases are very hard. If it happened in a hospital, maybe there'd be a chance, but . . ."

"It's too early to tell though, isn't it? It's only been a couple days."

"Five days."

How had five days passed? On the first, she'd left work and spent the afternoon—and then the night—in a bar. She stayed home the next day. She might have made it in to the office Wednesday, but she couldn't be sure.

"What's the doctor say?"

"Hang on." Roberta started up a blender. "They said there's very little brain activity!" she yelled over the motor. "But there's some!"

Just like Roberta to sound so flip in the middle of a crisis. She hid her pain like a cat.

It didn't make sense to Gretchen. Marty's treadmill was the only piece of furniture in his office that stacks of paper didn't cover. Early birds could hear the quick thumps of his feet at seven o'clock in the morning. At the *Crier*, he even had a standing desk that kept his laptop close by.

"I'm saying"—Roberta killed the blender—"that we need to prepare for the worst. I want to talk to you about his obituary. Come over tonight. See the kids . . . Say seven o'clock?"

Gretchen reached the bus stop. Mermaid Avenue was not far from the beach. She wanted to walk into the water. "I'll be there."

Just then, a seagull landed on top of the bus-stop map and showed her its profile. Its pale yellow eye fixed itself on her face.

"I'm in no mood to cook, but we'll get bagels and lox and an antipasto from Gregorio's. Sound good?"

The gull held something in its beak. She took a step closer.

"Honey? Are you OK?"

White feathers sprouted up from its wings. Dirt caked his underparts. His gray back and dark yellow beak gave Gretchen a feeling of foreboding.

"One yellow eye," she said. The bird turned fast to face her head-on and dropped something at her feet. "See you at seven," she said and hung up the phone.

She grabbed the object as the gull let out one shrill squawk and rose. It flew back down the block toward Dabrowski's, stopped a few houses down on a gate, and glared at her.

"What the—?" she said to it.

It squawked again, puffing out its feathers, and stretched its long black-tipped wings.

The bus groaned, lumbering up the avenue. She looked at the object in her hand—a key, copper, scratched, a yellow ribbon laced through its hole.

The seagull took off. Gretchen followed it back up West 28th. Every few houses it turned and taunted her. Then just as she reached Dabrowski's—her lungs burning, sweat wetting her underarms—the gull cried once more and rose over her head so high it disappeared. The day was clear and bright. She watched the sky.

I'm saying that we need to prepare for the worst.

"Hey!" someone yelled from down the block.

A boy stood a few houses over toward Neptune Avenue. His scrawny frame tipped from the weight of a sack of laundry slung over his shoulder. Gretchen ignored him. Surely this bird didn't know her, didn't know Dabrowski. Surely the bird was not taunting her. But she pocketed the key and searched the sky just the same.

"Hey!" The boy let the sack fall at his side. "Hey, lady!"

He looked twelve or thirteen, with slicked-back black hair. He wore a Nirvana tour shirt from before he was born, black Chuck Taylor high tops. A silver stud pierced one of his ears.

"You're the reporter, right? I thought I missed you. My mom sent me for the laundry." He talked fast in a high voice, his Brooklyn accent so thick it seemed exaggerated.

"Why were you lookin' at the sky like that?"

"Just watching a bird."

"Hopefully not her bird." He jerked his head in the direction of Dabrowski's. "She's a nut."

"You know Mrs. Dabrowski?"

He nodded at the duplex. "My house." He bumped the bag of laundry up against a gate and crouched down. "Can you come down here?"

She looked back at Mermaid Avenue for the bus.

"I'm Jaime." He reached a hand up to shake. "If my mom comes out and sees me talkin' to you, she's gonna let me have it."

Gretchen looked around. The block appeared deserted, but she crouched next to him all the same and shook his hand. "I'm Gretchen."

"I know. Dabrowski's been talking on the phone all week about you coming. Clever way to get down here, I gotta admit."

"What?"

"Listen, I got some information for you."

So it's this kind of encounter.

When she was at the *Crier*, people wandered in day after day with their implausible or uncorroborated or just plain unpublishable story ideas. Someone's cousin was always seeing Bill Clinton at the Greek baths, and someone else was always privy to 9/11 before it happened, and someone else was always seeing some Revolutionary War soldier prowling Bowling Green at night. And Marty always invited them into his office, gave them a chair and cup of coffee, and listened to them. He usually declined the offer, but nearly every time, the person left happy knowing they could return with another idea. "What most people want most in life," he had said, "is to be heard."

She closed her eyes.

I'm saying that we need to prepare for the worst.

When she opened them, the boy squinted at her with a perplexed expression on his face.

"OK," she said. "Shoot."

"Three months back, we brought my grandma to the emergency room when she was sick. She had the flu or something. We would have kept her home, but she had a kidney transplant earlier in the year, so we wanted to be safe. It was Fourth of July. People were coming into the ER all kinds of messed up. Fingers blown off by firecrackers, drunk driving wrecks. We waited for five hours." He told the story fast, like he had prepared it ahead of time, practiced it in the mirror.

"When they finally saw her, they wouldn't let my mom go in. They took Grandma all alone. And we waited there all night, didn't hear anything till around five. A doctor came and said she's been admitted. For what? She was dehydrated and had a fever. She was *seeing things*." Jaime made air quotes around the words. "Mom demanded to see her, but the doctor kept saying the same thing. She's in good hands, blah blah blah."

Gretchen hadn't been to visit Marty in the hospital. She'd figured he'd be out by now.

"Then my mom got upset and started yelling. Security came and kicked us out. We went home and tried to sleep, and we went back. We got nowhere. They said she's not even in the system! Like any trace of her disappeared! Three days later, we got a call." He paused and looked up, his eyes dry but grave. "She died."

Gretchen felt again like walking to the beach and into the water. She could do it in one straight line.

"I have to go," she said. "I'm sorry about your grandma. We only do obits on people with a public profile. I hope you get everything figured out."

"You don't understand what I'm saying. What I'm telling you is—"

"Jaime!" a woman called, her voice musical.

"That's my mom."

"Jaime! Home!"

He took something out of his pocket and pressed it into Gretchen's hand. "Her name was Dominica Padilla. Don't get up till you hear the door shut." He hoisted the laundry bag to his shoulder and shuffled under its weight back to the duplex. "Coming, Ma!"

The door slammed. Gretchen's head swam with information.

Dying of the flu? And which hospital? She put her hand in her pocket and felt the key.

I'm saying that we need to prepare for the worst.

She crossed the street and jogged toward Mermaid Avenue. She had to get out of Coney Island. And fast.

TWO
Author's Note

I'm not the best person to tell this story, but I'm not the worst either. I've spent the better part of my adult life studying the subject and all of her precious, gobsmacking particulars.

I'm a newsman, but let me get this out of the way early. This account relies on the highest standards of reporting. We're talking hundreds of hours of logged tape from eyewitnesses; interviews with local and state investigators about everything from campaign finance fraud to medical malpractice; and meticulous research about the ins and outs of Medicaid, corporate lobbying power, nonprofits and for-profits and everything in between. But my account is tainted by my deep and abiding love for and utter frustration with the subject of the investigation; that is, Gretchen Binacci Sparks.

I write this in February 2016, when I and everyone else are already suffocating in the heat of the presidential election. "I want to bury my head in the sand until November the 9th," my mother said on the phone this morning. I do too.

The most hilarious falsity peddled on both sides of the political arena is that they want "unbiased news" that shows "both sides of the story." The truth is that unbiased news—or as we journalists like to call it, news—has one single loyalty: the facts.

I said I am a newsman, but I am also a poet, so while the facts concern me, so does the capital-T truth.

Gretchen believed the facts could tell the whole story. I never agreed. Too much poetry is happening all around us—in the asthmatic wheeze of the cat beside me, in the smell of roasted peanuts sold for two bucks a bag on Broadway. And it's this stuff that gets lost in the twenty-four-hour news cycle. And it's why Gretchen Sparks was born to tell us the news.

"No bells, no whistles," she'd say as she edited my copy in her cluttered cubicle at the *Village Crier*. "If you wanna be a poet, go live in the woods. We write for the average Joe."

Ah Gretchen, it is impossible to tell your story without poetry.

The last time we spoke before she left me, I asked her, "Don't you ever want to get back to who you were before Dominic died?"

"That wasn't me," she had said. "That was another Gretchen."

But oh! The Gretchens I have known. Gretchen in glasses on the toilet, wearing a flannel shirt and knee socks, panties down around her ankles, crossword puzzle in her lap. "Raaaaaaj! Bring me some toilet paper!"

Gretchen in July, hair in two braids with short bangs. She sits on a picnic table at City Island and dips fried clams in melted butter. Behind her, a plane tows a Tom's Lobster Shack banner across the clear blue sky.

Gretchen in the morning, sniffling. Her hair stuck up in a bed-head mohawk, breath sour and eyes watery, her voice at its raspiest first thing when she sits up, rakes her hands over my chest, and says, "Coffee, Raj, coffee," until I obey her.

Gretchen in college, with cat-eye glasses. She clears her throat and asks Dean Willoughby again whether he knew the identity of the alleged masturbator before addressing the college of Arts and Sciences, and Willoughby, that snake, calls her "dear" and says she should get back to reporting on the campus sororities. Gretchen digs in and jots down every word in shorthand to publish later in a scathing editorial. Who learns shorthand at NYU? you wonder.

Gretchen Sparks.

Gretchen at fifteen in Mr. Gomes's Algebra II class, hair dyed Manic Panic Purple, eyelids encrusted with glitter, her Discman in her lap. With earphones trained up her black hoodie—the one with the Hole patch on the breast—to her small pierced ear. Her head tilts into Courtney Love's voice, knowing the words, feeling them, and then someone tosses a note onto her desk and she drops everything to read the balloon-letter scribblings of her third best friend in the world, Jessica Cardinale.

"Gretchen," it reads, "Nuno Cordero totally wants to make out with you."

Gretchen at the *Crier* standing beside Marty's desk. She leans over his shoulder and reads and nods while the rest of us pretend not to notice that he has groomed her from the start for greatness and we are lucky to witness the rising star. But she deserved every bit of his confidence and our envy because the girl could write. She hated adverbs. She rarely strung together a simile and never messed with wordplay—how she hated my puns!—but her prose was the simplest and purest of jazz ballads; like *Body and Soul* or *Summertime*, it was the song you didn't know you craved to hear but that caught in your ear and came back to you when you needed it most.

Gretchen at twenty-two sitting at a café on the Bowery reading a paperback copy of Nellie Bly's *Six Months in Mexico*, pencil poised over the text, her mug of coffee forgotten—the mark of her lips on the rim in All About Grape lipstick by Clinique that her ma got in a Macy's bonus—her glasses smudged, the world moving fast around her, but Gretchen, locked in an embrace with a passage that would not let go, suddenly jerks her head up and looks across the room . . .

At me.

Drinking Darjeeling and scribbling in one of my innumerable tablets. And I, emboldened by the suddenness of her head-jerk, somehow get up from my chair and sit directly before her. I have never seen her before in my life. I have no plan. I am almost still a virgin. She says, What are you writing? I say, Poetry. She says,

Why would you want to do that? I say, I'm not really. I am trying to meet women. She laughs, and my life begins.

I'd prefer to leave her be, to make my mother very happy by marrying a woman less narcissistic and more generous with her love. But Gretchen Binacci Sparks grabbed me that day in the Bowery café, and she hasn't put me down since. I'm suspended in midair, even now, in this beach bungalow where I've come to get it all down. There's a calico cat at my feet, and I sit with my notebooks and her notebooks and Marty's notebooks, piecing it together because the news has failed to tell her story, which makes me wish she'd show up just so I could say I told you so.

My name is Raajen Patel. This is the story of Gretchen Sparks.

THREE

In the time before Dominic was killed—and even in those first weeks at *Metro* after—the newsroom beckoned Gretchen, ignited her senses, put her in the zone, in her element, doing what she was born to do. The ringing phones; short, sharp conversations; pages turning; keys clicking; the occasional shout across the cubicles with a question or an exclamation—it all thrilled her. Especially *Metro*. Its mammoth newsroom holds 250 staffers with twice as many employees on the floor above and the floor below.

Even before her brother died, when Gretchen worked at the *Crier*, she'd arrive late, in a huff over some misstep in the morning—a spilled coffee, a stalled subway car, a headache that kept her up half the night—but when she got settled in to review the day ahead, her anxiety evaporated. She made calls, hammered out drafts, dashed back and forth to Marty's office, headed out for an hour to a meeting, grabbed a quick lunch, and delved back again to work with unfailing rigor.

But today, and nearly all the days in the time since, Gretchen slouched in her chair and covered her face with her hands.

"How's the investigation going?" Stewart, first name Jeff—but no one used first names at *Metro*—looked down at her from his cubicle. "Catch any criminals?"

Gretchen groaned. "I swear to God."

"What?"

"Go away."

"What's the matter?"

15

"You."

"There's a new girl. Gunderson and I are on our way out to talk to the mother. We'd ask you to join but know you're on a hot tip."

For what felt like the thousandth time, she wished Marty hadn't written her assignment on the whiteboard in his office. She powered on her laptop. Yawned. "They learn anything new?"

Stewart put on his jacket. "Cops aren't leaking anything. D.A. has sealed the files. What was that lieutenant's name? The one you got so cozy with when you were downtown?"

She rolled her eyes. Gretchen had no friends in the NYPD, and Stewart knew it. She did a story years before on New York's finest systematically failing to file paperwork related to sexual assault claims and discouraging women from reporting rapes. It got picked up by all the major papers—including *Metro*, including *The Washington Post*—and won her an Alty. Marty had submitted it for a Pulitzer.

Gunderson's head appeared from the adjacent cubicle. "You ready?" he said to Stewart. He didn't even look at her.

"Ready," Stewart said.

She signed into her administrator account for Borough Features. Of all her petty responsibilities at *Metro*, moderating the comments had to be the most demoralizing. Her recent listicle, FIVE GREEK PASTRY SHOPS IN ASTORIA THAT WILL MAKE YOU SAY *OPA!* had lit up overnight with good-natured suggestions that devolved into a political feud by morning.

HonestPatriot54 wanted fewer Greeks in New York—"Keep socialism out of the U.S.A.!" QueerSaturn1989 thought HonestPatriot54 should read a book for once in his life. Blessed4Life let loose a string of anti-Semitic rants at four in the morning.

Gretchen denied Blessed4Life, approved all the rest, and moved on to a profile on a high school football team in Staten Island. When she went out to interview the team, the coach steered her away from the Black and Latino players, who, she noticed, wore banged-up helmets and threadbare jerseys, a contrast to the shiny new uniforms the white players wore.

That could be a story.

But she had quieted her instincts and written the story she was assigned. Fans of other teams, mostly the parents of the players, took to the comments to trash-talk Washington High. She never understood the appeal of team sports. With nothing left to moderate, she opened a fresh document.

MARTY MITNIK, FAMED METRO REPORTER, DIES AT 55

Her fingers caressed the keys, as if casting a spell on them to write the obituary for her. She groaned and grabbed her notepad.

10 REASONS QUEENS IS THE NEXT BROOKLYN
10 REASONS THE BRONX IS THE NEXT QUEENS
THE ETERNAL DEBATE: JOE AND PAT'S OR REGGIANO'S
HIDDEN GEMS OF JACKSON HEIGHTS NIGHTLIFE
THE SPOOKY HISTORY OF DEAD HORSE BAY

She leaned back in her chair. Her thirst for news and snappy prose seemed permanently sated. She could churn out listicles and fluff for days.

> *Marty Mitnik, Pulitzer prize-winning jour-nalist of the Metropolitan,* NYC Daily, *and the* Village Crier, *died TKDay at Mount Sinai Medical Center.*
>
> *His death, following a cardiac episode on Oc-tober 5, was confirmed by his wife Roberta Krom, translator and professor of Russian Studies at City University of New York.*

That was the easy part. But when she tried to continue, a pain gripped her side. She opened her bottom drawer just enough to peek inside at her pint of Jameson.

"Sparks!"

She slammed the drawer as a document landed on her desk.

"Where are we with the obit."

All of Susan Conway's questions ended in periods. She was not a person whose time you wanted to waste. As a lowly junior reporter, Gretchen normally didn't interact with the managing editor much, but with Marty gone and the news team without a leader, the other editors split his workload, and Conway bore the brunt. Gretchen closed the notepad containing her blog brainstorm. "I'm working on it."

Conway raised her eyebrows and nodded to Gretchen's laptop. "Let me see what you've got."

"I've been reading a lot of his work, making notes. I'm going to Roberta's tonight to talk with her. About to get in touch with some old colleagues of his . . ."

"You haven't started writing," Conway said, her short nails tapping on the desk. Gretchen stared at the blank screen.

"Sparks!" Conway said.

"Yes! Conway!"

"Have you. Started. Writing."

Gretchen's face grew hot. "I've been trying."

The managing editor frowned. "If this is too difficult, given your relationship with Marty—"

"No! It's not. I got it. I had to go to Coney Island this morning for a Borough story, but I'm on top of it." She took a look at the paper Conway had tossed on her desk. It was a list of about a dozen articles Marty had written. She knew them all: the comptroller scandal he broke in 2013, the exposé on Bronx nursing homes, the Riker's guards—the best of Marty's investigative journalism from his years at *Metro* and the *Post*.

"We'd like you to include each of these."

"How am I supposed to write about twelve articles in 1,200 words about a man's whole life?"

"That's what the publisher wants." Conway looked at her watch. "Work them in." She turned away and then stopped. She stooped down a bit to Gretchen's eye level. A centimeter of graying hair marked her roots, and her rose perfume made Gretchen crinkle her nose. Conway's sharp eyes softened behind her glasses. "I know you've known him for a long time." She put one hand over Gretchen's and gave it a squeeze. "And I'm sure it's terrible to write this before he dies. But Sparks, write the damn obituary, or I'll find someone else to do it."

By six o'clock, she had banged out the most sanitized obituary that ever was and sent it over to Conway. Her phone rang five minutes later.

"This could be an obit for someone you've never even met. We have you on it for a reason. Try harder."

The reason was Roberta Krom. She requested that Gretchen write it. She still somehow trusted Gretchen to write well and with sincerity. Gretchen wanted to be home with a bottle of wine and some old episodes of *Law & Order*. But Marty's place was on the Upper West Side, and Roberta was getting an antipasto.

In her bedraggled tan trench coat, Gretchen walked west through Union Square, bag slung over her shoulder, hands in her pockets. Autumn smelled like death.

She rounded the corner onto 14th Street. A man walked toward her: baggy jeans, Knicks jersey. He flashed CDs in her face. "Two for one. Ten dollars. Double album. Help a brother out."

Gretchen had a studied reaction to solicitors and panhandlers. Head down. Don't make eye contact. Keep walking. She moved to the right to dodge him. He moved with her. She darted to the left. Blocked. "Hey, I'm not interested." She laid her Queens accent on extra thick. As she said it, a black sedan pulled up to the curb and the man put his arm around her shoulders and reached toward her bag—gently, like she were a celebrity and he was shepherding her away from her rabid fans.

"Hey, watch it!"

With surprising fluidity, the man opened the car door and pushed her in. The door slammed behind her.

Gretchen rattled the door handle as the car pulled away. Through the tinted window, she just barely saw the guy fading into the rush-hour crowd. The cold tanned leather of the back seat smelled like suntan oil. A tinted divider separated her from the driver. She tried the door again, the window. She scooted over to the other side. Locked.

"Let me outta here!"

"Calm down," someone said from the front seat. "Though I like a woman with some fight."

"Where are you taking me? Who are you?" The car pulled onto Fourth Avenue heading south. She reached into her bag. Notebook, laptop, wallet, recorder, business cards, stray receipts. Where was her phone?

"We got it, sweetie. You'll get it back," a woman said, her voice raspy and breathless, like a midcentury movie star. The car stopped. Gretchen banged on the tinted divider.

The rear door opened, and a tall woman slipped onto the leather seat. She had skin the color of sand and a mane of chestnut hair. She wore white cotton pants and a long-sleeved leotard—*Is that back in style now?*—with a sweetheart neckline, a white shrug, and nude high heels.

She smiled. "Hello, Gretchen." She was the source of the tanning-oil-and-piña-coladas smell. The car pulled away from the curb. Gretchen fidgeted with the locks, tried to open the sliding window of the divider. Locked too.

The woman rubbed Gretchen's shoulder as if the two of them were old friends who ran into each other on the street. "I bet . . ."—she looked Gretchen up and down—"I bet you're a native New Yorker. Yeah? What is it? Staten Island?"

Gretchen narrowed her eyes. She had fought girls in junior high school with a pretty balanced win-loss record. This woman was tall and had long nails. But who was in the front seat? She slipped her hand into her purse, clicked on her recorder—just in case.

"I told you, Gretchen. Ralphio took your phone and gave it to Maurice." She raised her voice, projecting toward the front of the car. "Didn't he, Maurice?" He didn't answer, but the woman nodded her head and, smiling, mouthed the words, "He did."

Gretchen's dead brother had a way of describing people as birds, horses, or muffins. The woman was all horse—her hair thick, her shoulders toned, her face long, and her cheekbones high. When she smiled, her full lips parted to reveal white-picket-fence teeth. She reached in her bra and took out her phone. Her hands were immaculate, tan like the rest of her, and thin, but not bony. Her manicured nails clicked on the phone's screen. She wore rings—gold and silver that glittered with gems. Gretchen thought of Mrs. Dabrowski's ringed hand on the screen door just that morning. It felt like such a long time ago.

"I am not," Gretchen said, "from Staten Island. How do you know my name?"

"How 'bout I ask the questions, Gretch. Mind if I call you Gretch?"

"Very much."

The woman had downturned hazel eyes. Her sing-songy voice was decidedly Brooklyn, her vowels almost as long as her eyelashes. "Oh, here it is." The phone displayed a picture of Gretchen crouching on the sidewalk with that kid—the one with the dead grandma—that very morning.

"Why do you—?"

"Why don't you tell me what you were doing down in Coney Island this morning?" Gretchen's hands fidgeted with the strap of her bag. "Who took that picture?"

The woman pouted her lips. "What did that kid say to you?"

"I'm not telling you a damn thing till you tell me who the fuck you are."

"I saw you at the Padillas', Gretchen. And if you must know, Maurice has excellent eyesight and could read your name and job off your name tag."

"I don't know the Padillas. I was out there to interview Darlene Dabrowski."

The woman rolled her eyes. "Who the hell is that?"

"A lonely old lady who thinks a seagull is solving crimes. If you've got a problem with that, you'll have to take it up with her."

"I saw you talking to the kid. You know them."

"I've got one of those faces. People always wanna talk to me." The car was about to get on the Manhattan Bridge.

"Right," the woman said. "At the *Metro*. What are they paying you to go peeking into other people's lives?"

Gretchen sighed. "I told you. I was investigating Dabrowski and her bird."

"I looked you up, Sparks. You've got a Wikipedia and everything. Not too shabby for a girl your age. You were sure writing a lot of articles back in 2010, 2011, 2012. Going after the cops. I remember that story. My husband read it to me over breakfast. You even won some awards. And now? What happened to you, Gretchen Sparks?"

"If you were gonna hurt me, you probably wouldn't be back here talking to me, letting me see your face. So if you're not gonna hurt me, and if I don't have any information, why don't you let me out?"

The car crawled along the bridge. The woman looked out the window for so long that Gretchen wondered if she had been forgotten.

Then she said, "I always take the Manhattan because I love looking at the Brooklyn. People say, 'Vita, why don't you like taking the Brooklyn? It's so pretty.' And I say, 'I like taking the Manhattan so I can *see* the Brooklyn.'"

"Vita?"

"Write it down in your little notebook." She slouched in the seat. "I'm depressed."

"This is kidnapping. I'll be filing a report."

"No you won't, Gretchen. You know why?"

"Why?" The car got off the bridge.

"Because the NYPD hates your guts." She knocked on the window. "Pull over, Maurice, preferably somewhere our friend will be hit by a bicycle as she exits the vehicle."

"I live in Manhattan," Gretchen said.

"Well you shouldn't. You should live in Brooklyn. The county of Kings." The car stopped, and Vita opened the door. She stepped out, one long leg at a time.

Vita stood a whole head taller than Gretchen. The passenger side window rolled down, and Maurice, whom Gretchen finally saw—Black with gray eyes and a goatee—held out her phone. "Oh!" Vita said. "Of course. I'd forget everything without

Maurice." Vita handed it to Gretchen and smiled. "Gretchen, I wish I could say that it's been a pleasure." She got back in the front seat and waved as the car darted out in front of a cab.

Cars, buses, honking horns, cyclists weaving in and out of the fray like lunatics—all contributed to the hell hole of Flatbush Avenue at rush hour. To express her irritation, she used a phrase picked up, no doubt, from the Italian side of her family.

"Christ on a fucking crutch."

Gretchen crossed the street to catch a cab back into Manhattan.

FOUR

Marty had collapsed in the stairway on Monday morning before Gretchen had arrived at work. Trucking upstairs to breeze through the sales department, sometimes with a few dozen donuts, was part of his ritual. He rarely had any business with the staffers. But he made it his business to cross paths with them each morning. Someone two flights up had heard him fall. Janet in HR brought the dusty defibrillator and managed to get his heart going until the paramedics arrived. Without her, he would already be gone.

Gretchen had last spoken to Marty at lunch on the Friday before. Hers was an unceremonious tin of mixed nuts. She kept her desk neat and impersonal—two bins for incoming and outgoing work, a pen holder, a stack of the most recent issues of the paper she might need for reference. If she quit tomorrow, there'd be little evidence that she was ever there. Open on her computer was a document containing the listicle about Greek pastry shops, written by one of the interns—an Ohioan named Brooklyn. Gretchen turned to her crossword puzzle. Marty had been busy all week—and was out—so she'd been solving it solo. The many empty squares seemed to form a frown.

"Sparks!" Zaiden, another intern, hadn't bother to look up from his phone when he addressed her. "Marty wants you."

"He's back?"

She looked back at the crossword. *One-named athlete whose real name is Edison.* She could never get the sports ones. She dropped the pencil and rose from her desk. As Gretchen passed the Pit, she shuddered. The handful of unlucky interns and part-timers entered subscriber data into yet another new system, one that would finally shepherd the paper into the twenty-first century. She had almost been relegated there too. But Marty had fought for her.

"Gretchen!" Marty said with a mouthful of gyro. "Come on in!"

"You want it open or closed?"

"Closed, for God's sake. If people don't stop dropping in, I'll never eat this thing." He took another bite. His head was just visible behind stacks of papers and books and envelopes that teetered and swayed.

"Why don't you get the interns to go through all that?" She gestured to the mess.

"They're idiots." He picked up half of the tallest pile and set it on the floor next to his desk.

"Or Felix, your secretary. I believe it's in his job description."

"Too risky. He wouldn't know what to toss and what to keep. And he prefers the title administrative assistant." Marty sat back in his chair. His kind, small eyes had bags beneath them. He had recently gotten a haircut, and it made the thinning of his widow's peak more apparent. A smear of tzatziki sauce occupied his shirt pocket.

"Ahem." Gretchen brushed the same spot on her own shirt.

"Ah!" Marty found a napkin and dabbed it, spreading it further. He waved his hand. "I give up. How's Suzie? She treating you right?" Nobody in the office called Conway by her first name, and nobody but nobody called her Suzie. But Marty was that way with everyone, the charmer.

Gretchen shrugged. "She barely notices me."

"You got my email about the Borough story? Bird Lady thing?"

Gretchen fought the urge to roll her eyes. "Yeah. Going out there Friday morning. If I'm honest, it doesn't sound very plausible."

Marty chuckled, throwing his head back. "But how delightful

if it were true! Make sure you call Cyrus Amos. I know he'll give you his two cents. Some local color."

"Isn't it colorful enough already?"

"I've known Cyrus for years." He took another bite and talked through it. "What a character." He wiped his mouth with a napkin and cleared his throat. "Next, Roberta wants you over for dinner next Friday. She won't take no for an answer."

"Let me check my—"

"She needs to feed people. It's like the food passes from you to her and keeps her strong."

"I really haven't been feeling up to—"

"My little teenage princess grows more beautiful and more devastatingly cruel every day." He opened a can of store-brand diet cola. "She needs a role model. She loves you."

"She loved me when she was seven. Teenagers are a different story."

"You're telling me."

"I guess we'll find out next Friday then."

"Third. I'm putting together an investigative team. You want in?"

Her face flushed. She looked behind her and around the room. "You mean me?"

"Yeah! You."

"Marty, I don't know. I'm very happy doing the work that I do."

"The work that you do is shit. An intern could do it."

"I'm finding the human element. You always said that's what the news is all about."

"Gretchen, you're sifting through shit for turds, and we're getting you back on track. There's a reason I have you covering Bird Lady. But I can't tell you about it yet."

"Oh?" She leaned forward.

His eyes lit up. "I'm working on something. Maybe something big. I don't know yet. I'm meeting a source this weekend. You and I will talk Monday morning."

It had been a long time since his last investigative story.

26

Gretchen knew how much they took out of him, mostly because, as news editor of *Metro*, he couldn't get out as much as he needed. Last time he worked with Gunderson and the darling boy squad, he had to be reminded to eat and missed his kid's graduation.

Gretchen sighed. "Are you sure you should be moving on this right now? Give it to the boys. They'll do a good job. You need to take it easy."

"They're good. But this will require some massaging." He groped the gyro and wiggled his eyebrows.

"Does Roberta know about this new story?"

"No. And you're not going to tell her. She's on draft two of the Stepanov translation and the now-ancient Mr. Crumb is giving the publisher hell."

"Crumb?"

"He did the first one back in the sixties. Anyway. She doesn't need the stress. I'm taking it easy. And that's why I'm telling you this. I need to work with someone I can trust. Someone good with documents. And besides, I can't be trekking to Coney Island early in the morning. But you can. So I'm sending you."

"So Bird Lady . . . she's part of it?"

"Oh God no. She was a happy coincidence, which I found in my letters, I might add!" He mopped his forehead with the napkin. "You won't have the byline. I'm telling you that up front."

"Big surprise." She crossed her arms.

"I know, I know. But Gretchen, I have something important to say that's long overdue. I know it's been hard for you here, the transition. *The Crier* was freedom. You were the big fish. I had more time to mentor you."

"I'm just giving you shit. You know I am very happy to be here."

He waved his hand and sipped from his cola. "That's not what I mean. I want you doing big work. I want to see your byline on the front page of *Metro*. But it takes time. I know two years feels like time, but it isn't. And I can give you a contributor's note on this one if we get it right."

A contributor's note was nothing to turn your nose at. Marty had that conspiratorial look in his eyes that she hadn't seen since they were downtown. That look had once made her heart rate rise with possibility.

"I can't get into details right now. We have to get it right." His phone rang. "But we have to be careful too. I don't know these people." Marty held up one finger and answered the phone. "Suzie! Yes, I'm back. And of course I read it. I'll be down in ten . . ."

Gretchen let herself out and went back to her desk, where a fresh round of copy awaited her for fact-checking. She finished her lunch, her mind spinning. "Oh!" She'd jumped up, snatched the crossword, and darted back to Marty's office. He wasn't great at the sports ones either, but he was better than she was. "A one-named athlete whose real name is Edison," she'd read as she walked into his office again.

But he'd already left.

Miss!" the cabbie yelled. "Miss, we're here!" Gretchen opened her eyes. "You paying with cash or card?"

She looked at her watch. It was nearly eight o'clock.

The hallway leading to Marty's apartment had the same old smell of paperback books and Murphy Oil Soap.

Roberta flung open the door. "Gretchen!" She smiled, hugging her close. "Come in, come in. I didn't realize it when we spoke, but we had already invited you for dinner last week. Did Marty tell you? Let me take your jacket and bag. Gosh, that's heavy!"

Gretchen's anxiety melted away as she stood in the foyer with Roberta fussing over her. She recently read that saying "thank you" instead of "I'm sorry" could work wonders on one's outlook.

"Thank you for waiting for me. It's been a weird day."

"It's been a helluva week for all of us. Becks! Sam! Gretchen's here!" Roberta hung up the coat and stowed the bag on a bench. "Let me put out the lox. I have just a simple meal. Hope that's OK. Have a seat. Relax. You've had a long day."

Marty and Roberta had the kind of apartment that made you forget you were in New York, but which couldn't exist anywhere else: huge by New York standards with all the prewar details that renters coveted. Hardwood floors, high ceilings—the kitchen's was made of copper—decorative moldings, an octagonal dining room. In the living room, a fire crackled in the hearth. Bookshelves lined the perimeter. A tapestry covered the television—"Out of sight, out of mind," Roberta would say—and velvety sectionals and armchairs invited guests to sit and never get up.

Marty's big desk, the sole mess of the house, sat in the rear corner, covered in books and DVDs and VHS tapes, a copy of *Julius Caesar* open beside *The Deathly Hallows*, seventh in the Harry Potter series, a bookmark sticking out at midpoint. She smiled. What a mess. Mail addressed to *Metro* was sprawled around the books, Marty's notes penned on the envelopes if he thought it worth following up. His tiny script was nearly indecipherable. Often he couldn't read it himself and asked Gretchen to translate it. His pocket-sized reporter notebooks were everywhere. Some stone pieces of a chess set randomly stood at attention like sentinels. A deck of cards and a set of dice added to the clutter. She touched his leather chair.

"Why can't I eat in my room? It's not like she's *my* friend," Becky said from the kitchen.

"If you want to keep that phone of yours for a whole twenty-four hours, you'll quit your bellyaching and put your heinie in that chair."

Gretchen picked up a few envelopes. The first looked like it had been ripped open by a claw. He wrote, GRAND CONCOURSE? BAXTER? CHECK WITH M. On the second, the address typed neatly on what appeared to be an actual typewriter, he had scrawled, GIVE TO GUNDERSON. GO BIG.

Ugh, Gunderson.

Next, a blue and white political mailer advertised some state politician named Dana Quinn: PROTECTING WHAT'S OURS,

FIGHTING FOR WHAT'S RIGHT read his slogan. She rolled her eyes. The midterm election couldn't come fast enough.

Gretchen made her way to the dining room. Roberta's simple meal was a lavish spread: bagels and a variety of cream cheeses; the driest, saltiest, best lox on the West Side; capers and red onion slices; the reddest, juiciest tomatoes; and Georgio's antipasto. Bagels and lox were never a big thing in Gretchen's house. Marty had introduced her to the sandwich she now loved. She realized she hadn't eaten since a ten o'clock turkey sandwich from the machine in the break room.

She took a seat next to Sam. She could hardly believe it was him. Even sitting, he looked several inches, maybe even a foot, taller. A spray of pimples erupted from his chin, and his dark curly hair grew past his ears and fell to his eyebrows. Gretchen tried not to stare at the thinnest, shortest beginning of hair under his nose. Roberta and Becky bickered in hushed tones.

She swallowed a lump in her throat and reached for a bagel. Roberta returned, poured Gretchen a glass of wine, then one for herself. "Everybody got what they need?"

Gretchen nodded. The kids sat brooding.

"Good! *Es gezunterheyt!*"

"Mother," Becky said. "No one here speaks Yiddish, including you."

"I speak some Yiddish."

"And we haven't even been to synagogue since I was ten." She rolled her eyes. She had Marty's triangular eyebrows, plucked thin.

"Do you plan on eating?"

"No," Becky said.

"Suit yourself. Sam, let me get you a bagel, sweetie. You want scallion or plain cheese? You want lox?"

He shrugged, as if the decision wasn't his to make.

"OK. I know how you like it." She spread on a generous schmear of cream cheese and piled it high with fixings. Then she spooned out the antipasto: romaine and provolone, salami and prosciutto and soppressata, roasted peppers and pickled mushrooms. Then she dished out just as much to Gretchen.

Gretchen made a few attempts at conversation with the kids, none of them successful. Becky asked to be excused after a few bites, and Sam followed.

After they left, plates in hand, Roberta said, "Now tell me about this dead end you were on when I called this morning."

Gretchen relayed the story. Roberta laughed at her impression of Mrs. Dabrowski, with her pudgy ringed fingers fidgeting as she smoked, and the "bird house" nailed to the fence.

"What are you gonna do? You can't write that. Marty would simply die! I mean—oh. Oh, Christ."

Gretchen took a gulp of wine. "I'm sorry, Roberta. About everything you and the kids are going through."

"What?" Roberta tilted her head toward the living room. "Becky? She's in a phase, that's all. We spoiled her, and now we're paying the price. It's Sam I won't know how to handle alone. Becky was hard enough with all the drama about her period. But I don't have any experience with this." She made a jerking-off motion under the table.

"You're avoiding the topic," Gretchen said. "I meant grief. I don't need to tell you how much this will change them. After my brother died, my sister Nicola brought my mother to her knees."

"How long did it last?" Roberta said.

Gretchen laughed. "It's still happening."

"And she's in college?"

"Well. It's different now. She's in school. She's finding her people . . . sort of. She's on the journey."

"At least in college they get their own lives. And they're out of the house!"

"I couldn't believe Ma let her live in Manhattan. I commuted every day from Kew Gardens. It's a testament to how insane Nicola makes her."

Gretchen nibbled at an olive—the big green buttery kind she loved. Using the tongs, she sorted through the antipasto for more.

"And how about you?" Roberta asked. "Were you hell on wheels as a kid?"

Gretchen laughed. "Something like that."

"But you and your brother were close. That can act as a buffer sometimes."

Gretchen paused and put the tongs down.

"I'm sorry," Roberta said. "Should I not talk about him?"

It was the most normal thing in the world for Roberta to ask about her brother—especially when Gretchen brought him up in the first place—yet the question knocked the wind out of her. She took a breath. "It's OK. Dominic and I *were* close. And he got along with everybody. Golden boy."

"That must have been hard on you."

"No, actually. It never was."

"Marty had said recently, he said, 'Gretchen's getting back to herself again. I can feel it.'"

Gretchen put her hand over her face. The day had been too much, waking up so goddamn early, the seagull, the kid and his grandma, being kidnapped by that crazy woman. Roberta moved over a seat and put her arm around Gretchen.

"Is he really going to die?" Gretchen said.

"They said it would take a miracle."

They both laughed to keep from crying.

FIVE

Along line of Italians and Germans, Koreans and Chinese, yuppies and hipsters snaked out of De Marco's Italian Delicatessen. They craned their necks toward the case of meats and cheeses and the big jars of pickled eggs and pig ears and watched the last soppressata disappear into a piece of butcher paper. Next door, a cell phone store blasted pop music, and a bored teenager held out a glossy flier. Food cart vendors hawked gyros and shish kebab, piles of onions smoking from the heated carts. A group of Hasidic men moved in a cluster toward the synagogue down the way. Gretchen pushed past all of it, head down, eyes narrowed.

She didn't stop till she reached Heltzel Konditorei. She could not help but peek into the display case at the heart-shaped *lebkuchen* with icing piped perfectly around the edges, the shiny brown toffees, the tight little *marzipankartoffeln* balls her Grandma Ada used to put out on the living room coffee table when Gretchen was a child.

Ada had been a force, and her story was the stuff of legends. She was born in a village in Germany in 1911. Before the war, she had been a columnist for a Berlin newspaper. When it devolved to Nazi propaganda, she said *tschüss*. Her pregnancy allowed her to make a graceful and unsuspicious exit. After leaving the paper, she got involved with an underground group of intellectuals that circulated anti-regime pamphlets. Hugely pregnant but stronger than ever, Ada penned manifestos and scathing rebukes that were eventually hand-copied by other subversives and

33

distributed in small batches across the Reich. By all accounts, she was a firecracker, fiercely smart, with a deadpan way of describing the most horrid of her country's sins.

And Grandpa Hobart worked as an engineer for an airliner, so you can imagine what kind of stuff he was into under the Reich. Quiet, mild mannered, analytical, he had begged Ada to give up the writing. "Please, we have a daughter to think about now."

"And the rest of the world can go to shit?" she had replied.

But when the rebel courier who would collect her writings was found shot in the head, Ada relented. She strapped a feverish baby Grete to her chest and got out.

"I'll follow you," Hobart promised. "I've sent word to Dieter. He'll be waiting for you." He kissed his little girl goodbye and loaded them on a cargo ship that smuggled, along with Ada and Grete, degenerate artwork to New York.

The baby died en route, and Ada arrived bereft to her brother-in-law's hovel in Queens. A year later, she completed her first book, a novel called *The Pamphlet*.

Once, Gretchen thought herself cut from the same cloth.

The bell on the door chimed as she entered Heltzel, and the unsmiling cashier plunked two *marzipankartoffeln* into a paper bag. Outside, the sun warmed her face until she reached the house.

The English Tudor on the corner of 120th and 86th was the prettiest on the block when she was growing up. The mix of brick and bright cream siding stood out, even among the other Tudors. For Gretchen, her home was a source of pride, and her father felt the same way. He labored for it, painting it, replacing the roof, slowly but surely making repairs as needed on the little house.

But now, it hadn't seen a fresh coat of paint in years, and Japanese honeysuckle grew up the brick facade. The red shingles curled off the roof. The overgrown yard, which her father had so closely tended, sprouted weeds and accumulated yard waste. Leaves covered two algae-ridden bird baths.

She picked up the newspaper from the doormat and stood on the porch. She could hear the TV going. She combed her hair with her fingers, checked her teeth in the reflection of the glass door, took a deep breath, and rang the bell.

The door swung open almost instantly. "Why'd ya ring the bell? You have a key, don't you? Unless you threw it away. Wouldn't be surprised. Come in. Let me hug you." Carla smoothed Gretchen's hair, cupped her cheeks, and peered into her eyes, as if she were trying to judge a lie from the truth. That was her form of a hug. She raised a penciled-on eyebrow, moved her hands down to Gretchen's shoulders and then to her waist.

"Come on, Ma. Hug's over."

"I just want to get a look at you before you're gone again," Carla said, her black hair up in a white handkerchief, her maroon lipstick drawn on in two peaks. "Time to get your nails done." She examined the scraped-away polish.

"Ma!" Gretchen put her hands in her pockets. "Will ya ease up? Jesus."

"Don't you Jesus me, young lady. I've been waiting all morning."

"I told you I'd come at eleven-thirty. It's eleven-fifteen." Gretchen made her way to the kitchen, Carla following on her heels.

"You know how anxious I get when I'm expecting visitors, even if it's just my ungrateful daughter. Sit down. I'm judging you haven't eaten a thing."

"I ate breakfast." She took a seat at the table, which was set with five placemats, like the family members were all still alive and under one roof. The coffee maker sputtered.

"Ha! Breakfast is not a cup of coffee and a birth control pill." Carla moved to the stove and began to stir a pot of sauce. "We've got forty-five on the sauce. I was thinking of frying some rice balls, but in the meantime, I picked up those toffees you like so much. I don't know why I did—that old banshee is so rude. But you know me—I'll do anything for my children." She moved fast from sauce to fridge to coffee pot, pouring Gretchen a cup

35

and using a tiny pair of tongs to extract three toffees from a tin. "You get three now, three after lunch." These niceties would demand their reward sooner or later. That was just Carla's way.

"How's your sciatica?" Gretchen said, figuring they could get those complaints out of the way first.

"Are you kidding? It's torture. I've been very worried about you girls with this kidnapper aloose. Very worried. You haven't returned any of my voicemail messages."

"No one leaves voicemails anymore. Text me."

"Text me, text me. That's all you girls do is text. It hurts my hands." Carla put down two mugs, a carafe of creamer, a sugar bowl. "How's the boss?"

"He's in the hospital. Roberta says it doesn't look good." Gretchen's eyes widened. "Is that Daddy's mug?" She wrapped her hands around the last of the glazed stoneware they'd had when she was a kid, big and wide so the coffee would cool fast because her father didn't like it hot. "What's this doing here?"

"He didn't take it." Carla shrugged. "I'm surprised you haven't noticed before. I use it quite regularly. Cools the coffee down faster." She clapped her hands together. "Now! I picked up the ground round this morning at De Marco's before it got swarmed, and I've already gotten to work chopping peppers and onions. Turn that TV off, please. I keep it on when I'm lonely, which is all the time, you should know. But now that my Gretchen's here I can give her my full, undivided attention."

Gretchen poured the coffee. Carla was back to putting cinnamon in it, which would get tiresome every day, but right now it made her feel like Christmas was coming. She switched off the TV with the remote. "I'd like to bring him the mug."

Carla had her hands in the meat. "Don't bother. He doesn't care about a mug. Who cares about a mug? Him? He won't even remember. Here, toss those onions in. Don't let 'em make you cry. Ha!"

"He should have it. Even if he doesn't remember."

Carla pursed her lips. "That woman will just steal it."

"What woman?" Gretchen said. "Marta? Why the hell would Marta steal a mug?"

"Watch your mouth." She mixed the meat vigorously. "She steals."

"You haven't even been over there in months."

"Because I don't want to get robbed."

There would be many battles today, but where to start? "Do you think she enjoys dealing with you? Elder care costs a lot of money, and she's very reasonable. And she speaks English! When Dominic and I found her, we were—"

"Oh, don't bring your brother into this." Carla shook oregano into the bowl. "Lord, she's testing me! It's her and Nico. Always the girls. They test me, Lord. They test me."

"You can't judge people based on where they come from. It's just"—she threw her hand in the air—"stereotypes! Like that all Italians are in the mafia."

"All Italians *are* in the mafia! Except for us." Carla shook bread crumbs into a pie plate. "You hired Marta. You can deal with Marta. But you're not bringing anything from this house over there to be stolen by her."

Gretchen dumped the rest of her coffee in the sink and squirted dish soap into the mug.

"Honor thy mother and father, Gretchen. Remember that one?" She pointed to the ceiling. "He sees you and He knows."

"Yeah, yeah, yeah." She wrapped the mug in a clean dishcloth and put it in her purse.

Carla pointed at her. "Stir the sauce."

"Besides," Gretchen said. "I've been reading a lot about it. Sometimes belongings trigger memories, or even feelings about memories. Maybe it would spark something."

Carla frowned. "Dementia! Ha! If you ask me, he doesn't want to remember."

Gretchen stirred the sauce, and they were quiet. It was this smell, this sauce, that was home to her, even as she tried to evade every sense of the word. Garlic, tomatoes, onions. So simple. She dipped the wooden spoon and drew just a teaspoon of sauce.

Carla handed her a crust of bread. Sauce-bread, they used to call it. It was the only thing they were allowed to eat for two hours before dinner. And even then, they had one small piece each.

"You know," Carla said, "you could make the sauce at home if you would move into a bigger place."

"Ma. Can't we just enjoy each other's company?"

"I do enjoy! I am enjoying! I'm just saying, if you wanted to move to, I don't know, Long Island City or even Astoria, be closer to home. You could have a nice place with a yard and a real kitchen and a bathtub if you would only get out of that closet you live in."

Gretchen put the spoon down. "I live in the city. I will always live in the city. Living in the city means I get to come home. To you." A door slammed upstairs.

"Again with the slamming! These people—it's all day long. Up the stairs, down the stairs, doors slamming."

"Have they been paying on time?"

"They pay," Carla said bitterly. "And I can't even sit in my son's bedroom. Of course, had I known . . ." She cracked two eggs into a small bowl. "Turn the rice off."

A few years before he died, Dominic had convinced Carla to renovate. He did a lot of the work himself. Relying on YouTube videos and the advice of hardware store employees, he added a kitchen upstairs and walled off the staircase so Carla could rent it out. Since then, she'd never been happy with a single tenant.

Gretchen turned and took a good long look around the house. Carla kept it neat. Neater, in fact, than it had ever been when her father lived there. Two glass end tables crowded the plastic-covered loveseat. A dainty bowl of stale breath mints displayed themselves beside a half dozen choice Hummel figurines on the glass coffee table. The beige carpet was worn but clean; it showed marks from the vacuum. Photos lined the walls, pictures of her and Dominic—Nicky, they called him when he was alive—and much later, their sister, Nicola, found her way into the frames. Carla had moved the wedding picture to a spot beside the large display case. Beneath it, Gretchen could still see the shadow on the wallpaper from her father's desk. Gretchen's eyes wandered around the living room, then the kitchen. Something was different.

Carla bumped Gretchen's hip and stepped in to fluff the rice, humming to herself, and Gretchen finally took a good look at her. She was always a slight woman. She had bad teeth—and worse gums—but the skin on her throat was still supple, her eyes sharp and dark, her nose severe. Gretchen, with her fair skin and light hair, once longed for olive skin and thick wavy locks, but she grew to love standing out from her dark-eyed siblings. *Sonnenblümchen*, her Opa used to call her. *My little sunflower.* But the mark of Carla was unmistakable: Gretchen's dark eyes caught all the shadows in the world. "Thank God," Carla would always say. "How else would they know you're a Binacci? The deep guinea eye comes all the way from Calabria."

In the time since Dominic died, Carla's own eyes had taken on a new depth. She clenched her jaw when her face should be resting. When she wasn't cooking or doing the crossword or scouring the kitchen, her hands just didn't know what to do with themselves. They fidgeted up to her forehead, pulled on her ears, or fussed with her hair.

The oil hissed in the pan as Carla plopped rice balls in to fry.

"Ma," Gretchen said, placing a hand on Carla's wrist. "I'm real proud of you for taking down the newspapers. Don't think I didn't notice."

Carla shrugged and, with one quick flick, had her hand back in the egg wash with a rice ball. "Have you talked to your sister?"

"Not in about a week." She glanced at the clock. Already noon.

"Well, go see her. God knows she could use a role model. You're not ideal, of course, but at least you're not *lesbian*."

"Why do you have to bring that up?"

"Because she's doing the lesbian studies, and I just want someone around to remind her of what's *not* between her legs. Not that you have a man to show for yourself, but still."

"Jesus."

"Oh, she takes Your name in vain!"

"Will you quit the performance?"

"Lord, save both my daughters!" She strained one brown rice ball with a slotted spoon. "Get the paper towels."

"She's not 'doing the lesbian studies.' It's just plain old gender studies. And it's offered at pretty much every liberal arts college and has been for decades."

"Ah, you see. That's the problem." Carla plunked a rice ball onto the plate. "They fill their heads with this nonsense about a woman's role. Then they all turn lesbian and it's a big gay fest." The oil seeped through the stacked paper towels.

"Turn it down, Ma." Gretchen hadn't had fried food in weeks, and the smell was intoxicating.

"Everyone has an agenda!" Carla squared her shoulders. "And I will not remain silent while Nicola shows her vulva to every coed below 14th Street."

"Jesus Christ."

Carla looked to the ceiling. "Lord, save her!"

"She's actually very shy," Gretchen said. "She doesn't date much."

"Lord! I repent for the sins of my daughters!"

The rice balls spit in the pan.

Gretchen let the screen door slam and stormed into the backyard. She heard the television turn on.

Part of her longed for some familiar spot on the property that would comfort her. But the family was too old for abandoned swing sets, had been through too much to leave vestiges of the past laying around to be mourned.

She dragged a lawn chair under the maple tree and looked up at the leaves. The sun shone through them like they were pieces of stained glass. She listened to the neighborhood: someone hosing off his driveway, a car alarm in the distance, a bar of salsa music carried out of a passing vehicle. She rubbed her eyes and then she took out her phone. For a moment, Dominic's absence was a sharp ache in her chest. She would have texted him right now to blow off steam. Or he'd be close behind her, striding into the yard to convince her to go back in and eat rice balls and joke about Father Grimes's hangover or Aunt Jana's watery borscht or Nico's list of sins they had found taped to the underside of the telephone table—which hilariously included MASTERBATTER and BAD SPELLER—or any number of family facts that he spun into comic gold.

At least the newspapers about his death had come down— the obituary, too. But every visit, she and Carla still argued about the same things. It made Gretchen tired.

"She's a difficult woman," Oma Ada had said one Easter after a big blowup. "But you are a difficult woman, too." She had cupped Gretchen's chin and kissed her on the forehead. "My Grete. We are all of us difficult women."

"Yeah, Oma, but Ma is the worst."

She had raised her eyebrows. "Maybe she is. But she is your mother."

SIX

Vita Pozi Quinn touched up her lips with a squirt of tinted lip gloss. She pursed them together and looked over at her husband next to her in the back seat of the black Mercedes Benz. "What's on the menu tonight? I could eat a pregnant horse."

She turned back to the gold-plated mirror she kept in her tiny clutch. Her eyes had the effect of making her look languorous, like she was always just waking up from a nap. She blinked and opened them wider. What's this? Two light creases—smile lines back again. This tired old campaign demanded too much smiling. Just a smidgen of Botox could fix that. She adjusted the straps on her cream Bardot dress, positioning them perfectly on her shoulders that shined like snowy mountaintops. Then she smoothed a flyaway back into her bountiful bun.

Dana Quinn worked his fingers on his phone. His hair—dark, freshly cut, with that shock of gray he'd had since childhood—curled just enough to make him look boyish. He wore the slim cashmere suit she had bought him years before, which he doted upon so much that he only brought it to his father's dry cleaner in Greenwich. At forty-two, Dana looked just as good—no, better—than when she married him. She ran a finger along the lines around her eyes and put the compact back in her purse.

"Hello? Am I alone back here?"

"Just go easy on the wine tonight," Dana said. "And stay off that phone."

Typical. She shifted in her seat. "Will there be press?"

42

He threw her a glance and then looked out at the traffic.

"There's usually press." She went back to drumming on the window. A line of preteens skirted down the sidewalk in front of the Chrysler building, bubbly, posing for selfies. A group of Asian tourists, cameras around their necks, toting Red Lobster bags of leftovers, struggled to pass. "Why couldn't you choose a different place? Times Square is like being inside a commercial for hell that you figure out is actually hell."

Dana opened the window of the tinted divider. "Can you at least go up 44th? Christ. What do you expect on a Saturday?"

The driver eyed him briefly in the rearview mirror.

"Don't you nag Maurice." Vita smoothed her hair back. If there would be press, she hoped they'd get it all out of the way early while everything was still fresh.

"If he would navigate the city with a modicum of intelligence, I wouldn't have to."

"Forty-fourth goes east, darling. And Grand Central is in the way anyhow."

"Don't you think I know that?"

"Clearly." She checked the time. "I thought you said it started at six."

"It did start at six. We arrive at six-twenty during cocktails."

Maurice changed lanes, bypassing the row of cabs at Grand Central. He took a right on Madison.

"Finally." Dana leaned back, his hand drumming the upholstery. "Will you spit out your gum before going in? This isn't *The Real Housewives of Brooklyn*. And no flirting with the waiters."

"You know what? This attitude"—Vita circled a finger from Dana's head to his toes—"is not acceptable. And it's not senatorial." She knocked on the glass divider. "You got a tissue up there, sweetie?" A tissue appeared. She spit out the gum and stuffed the tissue in the front seat's pocket.

"Don't be a slob," Dana said.

"You're just nervous, baby. You're gonna knock the socks off these rich snobs."

"I am a rich snob. Can you please remember that when you're on your high-and-mighty middle-class horse?"

"My *upper*-middle-class horse," she said, "is the reason you're here right now. And don't you forget that."

"Right. Because you're such a seasoned political analyst."

"Maybe if you stayed in Connecticut with that silver spoon up your ass instead of slumming in Brooklyn, I could have voted for Barack Obama and lived out my life in peace." It was a running joke that had at some point stopped being funny.

"Vita." He turned to her, his eyes suddenly soft. "I don't want to fight with you."

"Then don't be a dick." The car pulled up to the curb and stopped. "You're gonna get everything you need from these people 'cause you always do. And in November, you're gonna beat the pants off that old wifebeater." She reached to straighten his tie.

"I really need this dinner to go well."

"It will. Who are these people?"

"Doctors."

The door opened. "Should be a blast."

Despite her protests, Vita knew the Algonquin was the perfect place for a campaign fundraiser: small and intimate, but packed with history and nostalgia. Vita was tired of campaigning. The lunches, the parties, the endless phony conversations with the wives. During his first campaign, she had loved schmoozing, smiling, even stuffing envelopes and asking for campaign donations from various ladies' clubs.

"Well, here's the man of the hour." Harlan Vittles pumped Dana's hand and leaned in to whisper in his ear. Even in the flattering lighting of the parlor, Vittles's fleshy face was cavernous, scarred from acne of another era, his eyes two dark beads. Vita wondered if he had a tracking device on Dana; he always seemed to be lurking around.

"Vita," he said, "you look as lovely as the day is long." His Tennessee accent drew out the vowels. He leaned in and kissed her, his lips papery on her cheek. She gritted her teeth so as not to flinch. "Y'all are just in time. Come on, over here."

He led them to the center of the parlor. "Ladies and gentlemen," he said, "if I may have your attention."

The crowd of doctors and spouses hushed and turned toward Vittles.

"When I came to New York City all the way from Tennessee ten years ago to work at New York Presbyterian, I didn't know what to expect of you fine people. My daddy always told me that Southerners should stay in the South, and ever-who left would find a cold, cruel world. But even Southern daddies can be wrong." The crowd laughed. "In the course of the last decade, I've made the acquaintance of each of you fine folks dedicated to medicine. But we're hurtin'. Insurance companies are getting richer, and we're workin' harder for less, tryin' to do our best for our patients and maintain standards of excellence. It is my pleasure, my honor, to introduce the man who might-could be our silver bullet. Ladies and gentlemen, Brooklyn's District 22 senator, Dana Quinn."

The parlor erupted in polite applause. A waiter handed Dana and Vita glasses of wine. Vittles whisked Dana away. For a moment, no one looked at Vita, and she eyed the corridor to the restroom. Could she duck in for thirty minutes, until dinner was served? Dana began his stump speech, which she'd long ago learned to expertly tune out, and she backed away toward the lobby.

"Vita!" Linnie Vittles grabbed her by the arm. "Didn't you get dolled up!"

Vita didn't know what to say to that. Was it a compliment? A criticism? Did she dress up too much or too little?

"Hi, Linnie."

Linnie was at once frail and vigorous, with a waist so tiny that Vita suspected she wore a corset. The only thing smaller was her pea-brained head dwarfed by her oversized glasses.

"Look at us," Linnie said, gesturing to her bun, stiff with hairspray. "We're twins tonight."

Even though the Vittleses had lived in New York for a decade in the twenty-first century, Linnie still dressed like she was sitting in the parlor of a plantation in 1850. She wore a mint-green frock with a crocheted collar and billowing skirt—or skirts. Vita couldn't tell.

A young woman holding a glass of dark liquor didn't smile when Linnie grabbed her arm. "Vita, meet Patricia. Patricia's husband is an old friend, been in practice with Harlan for years. Isn't he, Patricia?"

Patricia looked just about as thrilled to be there as Vita. She shook Vita's hand, her eyes glassy, and excused herself, pointing across the parlor at no one.

"Y'all Yankee women ain't much for small talk." Linnie fanned herself as she led Vita toward the dining room. "On the other hand, her husband, Dr. Shears, is quite the charmer. She must be a"—she paused and pulled Vita in—"a cold fish."

Vita drained her glass.

"Not so fast, miss," a familiar voice said. She turned, and her face lit up. Howard Quinn stood before her, smiling. "Good evening, Ms. Quinn." He kissed her hand.

"I wasn't expecting you to be here tonight," she said to her father-in-law. "I woulda brought Boggle."

"Boggle is a perfectly acceptable game to play at a campaign fundraiser."

Linnie elbowed her way between them. "Why, Mr. Senator," she said, "Mr. US Senator Quinn. How wonderful to make your acquaintance. Twice the senator and twice as handsome as the son." She extended her hand dramatically to be kissed, her wrist bent and her cheeks flushed.

"Howard," Vita said, "meet Mrs. Linnie Vittles, the wife of Dr. Harlan Vittles who arranged this . . . party." She couldn't suppress a snort of laughter.

Howard stepped right in, turned the vain woman's hand, and shook it. "The pleasure is all mine."

Linnie's eyes widened in offense. "Well, you simply must meet Harlan. Now where did he run off to?" She scanned the crowd.

"If you'll pardon us, Mrs. Vittles," Howard offered with a smile, "I just flew in from Washington, and I haven't seen my daughter-in-law in ages." He didn't wait for a response but took Vita's arm in his and waltzed her to the bar.

"Thank you," Vita whispered.

Howard got her a glass of wine. "Happy to come to the rescue."

"I am so tired of that weird little shrew. Do you see the way she's dressed?"

"Like she's waiting for Sherman to come set fire to the plantation?" Howard laughed. "Oh Vita. It is good to see you."

"Good to see you, too. What gives?"

"Can't I come support my son while he begs for money?"

"Hate the sin, love the sinner. But I told Dana, after this campaign, I'm done." She lowered her voice to a whisper. "He was a wreck in the car. Just a wreck. I don't know how I'm gonna make it to November." The party was moving to the dining room.

"You'll make it all right. You're tough. And he needs you."

"I don't know how Cindy does it," Vita said. "Year after year, the fundraisers, the parties, the press." Dana's mother was, as Howard once described her, *Gray Gardens* with money"—eccentric and delusional and just able to keep it all together.

Howard looked around and whispered. "She was high."

Vita laughed.

"And I never made Cindy quite the center of my campaign."

"Well, South Brooklyn would never vote in a rich kid from Connecticut without a white-trash mobster's daughter like me."

"Here here." He clinked her glass with his. "Shall we?"

"Can't I stay at the bar and order fish and chips?"

"Come on." He gave her his arm. "You won't make me face a room full of Republicans on my own, will you?"

She guffawed, snorting, which was another thing she was not supposed to do on the campaign trail. When they entered the dining room, a hush fell over the party.

"My father," Dana said, clearly shocked. "Of course. Everyone, please welcome my father, Connecticut Senator Howard Quinn, and my lovely wife, Vita."

Polite applause and murmuring. Howard squeezed her hand and walked her to her husband's side at the head table. But they hadn't planned for the senator, and the waiters scurried for another place setting. Vita took her seat as the maître d' whispered to the campaign manager. A waiter attempted to scoot Harlan Vittles's place setting down to make room for Howard; Linnie's face darkened with fury; Dana placed a hand on the waiter's back and explained that his father could sit across the table because Dr. Shears's wife would be moving. Patricia, black bob and pencil skirt, scowled and went to the bar.

It all worked out just fine for Vita because Linnie Vittles was seated three whole bodies away. Instead, she had the attention of Dr. Shears and her father-in-law. Beside him, a cardiologist and her husband tried to exchange pleasantries with Linnie, who fidgeted with her napkin and stole piercing glances at Howard.

Introductions. Shaking hands. Toasts. Salads. Bread. Dana told the diners about becoming a New Yorker by marrying Miss New York—even though when they met eight years had already passed since her crowning achievement; and when they married, ten. He described how his vision of New York was anchored in its history of meritocracy and economic freedom. Then he spouted some new stuff about hospitals. There was always new stuff. When he met with old folks, he talked Medicare When he met with cops, he talked crime. When he met with guns, he talked guns. She wished he didn't meet with guns so often, but at this rate, she just wanted the campaign to be over.

The waiters brought out the main course dishes: plates of braised pork belly, strip steak and potatoes, grilled halibut. Dana had probably ordered her the steak.

Vita had barely eaten in two days, stressed as she was about Dominica Padilla.

Who is she? Why is her name written in Dana's planner?

And that raspy-voiced reporter know-nothing had been no help at all. With a pang, Vita remembered letting her first name loose to the woman. It had been reckless—and it felt good.

"So did you do private practice before you became chief of surgery?" she asked Dr. Shears—"call me Harry"—who was far too old for poor Patricia. Vita's place setting remained empty as the other diners cut into their food. Just when she was deciding whether she should say something, a waiter placed before her a platter of Brooklyn Lager Fish and Chips. She did a tiny hand clap, catching her father-in-law's eye. He winked.

"Looks like someone ordered off the menu," Harlan Vittles said in his lilting voice. "What is it, dear?"

Dana, cool as ever, smiled. "Vita loves her fish and chips."

Linnie made a quizzical face. "Now is that food native to Bay Ridge?"

"It's English, dear," Harlan said.

"You know," Linnie said, "I finally made it to your stomping ground last weekend. I never saw so many nail salons in all my life! And Arabs! I hadn't realized you grew up with so many Arabs. Bless your heart!"

Harry Shears said, "I love fish and chips. I could eat it every day," and launched into an ode to fishing that began in Florida and went on forever. She leaned in, asked follow-up questions, tried to pronounce all of her R's and soften her T's.

Early on, Vita had slipped into her role as First Lady of District 22 effortlessly. All those beauty pageants when she was a kid, sitting for hours at the salon while they curled her hair and stabbed her head with bobby pins. All those long walks along the length of their swimming pool. All she had to do was play a stereotyped version of herself. In Brooklyn, even on Dana's arm, she was still Vita Pozi of Bay Ridge. When she led a Bensonhurst ladies' book club, she wanted *Beloved*, *As I Lay Dying*, *Rebecca*. But she picked *Bridget Jones: Mad About the Boy* instead. She visited middle-school home ec classes instead of English classes and presented on decoupage instead of Dostoevsky. She won the Coney Island Nathan's hot dog eating competition two years in a row—and two years in a row vomited all night.

But that was all to gain votes—not money. To get money, she had to be someone else, someone she might get along with more, but whom on the surface she was poorly equipped to become. This Vita Quinn, wife of a rising star in the New York GOP, had to talk less, eat less, drink less, and never argue. She felt lucky to be stuck with Harry Shears. At least he was sweet. But Harlan was louder, and she realized that her father-in-law wasn't paying any attention to Harry's fishing odyssey.

"It will revolutionize cardiac research," Vittles said, "drawing more New Yorkers and Long Islanders and, yes, Connecticuters, toward the area, and property values will soar. It's a mutually beneficial relationship." As he spoke, a bit of pork belly hung at the corner of his lip.

"Mutually beneficial?" Howard cut in. "Who benefits? The trade-off for your fancy cardiac wing is American men and women going home crushed by medical debt."

"Dad," Dana said with a nervous laugh. "Let's enjoy dinner."

Howard leaned back in his chair and made a faint, almost arrogant laugh. "Meanwhile, you refer every patient from your own practice and never step foot in the halls yourself. I know how it works." He waved a finger at Harlan.

The vein in Dana's forehead throbbed, and his mouth clenched in an agonized smile. "Dad, please."

"And then what?" Howard raised his voice. "Your cardiac wing may be sparkling, but how are your dialysis machines? How many nurses and orderlies are on a shift? How many people are you funneling out on the street while they're still sick?"

"Dad!" Dana sprung to his feet. Harry Shears stopped talking. Everyone stopped talking.

"Now, Dana," Harlan said, always the first to break an awkward silence. "Your father is just passionate. Come, sit down."

"It's not passion, Mr. Vittles," Howard said. "It's the truth. You say you just want regulations loosened, just a little bit. UHA buys out another hospital, a better one than that dilapidated South Brooklyn."

"Dad, that's enough! Let's get some air."

"We're just having a friendly debate," Harlan said, looking around the table. The cardiologist and her husband looked ready to bolt for the door. Harry Shears searched the room for his wife.

Howard stood up and locked eyes with Dana. "He doesn't want progress. He wants profit. That's all United Hospitals Alliance cares about. If you get in bed with this"—Howard gestured to Harlan—"you won't recognize yourself when you get out." He dropped his napkin on the table, turned, and walked away.

"Well," Linnie said, forcing a hearty laugh, "isn't he just precious?"

Harlan stood. "Just a little family theatrics, folks. Please enjoy your meal." He gestured to Dana, and they walked toward the back of the room. The doctors shifted in their seats.

Linnie shook her head and sipped her spritzer. "My daddy always said, 'No politics at the dinner table.' He ran a tight ship, my daddy. Had to. He was a banker. That was in Virginia, of course, my birthplace and the birthplace of this great nation . . ."

Across the room, Harlan smiled as he spoke through his teeth. Dana's hands fidgeted along his belt and pockets. He nodded his head.

Vita summoned every ounce of strength so as not to tell Linnie Vittles to shut up. She looked at the cardiologist. "And where do you work, Doctor . . ."

"Why that's Dr. Robins," Linnie said, "of Beth Israel. And isn't it wonderful how she's risen through the ranks!"

Dr. Robins, one of the few people of color in the room, for a moment regarded Linnie with such complete disdain that Vita wanted to cheer. Then her face softened. She turned to Vita and said, "As I'm sure Ms. Quinn can attest, New York women are the most driven women in the world."

"You can say that again." Vita held up her glass.

Linnie hushed her. "Here they come!"

Dana and Harlan strode back to the table. "I want to apologize to you good people," Dana said, his voice clear and confident. "I know we all don't stand on the same side every time. As

51

I'm sure you know, I started off as a Democrat, like my father." He looked around smiling. "I am my father's son. But as Harlan said earlier this evening, fathers are sometimes wrong. And my father, whom I love and honor, is wrong about you. But I want to tell you another story."

Vita sat very still and looked up at her husband, her face placid, her hands in her lap. She had no idea how he was going to save this night. Part of her didn't care whether he did.

"I don't usually tell this story—heck, I don't *ever* tell this story." Dana cleared his throat. "When I ran for state senate in 2011, I was walking on air. My lovely Vita was by my side, as she is now." He put a hand on her shoulder. "And so was our son, Alexander."

Vita's heart sped up, and the corners of her mouth tried to fight their way down. "Alex turned eight that year. He was smart and brave, like his mother. Had just started third grade. He loved to swim and to build forts in the living room. There was nothing I wouldn't do to protect him. He was with us in the campaign office when the votes came in, asleep on a folding chair. The next day, he wore my American flag lapel pin to school, and he wore it every day after."

He took a sip of water and looked down at Vita, across the miles and years, an insurmountable distance forming before her very eyes as he spoke.

"The following summer, right after we'd finished up the legislative session and my first bill to step up Broken Windows had passed, we went down the shore for a few weeks. The future seemed big and bright. I remember Vita's big old beach hat she used to wear." He took her hand. She squeezed his in hers, as if that would stop him.

"And Alexander built a small town in the sand that first day. A post office and three houses. The next morning, he ran to the beach to see how it fared, but the waves had carried it away, leaving a clean slate. He tried again, this time making it more elaborate and detailed, adding a street, a cul-de-sac, and a school. And again, when he ran to the beach the next morning, his city had disappeared."

"Dana," she said through her teeth, "I don't think this story is appropri—"

"The town soon became a city with skyscrapers, stadiums, courthouses. Alexander made a new city each day of our trip that summer. Vita brought him tools that he used to make windows in houses and engrave the names of businesses into their storefronts. She helped him construct telephone wires with yarn and fill a coliseum with seashell people. Each city was different, with a new name, a new specific enterprise, a whole system of urban planning that blew our minds. Mind you, Alex had only seen one major city ever in his life! But he could dream, that kid."

Vita felt a chill run across her collarbone. Her hand went limp in his.

"Alexander didn't come home to Brooklyn with us at the end of the summer. Our baby boy drowned in the ocean. And the city he left, well, it was no city I wanted to live in. Not without him."

Linnie Vittles sniffled and wiped away a tear.

"But I have learned from him. I have learned that giving up is unacceptable. That building the same damn thing every day affords us no opportunity for innovation. No invention. No progress. I have built my career on Alexander's dream. I will stake my future on his dream. I will fight for his dream. I will fight for you."

Vita didn't hear the applause. The room receded in a flash of gold, everything zooming away like she took off on a roller coaster. She felt Dana tug her hand, felt herself rise to her feet, felt his lips on her cheek, his hands clasp her shoulders. She felt she should look somewhere, she should see something, but she didn't. It was as if she were standing on a dune of white sand that stretched as far as she could see in every direction and she sensed that no other form of life would be found.

"Mrs. Quinn? Mrs. Quinn." She heard an echo of his name. Her name. Was it her name or his? Quinn?

"Vita," a voice said, unrecognizable. "Vita, please. Let me get you a drink of water."

She looked around as shapes began to form. She heard chattering. She felt for something behind her, her chair. Someone took her hand.

"That's it," the voice said. It was warm and friendly. "Have a seat."

The energy in the room surged, and she saw Dana, her husband, her love, standing at the center, shaking hands with a tall man, then a short woman, then leaning into Harlan Vittles as he whispered in his ear.

"You had a bit of a dizzy spell, I'm afraid." It was the cardiologist's husband. His broad smile assured her that she was safe in this place, that this place was the place she was supposed to be. "But we all get them from time to time. Probably just stood up too fast. Here." He gave her a glass of ice water.

"Yeah," she breathed more than spoke. "Got up too fast." She drank the water, looking around.

Our baby boy. Didn't come home to Brooklyn with us.

"So many doctors in the room," he said, "but I have a feeling you're going to be just fine."

His wife beckoned him over. "Terrance," she said. "There's someone I'd like you to meet."

"Thank you," Vita managed as he rose.

B ack in the car, Vita closed her eyes. She wanted the deep black of a dreamless sleep. She heard Dana's phone vibrating. Felt the car pull onto FDR Drive and pick up speed. Heard in the pain of her inner ear the cry of gulls from that horrible day. Dana shifted in his seat.

"Vita," he said. "Baby. Are you awake?"

"Mmm."

"You looked pretty pale in there." He paused. She knew he was next to her, but she could not imagine that he were anywhere close. "I'm sorry I didn't warn you," he said. "I hadn't planned to . . . I hadn't wanted . . . It was my fucking father. He could have ruined everything. Baby. Can you please just say something?"

If he were to reach across the seat, if he were to draw her close to him and bury his face in her hair and kiss her shoulders, if he were to make that contact, it might be different. She heard him sigh, aggravated, shift in his seat, and take out his phone.

When they had met, the five years between them felt like nothing. Vita wasn't really middle class. She came from money, but a different kind of money. Her handsome father sold Porsches. They had two cars in the garage, sometimes three. When he got home from work, it was like Christmas for five minutes as he doled out candy and baseball cards and mood rings, and then he scarfed down dinner, changed out of his suit, went to his study, and closed the door. Sometimes he left again, saying nothing. But usually she heard his voice on his separate line, low and indecipherable, and wondered what he did in there.

Hers was that steamy seventies Brooklyn—*Saturday Night Fever* was filmed blocks from her house in Bay Ridge. Her mother, a five-foot-ten blond bombshell, strode down 3rd Avenue in tight bell-bottoms and crop tops. Her father wore platform shoes to work at the showroom, and Vita taught her little brothers the Hustle on the deck, the shiny Hitachi boom box thumping WPIX. She took jazz lessons at Lorrie's Essence Dance School and strutted, bumped, and funky-chickened her way through elementary school.

Her mother didn't take an interest in Vita until the summer of 1980, when Vita turned eleven and got her period at a friend's slumber party. The friend's mom sent her home with a box of tampons, which she hid on the floor of the bathroom closet behind the humidifier.

The fold-out diagram was perplexing. She tried to insert the thick cardboard applicator—sitting on the toilet, standing with one foot on the seat, and even getting down on the floor on hands and knees—but each time, the dry wad of cotton painfully failed to do its job. This went on for three days until Bianca, the maid, threw a pillow at her at seven in the morning.

"Come to the bathroom," Bianca said. "I'm going to show you how to use a tampon."

The lesson was informative, not only for its hygienic necessity but because Bianca gave her one last cryptic message: "And if next week, you want to explore more . . . Well. You're a woman now."

Vita didn't exactly know what that meant, but she found out soon enough. In the span of one month, her pubic hair darkened and grew, and her nipples turned the color of wine. Each night, she gazed at the poster of a disco-obsessed John Travolta that hung across from her bed.

One day that August, she was reclined poolside in her new string bikini, thumbing through a book, when her mother put down her daiquiri, strode across the deck, and grabbed Vita's breasts with both hands.

She dropped the magazine. "Ma! What the hell?"

"Shut up," her mother said, squeezing. "You, Vita. You are going to be a star."

Sixteen years would pass before she would sit on a fire escape in January, smoking Kools and glaring into a room full of trust-fund douchebags playing beer pong while a hockey game blared on the big-screen TV. Her boyfriend, Markey, had promised they'd make a quick stop to sell coke to the Dorito-eating, onion-dipping assholes. Greedy as ever, Markey dashed back out into the night when they wanted more blow, leaving Vita alone.

She had dressed for seventies night. She wore a denim jumper with bell-bottom legs and a halter top that made her look long, tall, and ready to disco. As Markey pushed her into the apartment, she grabbed the arm of his leather jacket and wouldn't let go until he maneuvered his way out of the hold and dashed to the stairway. When she turned around, a half dozen flannel-wearing, spiky-haired undergrads gaped at her.

Three hours later, she had one cigarette left and not even a subway token to her name. It was past one o'clock, and her friends downtown would already be wasted and have eaten all the E while she froze her ass off. She had to pee, but she had already fought off a groping, and the room smelled like farts and cheap cologne. She hugged herself against the cold and looked out at the quiet street.

The window slid open, and she turned.

"Look asshole," she started, "I am just waiting for Markey, OK? Don't mess with me." He was dark haired and fair skinned, probably an upperclassman. He didn't wear a T-shirt or flannel but a navy cable sweater. He pushed a mop of curly black and gray hair out of his eyes.

"Hi," he had said, climbing out the window. "I'm Dana Quinn."

She raised an eyebrow. What kind of kid introduces himself at a party by his full name? He extended his hand. "And you are?"

They didn't have sex that night, not after they climbed down the fire escape. Not after they jumped the turnstile and rushed down the steps as the 1 train screeched to a stop. Not after they slouched against the poles laughing or even after Vita unlocked her apartment door, turned on the lights, and put some water on for spaghetti.

As they talked into the morning, Vita had a feeling they'd have the rest of their lives for all that. "I just knew," she was once fond of saying. "And when you know, you *know*."

When Vita opened her eyes, the car was speeding across the Brooklyn Bridge, the silver cables stretching up in a perfect geometry. She reached over and took Dana's hand.

SEVEN

Carla was right about one thing. Gretchen's apartment was tiny. Sardine-can tiny. No-space-for-a-fridge tiny. Three's-a-crowd tiny. In an art deco building that went south with the trend. Mold climbed up the walls of the hallway. The roof leaked during heavy rain. She had to be careful not to trip on the curling linoleum on the stairs, all four flights of them.

But tiny she could deal with. Moving out to the boroughs she couldn't.

Gretchen lived for lower Manhattan, which she called the Nexus. Something was always happening—it was Manhattan, after all. But the West Village also had a sense of quaintness—of neighbors looking out for each other, of small businesses thriving—that reminded her, when she was really honest with herself, of Kew Gardens when she was growing up.

She occupied what used to be the janitor's closet. At a whopping eighty-four square feet, it held a toilet, a sink, a stand-up shower. She had just enough room for a tiny kitchen table, a coffee maker, a toaster oven. Her dad had built a lofted twin bed when she'd moved in eight years ago. She paid the rent in cash. The tenants in the apartments below her resented the janitor's absence.

The landlord did just enough to stay within codes. He knew all the loopholes, including the one that allowed Gretchen to live upstairs "temporarily." On the first floor, the Christopher Street Group of Alcoholics Anonymous held meetings around the clock, which made for excellent people-watching from her fire escape.

She dropped her bag on the kitchen table and stripped. The whole subway ride, she had thought about taking a shower. The morning in Kew Gardens did her in. Ma's guilt tripping. Nico's vulva. Her father's mug. And, of course, being in the one place where she could not avoid her brother's memory.

The previous night, she had passed out on Roberta's couch before she could talk to her about the obit, and when she woke up, there was a note that invited her to join Roberta and Josh at the hospital. She could hear some pop vocalist coming from Becky's room and had let herself out.

As the hot water sprayed her back, Gretchen thought of the woman. Vita. If the name was to be believed. Her audacious South Brooklyn accent, her manicured fingernails, the way she pouted when she realized Gretchen had nothing to tell. Tanning oil and piña coladas. Gretchen could imagine her teacup Pomeranian, with a sparkly pink collar, yapping up the dead as Vita did Jazzercise. Some burly alcoholic husband coming home late from the strip club and waking her up to make him a sandwich.

Then she imagined Roberta and little Sam sitting next to the machines that were keeping Marty alive, and she turned off the water.

She dressed in Saturday clothes—blue jeans and an oversized V-neck that slid down and showed off her shoulders. She poured a glass of wine, opened her laptop, and spread the clippings and the printouts from Marty's life on her desk. The crisp air flooding in from the open window and the glass of wine calmed her, a feeling she hadn't had all week.

Why had Vita been staked out in Coney Island at seven in the morning? Gretchen shook the thought off and turned her attention to Marty.

> *Throughout his 30 years as a reporter and editor, Marty Mitnik's commitment to investigative journalism matched his passion for fringe cinema, Shakespeare and food trucks. No story was too small, and no story was too big.*

She sipped the wine. Those two sentences felt true. The repetition of "no story" was choppy. She'd work on the language later.

A pebble plunked against the fire escape. Then another. Danny Russo's voice boomed up from the street. "Gretchen!"

She kept writing:

> *After 18 years on the Village Crier, transforming the struggling alt-weekly into the little paper that could, Mitnik took the helm of the newsroom at the* Metropolitan *in 2014, acting as news editor.*

Her phone vibrated.

> *A three-time Pulitzer finalist, Mitnik was uncomfortable receiving praise. But there was indeed much to praise. As a newsman, he could be aggressive, but he held his writers and himself to the highest ethical standards.*

Footsteps ascended the stairs.

> *He was a champion of the new. Though sentimental in other matters, he embraced online journalism at its start. He believed that journalism was for the people, and—*

He knocked on her door.

"Gretchen! Your window's wide open. I know you're home."

The past day and a half had been so bizarre that she'd forgotten about their standing afternoon date. Passing the bathroom, she checked the mirror and hurriedly applied concealer under her eyes, chiding herself for going to such lengths for Danny Russo. She put on the bra that had been drying on the windowsill. At least she was clean.

She opened the door. Danny leaned against the wall, hands in his pockets, like he was waiting for the subway but had no particular place to be.

"Hey, lady."

Gretchen put on a frown. "I'm working."

"On a Saturday?" He stood up straight, all five-feet-seven-inches of him. "I guess the news never stops."

"Nope." She crossed her arms. Danny wore cologne, too much cologne.

Sweat like a pig, smell like a god, he would say.

What she didn't tell him was that he smelled warm and spicy, a scent that made her think about fucking a cowboy in a barn loft, hay in her hair, moonlight shining through the window. A weird image born from her father's love of spaghetti Westerns and a romance novel she stole from Ma's nightstand when she was thirteen. But it endured.

He looked past her, as if peeking into a ladies' dressing room. "You got someone hiding in there?"

"No, Danny. I told you. I'm working."

"Aww." He pressed his hands to his heart and winced. "Can't you come out to play for a little while? Or could I . . . um . . . come in?" He had a tight little body, small but strong, and his style hadn't evolved since the nineties.

"Don't you have an AA meeting to attend?"

"It just finished. I thought about you the whole time."

"How's that working out for you?"

"Terribly. In fact, if it's not you, it's the bottle."

"That's not funny." She turned around. "I don't have any food. And all I have to drink is wine. And you have to let me work for another twenty minutes at least."

"No worries." He took a seat at the table and removed his worn Mets hat. He kept his hair long on the top and short on the sides, and because of the hat, it was always slicked back. "Just forget I'm even here."

Gretchen sat back at her desk. Where had she left off? He believed that journalism was for the people, and . . .

> *. . . his responsibility was to them—all of them. From the people sleeping in the park to those brunching on Madison Avenue, to Marty, every single New Yorker was his reader.*

Her phone buzzed. A text from Roberta of just two terrifying words: *Call me*.

She drained her wine glass and held it up. "Will it bother you if I have a glass of wine?"

"It's not your responsibility to keep me sober," he said and even brought her the bottle.

"Spoken like a true Big Book thumper," she teased. She had picked up a lot of the corny lingo.

He laughed. "Don't let me distract you."

"You could never." She turned back to the obituary but felt him over her shoulder.

"What are you writing?" he said.

She imagined the smoky night air, horses nickering below them, a crescent moon framed in the loft window.

She turned and gave him a searing look. He laughed, covering his mouth. He might have had good teeth before, but now they were chipped and stained after years of using.

"OK, OK," he said, bowing to her. "May I stand on your fire escape and smoke a cigarette, my lady?" His South Brooklyn accent made the imitation of an Englishman particularly funny.

"You may."

As he stepped out the window, Gretchen thought about the last time she'd promised herself she was done with Danny. After a solid two hours of fucking, they'd gone down the block to get a bite to eat at the Japanese hole-in-the-wall on Perry Street. She was famished and had nothing in her fridge. She didn't realize until they sat down that she had never been out in public with him. In the mirror on the wall next to their booth, she saw them: her in a sundress and boots—the first thing she'd thrown on—her shaggy hair messy, and he in his usual baggy jeans, brown T-shirt, and backward Mets hat, his cheeks acne scarred. When the waiter had come over, he ordered two miso soups.

That's it, she had told herself. You're playing with him.

Almost without realizing it, she opened her notebook to a random page and wrote:

VITA, SOUTH BROOKLYN?
DOMINICA PADILLA
JAIME (PADILLA?)
DARLENE DABROWSKI (BIRD LADY)

She ripped the page out and tossed it into the wastebasket. She turned back to the obituary. But as she traced the keyboard with her fingers, she smelled the smoke from Danny's cigarette. He looked out over the street, one foot crossed over the other, hands on the railing. The just-before-dusk, blue- and orange-streaked sky convinced her to close her laptop, power off her phone, and creep up to the window. The metal grate striped her bare feet with rust. She pressed her body against his back.

"Hi," Danny said.

"Hi."

After, Danny drew a finger along her hot-pink cheekbone. "Ouch," he said. "Does it hurt?"

"I wouldn't ask you to do it if I didn't want it to hurt."

"I know. But damn, Mama."

"I've asked you not to call me that."

He groaned and turned onto his side to look at her. "What goes on in that head, Gretchen Sparks?"

"I've had a fucked-up week."

"You wanna talk about it?"

"Not particularly."

"You mean not with me. I get it. I'll go."

She turned to face him, grabbed his wrist, and pushed his hand down between her legs.

"So it's like this," he said.

"Shut up."

Oma Ada was right. Gretchen Sparks was a difficult woman, to put it mildly. To put it honestly, she was capable of straight-up emotional cruelty. But she wasn't always that way.

63

And what Danny Russo didn't know was that Gretchen herself bore the brunt of her own criticism and contempt and loathing. She constructed the kind of walls around her that immigrations opponents can only dream about: titanium encased in concrete and encrusted with spikes. A fortification right up there with Hitler's Atlantic Wall.

Therefore, nothing would have surprised her more than her willful attendance the following day at the Bensonhurst Columbus Day Parade. Maybe it was the news about Marty. Maybe it was the looming anniversary of her brother's death. Or maybe she just didn't want to be alone, but she left the Nexus Sunday morning in Danny's 1995 Kia Sephia. The dashboard covered in Powerball tickets and scratch-offs, the floor littered with empty cans of Mountain Dew—this rusty, toxin-emitting piece of junk en route to a celebration of genocide was preferable to a day parked in front of her laptop writing an obituary for her not-dead-yet best friend. Who could blame her?

Kids wore "Italian Prince" and "Italian Princess" shirts, faces painted like the flag; high schoolers practiced their pageant waves from rented convertibles; middle-aged ladies wore approximations of premodern Italian dresses; priests came out in full robes; majorettes twirled batons while marching bands played upbeat versions of "On Eagle's Wings" and "Amazing Grace"; church congregations floated by on ships; acrobats sprung into formation; accordion players, their tunes drowned out by the rest, played anyhow; war veterans hobbled and shuffled and strode up the avenue. Gretchen held a tiny Italian flag in her fist and raised it high. Even when the Maids of the Milk passed, dressed like rejects of a Renaissance Fair, she cheered.

Everyone in Brooklyn must be here right now. And they're all so happy.

She should take Ma next year. She turned to Danny and kissed him hard on the lips.

"Whoa."

A hand grabbed her ass. "What the fuck?" She spun around.

"Grandpa!" Danny said.

A huge man wrapped his arm around Gretchen's waist. His breath reeked of beer and onions, and his waxy face glistened with sweat. "Wassa matta, Danny boy? Didn't ya fatha teach yada share?"

"Get the fuck offa me!" Gretchen yelled.

"A feisty one!"

Danny pushed him away from her. "What's the matta with you?"

"It's OK, Danny boy. Not my type anyway. Why doncha finda nice Italian girl, eh?"

"My family is from Calabria, you drunk shit," Gretchen said.

"Humph. Calabria?" He turned back to the parade as a dance troupe marched by. "Viva Columbus!" he screamed. "Show us da booooootiiee!"

Danny led Gretchen away, weaving between strollers and walkers and dogs. "Sorry about him."

"The alcoholic thing must run in the family."

"You kidding? That's nothing compared to what Grandpa's capable of. But more importantly, are you really Italian?"

"My mother is. My father's parents were from Germany. They escaped the—"

"Oh look!" He pointed down the block. "Here come the king and queen!"

The crowd around them roared. A float shaped like a gondola slowly came up the street. A man—handsome, she could tell off the bat—stood waving to the crowd.

Gretchen squinted. "Who is that?"

"Some politician. My mother loves him."

She read the words emblazoned on the side of the gondola. PROTECTING WHAT'S OURS, FIGHTING FOR WHAT'S RIGHT.

The same words she read on the mailer on Marty's desk. "What's his name?"

"Looks like he's gonna throw some stuff!" He waded into the crowd as the man threw a cascade of plastic cups and doubloons. The float passed, and a woman emerged from the other side. She turned to Gretchen, waving like a perfect beauty queen. Suntan oil and piña coladas.

Vita.

Her hair flowed past her shoulders. Her deep red blouse matched her lips. Dark green slacks coordinated festively with high-heeled boots. The man joined her, and arm in arm they waved to the crowd, all smiles and sparkling eyes.

Danny returned. "Those kids are merciless. All I got is a doubloon." He pressed it into her hand. She turned it over. QUINN 2016, it read, in green and red.

"I need to know everything you know about them." The float passed, but just before she was almost out of view, the woman turned and looked, it seemed, at Gretchen.

"Some local politician, I told you. My father hates him. Look, I don't follow politics, OK?"

"No," she said. "Her! What do you know about her?" She pulled out her phone and powered it on.

"Who, the wife? She was Miss New York years ago. She's still pretty hot." He pulled Gretchen toward him from behind and buried his face in her hair.

She pulled away. "I have to go." Her phone buzzed with texts and voicemails and emails. "Where's the nearest subway?"

"You know," Danny said, "you're really something."

EIGHT

"This is the last time"—Vita plunked her earrings onto her dresser—"the last time you parade me around. After November, that's it. You can find another mascot." Her feet ached from wearing the new boots. "I can still feel his slimy hands on me."

Dana slid his tie from around his neck. "Baby, I said I was sorry. There's very little I can do in a situation like that." He hung his tie in his closet, turned to her, and squared his shoulders.

"You could knock him out to start. These things are so fucking tight I could hardly breathe." She pulled off her slacks, picked up her brush, and yanked it through her hair.

"Will you take a bath? Calm down? You'll feel better."

She threw the brush at him. It missed and landed on their big empty bed with pillows arranged in a puffy pile, not a single crease in the comforter. "I am not a child!" Her chest throbbed with pressure. Rage strangled her neck. "You have been terrible to me for weeks!"

He unbuttoned his shirt. "Yeah? You used to love this shit."

"What?"

"The campaign. You ate the attention right up. I gave you a stage and you loved it."

Early that morning, she had woken up gasping, her heart going like crazy, like she used to in the first year after Alexander died. When she'd reached for Dana, she couldn't find him. She groped for him in the dark, panicked, taking shallow breaths.

"Is that what Saturday night was supposed to be? Me loving the attention of a room full of strangers who suddenly know how my son died?"

He rolled his eyes. "This was everything you'd been missing for years. Your very own beauty pageant with no competition."

"Fuck you."

"Oh, fuck me?" He extended his arms wide. "I'd be pleased! Maybe if you let loose a little of that sexual energy at home, you wouldn't have eighty-year-old drunks groping you in public."

She pulled on a tracksuit. "Why don't you go get it from Dominica Padilla?"

His eyes widened, and he sucked in his breath. That was all she needed to confirm her fears. She darted past him, out of the room.

T he gym was busy, the windows fogged up. She paused at the door and put in her earbuds to avoid a conversation with that busybody Mrs. Russo.

"Saw you at the parade this morning," Mrs. Russo said anyway, her voice a scratch on a record. "Senator Quinn looked so handsome up there."

Vita all but shuddered.

"How you doing, Mrs. Russo? Nails are looking great."

"Oh, you know Tina. Always wanting to do palm trees or pandas or whatever. Of course, Mike said I'm too old for it. But I like 'em." She wiggled her fingers. "How was the after-party? I wish I coulda been there with all the kids."

Vita paused. If she said something, Mrs. Russo's embarrassment would quickly sour into resentment, and she was the biggest gossip in South Brooklyn. But maybe a little gossip would bring Dana right down to earth. She narrowed her eyes. "Actually, it wasn't too great. Your father-in-law got a little handsy with me."

Mrs. Russo twisted her lips in disapproval. Then she waved the comment away. "Oh, you know men." She turned to the next customer, a young woman with music blaring from her earphones. "They're all the same."

"Yeah," Vita said. "They sure are."

She grabbed a pair of five-pound weights off the rack and found a Stairmaster looking out at Bay Ridge Avenue, just a block away from their brownstone. Vita had lived in the neighborhood all her life. Sure, she and Dana had visited Napa Valley and Chicago, Paris and Rome; her family went to Florida every year for a couple of weeks when she was a kid. And then there were the pageants all over the country, the hours spent in her mother's Camaro studying until she got carsick and puked, for which she had to endure her mother's rebukes, only to start studying again right after. Truck stop bathrooms with vending machines packed with Spanish Fly and flavored condoms, the look in men's eyes when she skittered past them on the way out to the car, the smell of gasoline and her mother's Salems.

But Bay Ridge, Bensonhurst, Dyker Heights—South Brooklyn was her home. Through the fogged-up windows of the gym, she could just make out the leaves on the trees, some already turning yellow. Two more weeks before they really popped. She scrolled through her music, settling on Gloria Estefan's *Cuts Both Ways*. As the first chords struck, she started to climb. It hurt at first. She had eaten a meatball sub at the parade—she had to, it was all part of the shtick. And now it sat like a rock in her stomach. A cramp formed in her side. The music picked up, she quickened her pace, her knees up, up, up. She lifted the weights with each step. Up, up, up, and her forehead broke out in sweat. Up, up, up.

Gloria crooned, her voice so rich with youth—Vita's youth. Her upper lip moistened with sweat, and her muscles burned.

The July day had been perfect. The beach was theirs, save for a few small groups far enough away that they provided only echoes of the rest of the world. Vita read a magazine and dozed. She wore the floppy beach hat to shield her face because she knew from her mother just what the sun could do.

Dana and Alexander were hard at work on a city that Alexander had drawn up over breakfast. They had already laid out a wagon-wheel grid and built the bank and the fairgrounds. As he studied it with Dana under the umbrella, he traced the curve of the river, looked up at Vita—his dark curls tousled in the breeze—and asked that summer question she had heard a hundred times. "Mama. Can I swim?"

"Swim!" she said. "Swim like a fish!" And he smiled, turned, ran down the beach toward the surf.

Dana lay down on the blanket, his head by her feet. He began to stroke her ankle and her calf. She regarded him: quite tan himself, his chest naked and his nipples encircled by curly hair that met at his sternum and climbed down his belly into his trunks. On their first morning in Cape May, he had declared that he would not shave; his beard grew with a streak of gray just like his hair, and Vita loved to lose her fingertips in it as they lay in bed in the morning, their bodies tangled, his cock hard against her leg.

His hand worked its way up to her knee. His eyes were closed, his eyelashes glittering with sand as he stroked her inner thigh. Vita looked out at the water, at Alexander diving into the crest of the waves, bobbing up, coming in with the break, and swimming out again. Over and over, her boy dove all that summer.

Dana flipped over on his stomach, put both hands on her shins, and looked up at her. She felt like a little minnow was darting around her bathing suit and up her spine. He bit the inside of her calf and ran his lips up to her knee. She closed her eyes.

This is my perfect life.

Then she reached for his hand and brought it up to her bikini bottoms, pressing it to her mound.

She slid off her chair onto the blanket. He stood, looked around. Their beach companions lay on towels and in chairs, oblivious to them and the rest of the world. Alexander dove and bobbed and swam. Dana loosened the umbrella from the sand and brought it down to the ground. He picked up Vita and sat her behind it, and he straddled her body from behind to where he could look to the left and see the ocean. He laid a towel across her lap and reached beneath it to stroke her inner thighs.

Vita's toes dug into the sand. Her head fell onto his shoulder and he kissed her neck. "You have to watch him," she said as his hands moved.

"I promise," Dana said.

His left hand groped her breasts, strong and hard, then light and then not at all. She let out a soft moan. She felt him, hard against her ass, and scooted closer into him. She moaned again, louder, and his hand met her mouth.

The sky was so blue, dotted with thin wisps of clouds. Her smell mixed with the smell of tanning oil, of sand, of salt. The sun covered her completely as her mind blanked.

V ita's phone buzzed as a text came through. "I'll be at the office," it said. "Don't wait up." She turned her phone over, checking her step count—4218, 4220, 4222. She bore down and breathed deeply. Every muscle burned.

NINE
Author's Note

"Nicky," Gretchen was always quick to say, "got all the brains. Nicola the looks. Me the fire."

I beg to differ. Gretchen was all that and more. She was the dew on the grass in the morning, the river rushing in the night, the lightning bolt that sliced me again and again into multitudes. She was, like the great Chilean poet said, "not only the fire." Her "whole body like an open hand, like a white cluster from the moon," her dagger wounded me in my roots.

I loved her, and sometimes she loved me too.

But, to humor her, I will admit that Dominic *was* sharp. A brainiac. He skipped two grades. They couldn't catch up to him.

"Two college tuitions at once?" their father had said, always planning for the future, when Dominic joined Gretchen in the third grade.

"I'll lose both of my babies at once?" their mother had said, always centering herself in the lives of her children.

Carla enrolled him in a gifted-and-talented nerd club through the Museum of Natural History that cost forty dollars a month, and the museum couldn't keep up either. He blew through every lesson and experiment and contest, second to none, rising through grade levels. He ate physics for breakfast, chewed up chemical equations and spit them out. He consumed information and beelined through med school.

So it's no surprise that the kid learned Morse code at eight years old, met the standard translation speed of 5 wpm—and then some—to get his Morse interpreter strip on his Cub Scouts sash, and found to his frustration that none of the other scouts had kept up with him. He sent signals out of his second-floor bedroom window with a flashlight to his indifferent neighbors and scanned the sky for a comrade.

His rise to stardom dimmed Gretchen. Fourth grade had been merciless. Everyone associated her with the brainiac. Einstein, they called him. Big Head. Human Calculator, or H-Calc, for short. Yet even as they mocked him, they occasionally paused and stood in rapture.

But Gretchen, always secretive, shut herself away in her room each evening for another reason. The girl, then ten years old, listened to *The Immaculate Collection* with her Walkman, a delinquent copy her rebellious babysitter had made her because she knew Gretchen could handle it. (Just thinking of her mouthing the words to "Justify My Love" gives me an erection followed by a wave of shame.) She softly sang along and studied a copy of *Morse Code Manual for Scouts* that she checked out at the library and never returned.

She studied and practiced and studied and practiced in secret each night after dinner.

Most of the time, Otto Sparks was high above the clouds in the cockpit of a commercial airliner. Carla had first fallen in love with his voice, which piped into the cabin as she fetched ashtrays and cocktails for passengers in 1974. She straightened her hair with an iron back then, wore blue eyeshadow, a short scarf tied around her neck.

You'd think Dominic would have found a willing Morse conversationalist in Otto. Sadly, he didn't.

But Gretchen. Gretchen learned code backward and forward, and it didn't come easy to her. Skilled in the arts, in synthesis and interpretation, she wasn't one for memorizing dashes and dots. It took practice and hundreds of flash cards, cassette tapes, and conversations with herself in her bedroom.

She might have practiced forever, perfectionist that she is, but Dominic talked of giving up his nightly ritual. He started studying German, to the delight of his paternal grandparents, and he took to staying overnight with them each Thursday. Their house sat kitty-corner behind the Sparks' Tudor, and if all went as Gretchen hoped, Oma Ada would tuck him into bed in the guest room and turn off the light at eight-thirty.

She waited. The minutes crept by. She flipped the Madonna cassette tape and watched the clock. Carla yelled up to her to go to sleep.

Finally, across their backyards, Oma turned the light off, and Gretchen opened her bedroom window into the blustery February night and angled her flashlight against the house.

— · —

The prosign for Invitation to Transmit.

— · ··   ·   ·   ·

Nicky.

She waited. She had tried the light on many nights, experimenting with angles and distance. She felt certain there must be a mathematical equation that would reveal itself to her through experimentation. She also considered asking Opa Hobart to watch for the light—he was an excellent secret-keeper—but she worried that even he would blow her cover.

Maybe he is looking for a flashlight, she thought, knowing full well that Oma kept two in the hall closet just outside the guest room.

She tapped out the code with the flashlight again, waited, her hands stinging with cold. The entire endeavor felt ridiculous. Why had she made a big secret out of the whole thing? Why hadn't she just told Dominic she would learn Morse code? He, with his generous spirit, would have happily practiced with her! Yet she insisted again and again on closing people out rather than inviting them in.

It must be ten below out here, she thought. She put one hand under her armpit because Dominic told her it was the warmest spot on the human body. She withdrew her hand and the flashlight and reached up to the window sash just as a light blinked to life across the yards.

They soon found they didn't even need flashlights. They could code by blinking their eyes across the dinner table while Carla lectured them. They could take the Lord's name in vain at Sunday School with a few taps on the table. They could taunt their annoying little sister with their secret language.

You up?
Barely.
You see the plane?
Yeah.
Dad?
No.
Think they'll divorce?
Who knows.

If they were friendly before, if they more than tolerated each other, they now embarked upon a friendship that would make those closest to them envious.

I, Raj Patel, should know.

Nicky—yes, I call him Nicky because I loved him too—was a rare person, one who understood darkness but hadn't visited its depths himself. He was her *person*. The root of the root. The bud of the bud. The sky of the sky. He was the fire she knelt beside to warm her hands.

And everyone else? Me?

Smoldering embers.

TEN

Gretchen paced across the twelve feet of her apartment. In one hand, she held the doubloon from the parade, warm to the touch; in the other, the cool, yellow-ribboned key that the crazy seagull dropped at her feet Friday.

She had been researching. Nothing serious, nothing that committed her to any of these people. But still. Pretty big coincidence that she'd found Quinn's mailer on Marty's desk the very same day that Quinn's wife had pushed her into a car and interrogated her about this Dominica Padilla. And on the very same day, some kid had told her about Dominica Padilla, a grandmother who had died in a hospital under suspicious circumstances. Gretchen believed in coincidences and chance, but this was too much.

She shifted the objects in her hands. The doubloon. The key. Two small objects, with no meaning to her, that she could just as soon drop into a curbside trash can and never see or consider again.

When had Vita noticed her outside Dabrowski's? She seemed unconcerned with her visit to the Bird Lady and absolutely obsessed with her five-minute chat with the kid. Had she even seen Gretchen enter or leave the apartment next door? And if Gretchen had not lost her mind and followed the screaming, taunting seagull back up the block, would Vita have seen her at all?

Leonard. Gretchen rued the name, the beady eye, the dirty underbelly of the fowl.

Vita, she had read online, was in fact a beauty queen—or had been, when her last name was Pozi. Gretchen found a single photograph of her from back then. She wore a royal-blue ball gown with a high slit up the side and puffy shoulder pads that gave way to skin-tight sleeves. She must have been no older than eighteen. Spiral curls, coffee brown—no surprise that she colored it now—sprayed out from behind a tiara. A perfect fringe of bangs framed her eyes. A banner crossed her chest. Her smile looked frozen on, her teeth sparkling white and framed by lips painted in perfect triangular peaks. The photo was old, grainy, scanned from a newspaper, and when Gretchen zoomed in, the smile looked more like a grimace.

She was like the ladies in Carla's church who attended every baptism, communion, confirmation, and funeral, whether they knew the families involved or not. They had the same strained look from smiling too much. Only, Vita was beautiful. Beneath all the makeup and eighties hairstyle, she had an effortless beauty and poise, a sex appeal both dirty and innocent. No wonder every kid in South Brooklyn had a boner for her back then.

Miss New York 1989 and second runner up in Miss America. Second runner up? The brief article said she scored highest in evening wear, swim, and—get this—oral examination. Not that the questions could have been very difficult. It also said that she planned to study literature at Brooklyn College. Had she ever made it?

A search for Dana Quinn heeded much more. From Greenwich, Connecticut—a rich bastard, of course—and son of US Senator Howard Quinn. Howard was a darling of the Left, Enemy Number 1 of the NRA and for-profit sector. His blood ran blue on every issue.

Dem darling Howard sent his son to Columbia, where at some point, somehow, way up on the UWS, he met Miss New York, the Bay Ridge Beauty and her feathered bangs. He practiced law for a few years and then followed in his father's footsteps—except for the whole political ideology thing.

But one thing didn't add up. The younger Quinn served District 22, and even a girl from Queens like Gretchen knew it was the whitest working-class district in the city. And racist, too. Even Danny would admit that. She looked up past district senators for 22, all older men, all from South Brooklyn, all standard bearers of the blue-collar pride.

So how in the hell did Dana Quinn, son of Howard Quinn whose net worth was estimated in the millions, get elected to a solidly working-class district where hometown pride was paramount?

Gretchen released her fists and looked at the doubloon, the key. She sat back down and put on her glasses. She stared at the grainy picture of Vita Pozi, age eighteen.

Her phone buzzed to life with a text.

R u alive.

She rolled her eyes. Was it so hard to type a question mark? She didn't expect much from her millennial sister. Nicola was in a phase that had started at fifteen and was still going strong through college. Brazen, emotional, she had always been a peacock, but since their brother died, she consumed attention like it was her life force.

Suicide threats? Check. Drunken accusations? Check. Fake pregnancy? Check, check, check. Nico had been an afterthought, born long after Carla got the operation that should have ended childbearing entirely.

"That stupid guinea surgeon," her father had said, right in front of Gretchen and Dominic at dinner when Carla shared the good news. Their father tore up the stairs and came down holding what looked like a makeup compact. He held it up in front of her face.

"It's unholy!" Carla cried and turned away from him.

Eight months later, Nico was born screaming and hadn't ever stopped.

Gretchen popped the seal on a box of wine. She had to start buying the good stuff, or at least the better stuff. Maybe she'd drink less if she did. She made her way out to the fire escape, the doubloon and the key in her hand.

Nico's incoherent string of texts from the day read like a prison letter from an abusive spouse.

> *How could u ignore my texts like this?*
> *I love u, don't u know that?*
> *I need u right now.*
> *Ur a real bitch.*
> *Come visit me!!!!*

And then: *I can't believe you're acting like this the week of the anniversary.*

She put down her wine and phone and grabbed the one dead potted plant on the fire escape. It had been so long since she'd watered it that she easily yanked it out by the roots, deposited the doubloon and key in the bottom, and stuffed the root ball back into the pot.

She checked her voicemail, heard Roberta's voice. "Gretchen, get over here. Marty's awake! He asked for you!"

That couldn't be. They had a small family—barely anyone lived in the city—but surely he had more important people in his life. She listened to the message again, and again, and by the fourth time, she was pulling on her boots.

There's a reason I have you covering Bird Lady, Marty had said. *But I can't tell you about it yet.*

The nurse pulled back the curtain. "We're packed full, as you can see. He'll hopefully have his own room in a couple days."

Marty lay in the bed, tubes tucked into his nose. Beside him a machine beeped steadily. The nurse approached his bed and checked his IV. The back of his hand was deep purple, the bruise spreading up his arm.

"It's normal," the nurse said, "for coma patients to have tremors, but his are severe. He lost the needle a couple of times." She put a pillow under his hand and smiled at him. "Now why do you want to get rid of that needle, Mister Mitnik? Don't you know we need to get you some fluids?" She pressed something on the machine.

Marty's bloated face held almost no color, his eyes swollen into fists, his hair sticking out. Even his pointy eyebrows drooped. The feeding tube pulled down the right side of his lip. His tongue was distended and lolling, blistered and coated in gray film. Gretchen swallowed hard and took a step closer.

"How long has he been asleep? You think I can wake him up?"

"Miss," the nurse said, narrowing her eyes. "He's under. If he wakes up, that's up to him."

"But Roberta said he was awake."

The nurse looked at her watch. "When did you talk to the family?"

Something was wrong. She knew it. "She left me a message this morning."

"You need to give her a call. Mister Mitnik went back under within thirty minutes."

"But he asked for me."

"That may be true, but look, visiting hours have been over. I'm gonna need you to come back tomorrow."

All at once an odor filled the room. Sulfur and sour. Gretchen looked at her friend. His waxy cheeks sagged toward the bed. That awful purple hand lay limp on the pillow. That body was Marty, but it also was not Marty. That body couldn't cackle, couldn't conjure a terrible pun, couldn't pound a treadmill at seven in the fucking morning. Her chest tightened as the elevator doors opened. She stepped outside into Union Square.

The day had grown blustery. Clouds gathered above her. The trees shook, making sounds like cellophane twisting. She had run out to the hospital without a jacket. She crossed the street and sat on a bench.

Christmas vendors had already set up their kiosks on the south side of the park, and a pumpkin patch had been set up on the north side. Children were everywhere, and they all shrieked. She got up and crossed the square, heading toward the south side chess boards.

I'm saying that we need to prepare for the worst.

She bought a pack of cigarettes from a kiosk and lit one with a match, felt the old burn of it.

"Excuse me, ma'am? Do you have a moment to save the children?" A perky college girl stood a foot away, her eyebrows raised in expectation.

"I don't."

"That's why I'll make this quick. Every day, children around the world are—"

"I said no."

"But Yonni in Guatemala City sleeps on a bed of wires. A bed of wires!"

"I swear on my mother's life, if you don't get the fuck away from me, I will push you into the street."

The girl flashed a wounded look. "You're a horrible person. Do you know that you're a horrible person?"

"Yes," Gretchen said. "I do."

S everal blocks and a shot of Wild Turkey later, Gretchen sat in a booth in the back of Cowboy's Village Pub. Her old stomping ground. Cobwebs hung from the ceiling like Spanish moss. Dust coated the fans and flew off in strings on rare occasions when the owner turned them on. The only beer they had on tap was Miller High Life. "The Champagne of Beers," Marty used to remind her when they got a drink after work. Cowboy's was part of the reason the *Crier* stayed open on a shoestring budget. It occupied the offices above the bar. The owner, Cowboy, loved the paper in the way a Tea Party Christian loves his daytime talk radio: it affirmed his views all the time.

Cowboy had blown in from New Orleans with Hurricane Betsy decades ago and never left. Didn't bring anyone with him or let a peep go about the money he brought—enough to buy the building and then some. He believed the secret to steeling himself against the tides of development and construction and *Starbuckization* was to be allergic to cool. So the first thing you saw when you walked in was the official presidential portrait of

George H. W. Bush. The second thing you saw was a shitty pool table that had a huge brown stain on the felt top. The third thing you saw was Cowboy hawking a loogie into a handkerchief. He stocked the jukebox with David Allen Coe hits. A trough of piss-gold ice in the men's room invited absolutely no one. Cowboy also got along with the cops and a couple good old boys at the Department of Health.

The bar wasn't full of assholes. Nobody had tried to bring their babies. It hadn't lost its touch quite yet. But a small group of college kids huddled around the jukebox. One had on a crushed fedora; another, a threadbare sweater that she probably bought that way. Someone got out a selfie stick. Gretchen rarely had a "What is the city coming to?" moment and had little patience for those stuck in some make-believe glorified past of "when New York was New York." Yet the sight gave her a pain. And Cowboy was old. Marty always said he had to be at least eighty. How long could he hold out? And besides, the new smoking ban meant that most of the people who hung out at Cowboy's were hanging out at home. It had been terrible for business.

She heard him coughing a couple booths down. "Cowboy!" she said. A moment later, he leaned his crutch against her table and sat down across from her.

"Girl, where you been?"

"You got that bourbon?"

"No, I ain't got dat bourbon. Is way over there." He opened his mouth wide and laughed, wheezing, and then coughed for too long.

"Don't you move," she said and strode toward the bar to fetch a couple of plastic cups and a bottle of brown liquor. She took some quarters out of the register and put them in the juke-box—put on Patsy Cline. She sat back down in the booth and poured them each a shot.

"Ha!" he said. "Anyone else go behind my bar, I'd shoot 'em. Open up the register? Bam! But you?" He banged his fist on the table. "Where you been at?"

Cowboy's thick glasses were greasy like his skin. His gray hair was cut close to his head, and he kept his mustache trimmed and his face shaven. He wore a maroon dress shirt, gray slacks, and suspenders.

Gretchen sipped her drink. "How old are you, Cowboy?"

He cleared his throat and leaned in. "You can't come around no more? Too good for your old friends, eh? Eh? But you wanna know how old I am."

"I feel bad coming around here." She poured another shot.

Cowboy grunted and waved her comment away like it were one of his cobwebs. "Nothing to feel bad for. I told that man to send you."

"Who? Marty?"

"He came in here Sunday last."

"He come alone?"

Cowboy sucked his teeth and gazed around the room, as if searching for the information.

"With a tall man, light skinned. Never seen him before. They sat right there."

Cowboy closed his eyes and nodded his head. Patsy Cline's voice filled the bar, and the barman dozed.

When Roberta picked up the phone, Gretchen felt guilty for waiting so long to call. Roberta's voice sounded deflated. Marty had been awake for twenty-four minutes. For twenty-four minutes, Roberta and Sam held his hands and felt his fingers faintly squeeze back. He couldn't talk really. He had a feeding tube down his throat still. But his eyes widened and he looked around the room.

"We started saying names. You know, he was an only child. His parents have been dead for years. But Sam said your name, and his eyes widened."

Gretchen didn't know what to do with that information, so she accepted it.

Roberta said, "He was so excited last weekend before it

happened." She paused. "He was working on something—stressed, up too late online, had a Sunday morning meeting. Sunday is our time. I told him to take it easy. That's why I wanted you to come over for dinner, to help me talk some sense into him."

Gretchen looked at the liquor bottle and tried to remember how much she started with.

"I'm on Borough Features. I don't get the hot tips."

"I still can't understand. He'd been exercising, right?"

"Every morning."

"And not eating off the carts?"

"Please. He never stopped eating all that shit."

Roberta sighed. "I'll come by *Metro* tomorrow afternoon to talk about the obituary. You'll be there?"

It would be Monday already. "Yeah."

"I'll see you then. And Gretchen? Let me know if you remember anything about his last story. I'd really like to know."

Gretchen put her head down on the cool Formica table. She knew it was filthy, that she was right now smearing dirt and germs into her acne-prone skin.

Bam! Cowboy slammed his hand down. "Gretchen!" he hollered. "You bring that old man 'round here next time, eh?" He hopped out of the booth, grabbed his crutch under one arm, and picked up the bottle of bourbon. "That's on me." He made his way up to the bar. "Closing time, folks!"

ELEVEN

The wind whipped the pennants on the bodega overhang as Gretchen attempted in vain to light a cigarette.

It was just as well. Her lungs felt ragged from smoking. Her eyeballs ached. If she got a migraine, she was screwed. She dug through her bag for her prescription—even with insurance it cost $10.50 a dose—and swallowed the pill dry. Her chest was hollowed out and replaced with a helium-filled balloon. She couldn't get enough breath, and her eyesight blurred. All of this happened right before a migraine that could knock her out for days. And not a fun, boozy knocked out. A lay-in-the-dark-and-cry kind of knocked out. A circular-saw-in-her-ears knocked out.

When Dominic died, she started with the morning drinking, the looting of Carla's medicine cabinet for Lortabs, the ill-advised sex with strangers. She was sure any undergrad majoring in psychology could make her easily. In fact, she knew one who would. Nico was an amateur psychoanalyst—among her many callings.

A text came in as she turned onto Christopher Street.

Y dont u luv me like he did.

When Nico picked up, house music blared in the background. She held the phone away from her head.

"Gretch-EN!" Nico sounded elated. "It's my big sister! Hang on! Hang on! Let me—I have to take this. I have to take this. OK. Get me a Long Island Iced Tea. Hang on, Gretch-EN!" Sound of wind and cars. "Thank you! Holy shit, I cannot believe you just called me!"

"How are you?"

"I am like blowing up everybody's shit tonight. I told Ma I was never going to have kids, and she said that I have to have kids because Dominic is dead and you obviously aren't going to, and then I said she shouldn't sell you short. You're only thirty! Or thirty-three?" She paused only to breathe.

"You've been texting me for days. What is going on?"

"I am so worried about you, Gretch-EN! Mom told me about your boss. Is he gonna be OK? Do you need me to come over?"

"No. I'm fine. I'm busy with work."

"You must be having to do so much more since he's in a coma. He's in a coma, right?"

"Yes."

"Holy shit! That guy has been around for like as long as I've been alive. Well, I've been wanting to tell you, I am learning all this crazy shit about Reagan and the Sandinistas and the Lost Girls of Juarez? Have you heard about them? Just random teenage girls are dead on the side of the road in Mexico, and no one cares about it."

"Well, I don't think it's that no one cares, Nico. It's that the drug cartels—"

"And the war on drugs? What the fuck is with that?"

A siren blared on Nico's line. "What about it?"

Nico let out a squeal. "Oh. My. God. Is that John Legend? John! John! Over here! It is not John Legend. Now that guy is looking at me like—"

"Am I really talking to you right now? Are you a real person? Or are you a meme?"

"OK, that was offensive."

"No, Nico. You are a ridiculous person. You cannot text me a hundred times a day. I will block you." The AA meeting was just letting out below Gretchen's apartment.

"You wouldn't!"

"I would."

"You would block your own sister?" Her voice cracked. "You would block me? All I ever wanted was for you to love me."

Gretchen rolled her eyes. "You're drunk. Are you with someone? I mean are you with someone who will take care of you tonight?" She dug in her bag for her keys.

"I'm with my friends."

"Good friends or asshole friends? Are you with Gabby?"

"Gabby is my bestie. She and I are going to—"

"She will leave you in a bar in Brooklyn without any money or a MetroCard so she can go have a threesome with your boyfriend and some whore. So I am asking again. Are you with friends?"

She whimpered. "No."

"Get in a cab, come here. I'll pay him. He'll take you home. I need to go to sleep. You have ten minutes."

She hung up.

"Damn," one of the AA guys said. He had a Kid Rock look and those terrible plugs in his ears. "That was some stone-cold shit right there. I hope nobody ever talks to me that way. Stone cold!"

"Mind your own fucking business." She turned the key.

When the cab arrived, Gretchen stepped out onto the sidewalk. The driver rolled down his window. "You paying?"

"How much to take her to Broome Street?"

"No, no, no." He waved his finger. "She puked. Out the window. Look."

Chunks of vomit streaked the back door. Nico was passed out, her face smooshed against the glass.

"OK, so the fare is what?" She ducked her head to see the meter. "Six bucks? That's another dollar-fifty to get her home? I will give you twenty dollars in cash right now if you just take her home. You can leave her on the sidewalk. Campus security will get her." She pressed the bill through the window.

"No ma'am. I'm sorry ma'am," the cabbie said.

"Please, just, twenty bucks. Take it. It's yours. Just get this girl home."

"Ma'am, I will take your money and give you change." He counted out singles.

"Fuuuuck," Gretchen said. She knocked on the window. Nico's eyes opened and she smiled.

"Fourteen dollars," the man said, pushing the money at her.

She took it, peeled off a single, and gave it to him. "Yeah, thanks a fucking lot." She opened the door and Nico spilled out of it. She sprung to life.

"Gretch-EN! It's so good to see you!" She put her arms around Gretchen's neck, pulling her down to the ground, oozing love.

"OK, Nico. Let's go."

"Did you know Libras are sun dancers? And I am a Libra?"

"Little help here, please!" Gretchen yelled. Stone Cold guy was happy to give a hand, and together they managed to take one arm each and move her toward the building, her boobs almost spilling out of her dress.

"Don't fucking look at my little sister's tits," Gretchen said as she unlocked the door.

"Are you always so scary?"

"Do you really want to know the answer to that question?"

They carried her through the door and wrestled her up all four flights of stairs. All the while, Nico babbled about astrology and someone named Javier. Gretchen kicked her apartment door open. "To the right," she said. They rushed Nico to the toilet.

Gretchen leaned against the wall, panting.

"Is she gonna be OK?" Stone Cold said.

She held out two dollars. "Yeah. You can go now. Thank you for your service."

"I couldn't," he said, and took the money. "If you need me to—" but she was already closing the door.

She rubbed her eyeballs. She felt like she had been awake for days. She stepped in the bathroom where her sister lay on the floor.

"You OK?"

"I think I haveta puke."

"All right. Come on." She helped her to her knees and positioned her head over the bowl. She gathered all of Nico's thick, black, curly hair and held it in a gentle knot. "OK," Gretchen said. "You're good."

At two o'clock in the morning, Gretchen stood in her kitchen. She had gotten Nico in her bed at one o'clock and petted her hair until she fell asleep. Her sister had a sweet face: round and smooth, her eyes just close enough together to make her look mysterious and secretive, the outside corners turned up, which Nico made more dramatic with thick eyeliner. Her nose was cute and round, her lips pouty. Nico looked like their handsome brother, but she had the personality of a blimp crashing through a city.

Gretchen had been so busy in college. Too busy to party. Too busy to let go. Was that why she sought oblivion now?

She washed her face and brushed her teeth and lay down, but sleep wouldn't come. She thought back to *Metro*'s recent big news stories, before the kidnappings. They had done the teacher's union negotiations, a lot on the MTA scandal—but that was all wrapped up.

Every time she tried to clear her head, some detail of the last three days crowded into her mind: Conway's warning, the goateed guy who drove Vita Pozi Quinn's car, Marty's meeting at Cowboy's.

She put coffee on. What if this story—this story Marty had been working on—what if it were something worth pursuing? If she couldn't sleep anyway, she might at least indulge her curiosity.

Coffee made, she sat down at her desk, opened her notebook to a fresh page, and wrote on the left, DOMINICA PADILLA (DECEASED), JAIME (GRANDSON). Off to the right, she wrote, DANA QUINN. And next to his name, VITA POZI QUINN. In the center, she wrote SOURCE??? MET MARTY SUNDAY MORNING? She drew two lines to connect Dana and Dominica to the source. But who was it?

She thought back to that Thursday before Marty's attack. She had been fact-checking for Gunderson—again—on his work on the comptroller race. She probably moderated the blog comments. Oh, and she put up that listicle.

And just before lunch, a copy of the *Always Free Coney Island Gazette* had appeared on her desk. A yellow Post-it said in Marty's handwriting, "DARLENE DABROWSKI—SEAGULL SOLVING CRIMES" and the phone number. The paper was mostly ads and arrest information, like the short piece about the man apprehended for jerking off under the boardwalk. No mention of this Dabrowski person or a seagull.

"What in the ever-loving fuck," she had said to no one.

Marty was in a meeting, and Features kept sending her corrections to check. By the time she had a minute to breathe, he had left for the day.

On Friday, Marty, his shirt stained with tzatziki sauce, told her he was working on "something big." She got drunk that night with a college friend she tolerated and had to go out to Queens on Saturday with a hangover to look at a nursing home for her father. Its name, New Horizons, was a rude irony. Looking at apartments in Manhattan for years had taught Gretchen a thing or two. Cockroaches scampered away when she opened a cabinet. The water ran brown when she turned on the faucet. The toilet's low pressure barely managed a flush. A big dry-erase board calendar labeled ACTIVITIES was nearly empty. The residents in the musty day room looked withered, and one reached her hands out to Gretchen when she passed. That was the last Queens home she'd bother with. If their father lived in Manhattan, Gretchen and Nico could easily visit him.

Saturday, she had a migraine and downed a bunch of NyQuil. She didn't mess with the alcohol-free shit. She drank the syrupy, cherry-flavored booze and doxylamine and passed out. She didn't wake up until three o'clock the next afternoon. She had two missed calls from Marty, both with simple voicemails: "Gretchen, give me a call." "Gretchen, Marty again. Call if you can." But she didn't. She stayed in bed and watched *Law & Order* and ordered the greasiest Chinese food in the Village.

And Monday morning, Marty collapsed.

Again she racked her brain about their last conversation. He was concerned about her, had that look of wanting to do more. He was eating that gyro and was covered in tzatziki sauce. She complained about the bird story. He defended his stacks of letters and declared Felix incompetent, which Gretchen had known from the start. He hinted that he was working on something, that she could get a contributor's note. What else? They joked, of course, about his mess, about the Bird Lady. He told her to call Cyrus, one of the many New Yorkers with whom Marty was enamored.

Then why hadn't she remembered it until now? What had he said?

Call Cyrus for a quote. For local color.

Cyrus was Old Brooklyn. Owned some kind of shop that had been open for ages. He was practically an institution in Coney. What was his last name? She scanned through her computer documents and found the folder marked SANDY from their coverage of the hurricane in 2012. Cyrus Amos. He worked with the city to coordinate cleanup after the storm. He had broken down doors where people were trapped standing on their kitchen tables and beds while flood water lapped at their toes. He owned the True Value on Stillwell Avenue.

She closed the document. What was she doing? None of this made any sense, and anyway, she should be working on Marty's obituary, not reading through years-old *Crier* stories.

But she pulled up Quinn's website again. He was predictable on most of the issues: for loosening restrictions on background checks for firearms, changing zoning to open up residential property to small businesses, revising state Medicaid. Against police body cameras. He was on the city's anti-terrorism task force. He voted red on most of the bills—but blue on one to increase the budget on state parks. It would allow for part-time lifeguards. Why would he go against the party on that one? She found the answer soon enough.

Quinn had a child who'd drowned in New Jersey several years ago. Alexander.

Such a studious name.

Not at all what she would have imagined that the beauty queen would name a child. She pulled up her Miss New York picture and remembered her at the parade, dressed in red, white, and green—like the Italian flag—waving on that gondola-shaped float. She'd had the same strained smile as in the picture, like part of her was clawing to get out from behind it.

How many marriages lasted after a thing like that? What else did she not know about Vita Quinn?

But the question was not what she didn't know about Vita Quinn but what she didn't know about Vita Pozi. Vita Quinn was the woman on the float who was "passionate about fitness and healthy living." Vita Pozi was the woman who had one of her goons push Gretchen into a Benz.

Gretchen thought back to Friday morning and the kid. He had been so adamant that she listen to him. But it was all somewhat of a blur. She had been on the phone with Roberta. She had chased the seagull. The kid had said something: *Clever way to get down here, I gotta admit.* Had Jaime been talking to Marty?

Was there anything else she was missing from that Friday? Anything Marty said? She checked her email and texts, but nothing. She opened up her calendar.

It was after four in the morning. Yesterday had been Nico's birthday.

TWELVE

Maurice Pershing's phone vibrated on his nightstand, and he smashed a pillow over his head until it stopped. Not thirty seconds passed before it started up again. When would Jalissa take the hint? They were done. She knew it. But her late-night-early-morning drunk-dials persisted.

On the third call, he switched on his lamp, picked up the phone, and squinted at the caller ID. The only thing worse than his ex calling late at night was this.

"Mr. Quinn?"

"Maurice. I hope I'm not waking you."

"It's three-thirty in the morning."

"And I hate to wake you. Really, I do. But I need a favor that requires some urgency, unfortunately."

As he brushed his teeth and washed his face, he thought about Dana's comment on the way to the Algonquin.

If he would navigate the city with a modicum of intelligence . . .

As if Maurice were not listening, and as if using the word *modicum* made Dana smarter. Superior. He dried his face and looked hard in the mirror.

When you gonna do something else?

He shaved, taking his time, dressed in the shirt he had just picked up from the cleaners, tied his tie. "You really don't gotta get all dolled up just for me," Vita would always say. But it wouldn't be *her* on the receiving end of Dana's insidious comments. Maurice made his bed, ran a brush over his head, an act more of ritual than practicality. When he put the brush back in a drawer, he caught a glimmer of something. A small vial of perfume hid beneath the tangled cord of his clippers. He brought it to his nose, and the spicy mix of jasmine and clove smelled like Jalissa, all right. She'd probably left it there on purpose. He put it in the shopping bag that hung on the bedroom doorknob with the rest of her things.

At least he'd found a spot on his block to park his Honda Civic. He put on Sade and set off. He pushed his visor up and caught a glimpse of the photograph he'd slipped into the elastic: his mother on the day of her retirement, her lavender blazer adorned with a corsage, her smile broad. He'd been able to send her and her best and oldest friend on a cruise along the coast of Mexico and to the islands. *The time of my life*, she'd told him when she returned, her skin glowing from the sun, the bags under her eyes finally diminished. Pancreatic cancer came out of nowhere, and a year later, they buried her out in Jersey.

He never minded being a mama's boy. When he'd lost his title and landed in the hospital for two weeks, she begged him to quit racing. She didn't have to ask twice. Maurice Pershing, the three-year Grand Prix champion and first Black driver to win in twenty-four years, traded in his hotrod for a Honda and started fixing cars. That's how the Pozis had found him.

On the phone, Dana had told him to double park and come around the back of the house—he'd leave the alley gate unlocked. The man rubbed his hands together as Maurice came in. He was wearing his preppy pajamas and bathrobe embroidered with his initials. He probably embroidered his initials on his underwear, too.

"Thanks for doing this, man," Dana said, embracing Maurice in some kind of half-hug, half-dap handshake. As if they were coconspirators in a game from which they'd both benefit. "My brother-in-law isn't right in the head—you know that. He's gotten himself into some trouble, like I told you, and I can't afford this bullshit so close to the election. I'm sure you can understand that." His breath smelled like sour milk.

"Sure, Mr. Quinn," Maurice said. "Sure I can." But he yawned in protest.

"Can I get you a cup of coffee at least?"

"I don't touch the stuff. Just tell me what I need to know."

"I'd go myself if it were appropriate. Just go down to the precinct and ask for Officer Martin. Martin. He's the one. And this is important." He reached to the counter and picked up a handbag, a light leather Gucci with a thin strap. "Martin will take you back, and when you're alone—only when you're alone—you give him this."

"Hold up." Maurice took a step back. "You didn't say anything on the phone about bribing a cop."

"It's not a bribe so much as it's a favor. You're just doing me a favor so Martin can do me another favor, that's all."

"Uh-huh. Sounds like a bribe, and to be honest, Dana"—he called him Dana now—"I'm not comfortable with making this transaction." He turned to go, thinking already of calling his uncle and begging for a door job at the nightclub in Jersey City. He hated Jersey City.

"My opponent is an ex-cop. Do you have any idea how fast this could ruin me? Besides, it's for Vita just as much as it's for me."

He stopped. Vita's flaws were many, but she had been good to him. Insisting on his hire, insisting on health insurance for him and his mother—a good policy that helped her die with dignity—insisting on raises and overtime, being semi-decent all the while.

"I'll never ask you for a thing like this again. This is a totally unique circumstance, and that's why I'll add a grand to your next check."

Maurice sized him up: his silk robe and his haircut probably cost just as much. "Two. Two grand."

Dana nodded. "Two grand," and stuck out his hand. Maurice took the purse and left.

THIRTEEN
Author's Note

We were friends first, college kids. She had things to do. She'd rattle off lists as we walked through Washington Square Park. "I have to get over to Tisch to meet with so-and-so about that fucking term paper; I have to call so-and-so and pry a statement from him; I have to study for Econ, proof the paper, storyboard my documentary, call my mother back, and I have to do it all by nine o'clock!" I—jogging to keep up with her long, striding gait, my arms full of her textbooks and the lunch I brought for us to share—nodded with each item on the list, praying she'd look over at me and pause, ask, "Are you free tonight, Raajen?" and set my heart alight.

But more often, we'd sit on the fountain wall. I'd let her eat most of the lunch, she'd read her newspapers, and I'd watch the world turn, waiting.

I cherished times she was sick and allowed me to care for her. When she'd be knocked out with a migraine, I'd fetch her prescriptions and make her tea. I'd microwave the rice sack and lay it gently across her eyes. I'd pet her head and savor the luxury of caring for her.

Her migraines began in adolescence with her period and over time increased in regularity. Sometimes they started with the aura, a small hole of light that grew and crowded out people and objects and danced around her vision, squiggly lines radiating from its center, a tingling in her arm. Then it advanced like knives attacking her eyes, like lead balls pushing outwards, like a scream that couldn't get out.

At seventeen she went in for an MRI. She brought her brain scan home and proudly displayed it in the kitchen on a disassembled Lite Brite. She pointed to an umbrella-shaped tangle of veins and declared, "I have a Venus anomaly!"

"Hmm." Nicky said. "Spell it."

"V-E-N-U-S. Venus. A-N–"

"Venus?"

"As in the second planet from the sun. Ever heard of it?"

He burst out laughing.

Her eyes narrowed and her cheeks reddened. "What's so funny?"

He fetched a pre-med textbook he had pilfered from a neighborhood college dropout, flipped the pages in the glossary, and turned it to face his sister.

"V-E-N-O-U-S, like veins. But they don't usually cause headaches. Look, it says right here, they're congenital—that means you were born with it—and almost always symptomless."

She snatched the heavy textbook and studied the definition. Then she dropped it on her brother's foot.

Even back then, Gretchen Sparks was stubborn. And she hated being wrong. And more than anything, she hated being laughed at. She stewed for days, studying the picture of her brain, tracing the Medusa head of veins with her finger. She raced home from school to complete her homework before a possible headache knocked her out. One night, she lay in the dark, a hot bag of rice over her eyes, and heard the tap of a pebble against her window.

"Not now." Another tap.

She inched the rice bag up and saw the flashing lights.

H-E-L-L-O, V-E-N-U-S

Still smarting from the slight, she ignored it.

A-N-O-M-A-L-Y.

An anomaly. An aberration.

  Gretchen. One that is abnormal or rare. Venus. The Roman goddess of love.

  Gretchen, born of seafoam with a tangle of veins in her skull.

FOURTEEN

Marriages end. Even the most ardent Catholic nonnas might forgive a husband and wife their separation after the death of a child.

Not Vita Quinn. The day after the funeral—amid the many casseroles and lasagnas and cold-cut platters brought to the house, her eyes so puffy from crying that she could hardly see— Vita decided she'd do what she always did on Saturday mornings. She would go grocery shopping. No matter that they had enough food to last a month. She put on a white romper that showed off her long legs and torso, slipped into a pair of platform sandals, wrapped a silk scarf around her head, and donned her biggest pair of Jackie O sunglasses. The July day was already sticky hot, and she blasted the car's air conditioner.

The bright lights of the Shop Rite floored her at first. It had been a week of dim lamps, of church candles, of the curtains drawn in her bedroom. Everything had been muted since that day at the beach. But now the glare of fluorescents on the tile floor, the creaking of the shopping carts, the many options from which she was supposed to choose were a funhouse, and she reeled from it, dizzy and amazed.

At the deli counter, she spied the mountain of oranges at the head of the produce section. When the guy asked her how thick she'd like the salami sliced, she could see his lips moving but could only hear the surrounding sounds: snatches of conversation, phones ringing, a paging over the loudspeaker.

There would be no more soccer games, no more cutting up oranges for the team of eight-year-olds to suck down at half time.

The deli guy spoke again, louder, but she heard only the screeching of gulls on the beach. She backed away into her cart and scampered to the restroom. Not enough air in the world to fill her lungs.

When she entered the house empty-handed, the smell of flowers made her gag. They had been coming since Tuesday: roses and lavender, hydrangeas and lilies, snap dragons and violets and baby's breath—the last of which just seemed cruel.

She gathered them in two trash bags and hauled them out to the curb. Then she made her way upstairs to wake Dana. The two drove to the cemetery in silence, parked the car, and trekked up the big hill to their son's grave.

Sitting on the top of the hill, she felt miles apart from her husband. They had barely spoken in days, moving through the house like sleepwalkers and putting on brave but somber faces when forced to meet the world.

"They say," Dana had said, his voice cracking, "most marriages don't make it after something like this."

"Don't even think about it." She took his hand. "For better or for worse, Dana. That's what we said. Remember?

He had smiled weakly and looked up at the trees.

Vita made two pledges that day.

She would never have another child. She would make her marriage work.

She thought of that day Monday morning as she waited on her front stoop watching leaves fall from the trees. Her hair had dried wavy the night before when she showered and crashed into the guest-room bed. It whipped her face in the wind. She had the BINGO game at the senior center at ten-thirty, leaving just enough time to check in on Dominica Padilla.

Maurice rolled down his window when he pulled up to the curb. His eyes looked red-rimmed, haunted.

"Late night?" she said. He put on his sunglasses. The chauffer was a short man, muscular and broad shouldered. He had a plain but pleasant face. A quiet man. If anything, Maurice was reliable.

"I can't drive you today."

"What are you talking about? Is this Dana? We've talked about this. You're my guy on Mondays, Wednesdays, and Fridays." She slid her phone from her purse.

Maurice glanced at the side mirror. "Look, I'm not sure you should go anywhere today."

"What has gotten into you?" She came around to the passenger side.

As soon as she closed the door, she could feel someone else was with them. Maurice rolled up his window and ran his hand over his head. He still had his sunglasses on. He had a dark bruise on his right cheek.

The warmth went out of Vita's hands, but she felt behind her for the partition's window all the same. She didn't know how, but since she was a teenager, she always knew when Julian was present.

"Hello, sister," he said. She closed the window.

"What the fuck is Julian doing in my car?"

"You're gonna have to ask him that."

She took a deep breath and turned in her seat to open the window again. Julian Pozi played with a zippo; his long white fingers opened it, snapped it shut, opened it, snapped it shut. He looked worse than ever, his pallor practically gray, his cheeks sunken in, his lips chapped and red. His eyes, close together and small, fell into the shadows under his brow. He grinned.

"What are you doing here?" She winced at her scolding tone.

"Just wanted to say hello to my big sister first thing on a Monday morning," he said, his voice cold but bright, like a snowstorm. He had none of Brooklyn in his voice. He was an alien—even to her.

"You need a ride somewhere?"

"Nowhere in particular."

"Just hanging out with Maurice then?"

"Tagging along with the popular kids."

She shut the window. Maurice shook his head and put on the radio, turning up the volume in the backseat.

"Did you want me to drive you somewhere?" He checked his mirrors.

Vita's hands snatched at her hair. "I am not fucking around, Maurice. What is going on?"

"I don't want to be involved. And I need the afternoon off."

"You can't roll up with my troubled little brother in the backseat and not explain anything."

"How 'bout we just drive around the block?" Maurice said.

"Fine," she said.

He pulled out onto Bay Ridge Avenue. "Dana told me not say anything."

"But?"

"But I've been up half the night and might just leave the both of you on the sidewalk and go on home." He sighed. "He called me around three in the morning. He had gotten a call from the precinct. They had your boy back there locked up."

Vita felt ice water in her stomach, but she said, "Julian is harmless."

"They said he'd been freaking some girls out at the club, hanging around past his welcome."

"Oh come on!"

"The club got three separate complaints about him this weekend."

"He's bad with social cues. All they have to do is tell him to get lost and he's no problem, but these girls, they feel empowered to lead a guy on." She shook her head.

"Lotta girls gone missing lately."

"If you think for a minute I'll let you talk about my family that way—"

"Forget it. I'll drop you at home."

She opened her mouth to protest but then shut it.

He turned toward her and took off his glasses. A dark bruise circled his left eye. "Dana wanted me to go get him. I said it wasn't my job. He said he'd make it worth my while and wouldn't let up, so like a fool, I get up and drive down here. Dana hands me a pocketbook and tells me to go to the precinct."

She brought her hand to her mouth. "You're kidding."

He shook his head.

"He bribed the police?"

"Two-thousand dollars."

"Jesus Christ. He's more worried about the race than he lets on."

"Yeah, he is."

"So where'd you get the shiner?"

"Oh, you mean the South Brooklyn Kiss?" He laughed. "One officer wasn't pleased about releasing your brother into my care and not seeing any of the profit."

"So he socked you?"

Maurice just sighed.

"Why haven't you dropped him off?"

"Dana told me to drive him around till I heard otherwise."

"Well you just heard otherwise." Vita opened the window. "Why are you getting yourself into trouble, Julian? What did Ma make you promise?"

"'Stay outta trouble, Jules baby,'" he said, imitating their ma in her last days, her breath ragged and voice barely audible. Then he faked a coughing spell and snapped the lighter shut.

"You know you got a lot of nerve sitting back there like you own the place after the crap you pulled."

"We wouldn't want anyone to find out, would we, Vita darling? Not in an election year!"

"We're taking you home."

"Say, Vita." He affected a Southern accent. "You wouldn't know any Southern gentlemen 'round these parts?"

"What?"

"Someone I might-could speak with about your husband's pursuits?"

"We're taking you home."

"I'd be obliged," her brother said, still Southern, "if you'd deposit me outside the nearest subway station."

By the time they got to Coney Island, it was nine-thirty. "Just thirty minutes," she had promised. "Then you go home, get some rest." The block, usually sleepy, showed signs of life. A few kids rode bikes up and down the street; a couple raked leaves in their tiny yard.

"It's Columbus Day," Maurice reminded her, parking in front of a hydrant.

"Right . . ." she said.

"There's something else you should know."

"Jesus," she said. "What else?"

"Your husband asked me if I had taken you down here."

"And you said . . . ?"

"I said no. But after today, I'm done with all this. I'll need to be looking for something else if all this craziness keeps up." He shut off the car, got out, and crawled into the back seat to sleep. A moment later, he opened the partition window.

"What now?" Vita said.

He handed her a sheet of paper folded in threes. "Looks like your brother left you something."

She slid it onto the dashboard and adjusted the front seat to give Maurice more room.

For a while, the duplex showed no sign of life, and Vita, for all her determined effort to get out there first thing, felt mounting uncertainty. She had come planning to confront her, to get to the bottom of things. Dana had already been gone when she woke up, and she half expected him to come darting out of the duplex, shirt untucked and face unshaven. Morning sex had been off the table since they'd lost their son.

Her knuckles rapped on the steering wheel. Could she really be sure this was the woman? Because surely, there was a woman. She had never snooped before. But the hushed phone calls and "late nights at the office"—when she knew damn well he wasn't there—

coupled with his renewed animosity toward her, propelled her to casually open his planner when she'd written Maurice a check.

Finally, the screen door opened. The kid came out. Always the kid. Coming and going. He was lanky, all elbows, reminded Vita of Julian when he was much younger, before he got all mixed up. He held a skateboard and jogged to the street. He looked down the block both ways—not a quick take for cars, but a long look in both directions. Vita slid down in her seat till she couldn't see. She heard him skate past, saw a couple drops of rain hit the windshield.

Julian. That's why she felt out of sorts. She would have to visit him more once she got all this sorted out. Then perhaps their encounters would feel more . . . normal? Nothing normal about Julian.

It was her fault, after all. In the past, she'd made time for him, despite Dana's protestations. Julian was a doting uncle in his own way. He treated Alexander like a little adult, never babying him, never patronizing him. And despite his uncle's awkwardness, Alexander adored him.

But Julian was bad for the campaign, bad for politics, so when Dana told Vita about his desire to run for office, she balked. Vita had kept Julian safe as a secret during her and Dana's courtship—not because she was ashamed of him, but because he was delicate. And even after, she didn't tell Dana his whole story. Dana wasn't from the neighborhood. He wouldn't have heard the stories about the girl who'd gone missing and was never found.

She told him everything, of course, when he'd decided to run. It was their first big blowout. The next day, two advisers set about planning how she'd improve her image, get her into the district's consciousness not as the sister of an alleged criminal but as the former beauty queen they once loved. And that meant a gradual but relentless separation from Julian.

Clouds gathered overhead, and a man sagged past the house. Clothes rumpled, jacket splattered with mud, he wore a yellow baseball cap and held a forty in a paper bag.

Such a shame.

The gate creaked when she opened it. A tall bush separated the two cramped porches.

The aluminum siding was gray and worn, and the red awnings above the doors were faded. The Padilla's side had a little bench next to the door that was chained to the railing, and a length of red wooden beads hung behind the screen. Vita stood there, unsure what to do next. She hadn't planned to get out of the car. She hadn't planned for Dana to step out on her. But, since she'd first read the name and address on a Post-it note tucked into the page for time zones in Dana's planner, every moment had led to this one. She raised her finger to the bell.

A screen door slammed. "Who're you looking for?"

Vita jumped.

"Over here," the same croaky voice said. She looked around, her hand over her heart. The bush between the front doors shook. A woman's pink face appeared through the branches.

"Who're you looking for?" she said again.

Vita backed away from the door, down the porch step. The lady on the other side of the bush wore a ratty brown robe, and a bunch of foam curlers flopped atop her head. She was barefoot, her ankles swollen and veiny. She puffed a cigarette.

"Nobody." Vita backed away toward the gate, light drops of rain falling now.

"Nobody?" the woman repeated. "Nobody's looking for nobody." She set the cigarette down in an ashtray that balanced on the railing and picked up a phone. Vita tried not to scowl at her. She was exactly the kind of woman Vita hated. Ugly, useless, stupid. Never did anything good for herself when she was young and now was too old to be of any use to anyone else.

"If you wanna talk to the Mexicans, you'll have to come back," the lady said, poking at the phone with her stubby fingers. She lifted it up in front of her. For a moment, Vita thought she was just farsighted, trying to bring something on the phone into focus. "Say hello to Leonard."

"Leonard?"

A bird shrieked.

She jumped again, this time tripping on a root protruding from the sad little yard. As she wrested herself up, a seagull landed right on the lady's porch railing.

Then the lady laughed. "Say cheese! Show us that beauty queen wave, Mrs. Quinn. I can see the headline already. Senator's Wife Stalks Coney Island Resident! Read it in *Metro* tomorrow morning!"

Vita bolted to the car, opened the back door, and shook Maurice by the knee. "We gotta go!" The rain started.

The lady laughed and shouted something to someone inside. Vita tore around to the front of the car, got inside, and slid down the seat. Her mouth was dry. Her head spun.

Maurice got in the driver's seat, yawning. "What happened?" He rubbed his head. "You look like—what are you doing down there?"

"Just drive, please!"

He turned on the car and signaled his intentions.

"Hurry!"

"She's taking pictures of the car."

"I know!"

They made it to the stop sign. "I think you can get up now," Maurice said.

She shook her head. "Wait. We have to go back. We have to get those pictures."

"Lady, you must be crazy."

"But—"

"I'm dropping you off and going home to sleep."

Almost absently, she took the folded piece of paper off the dashboard and opened it. She gasped.

"What? Your little brother left you a love note?"

Vita thrust the paper at him.

An enlarged photocopy of Gretchen's driver's license showed her glaring at the camera, glasses off, hair shaggy and unbrushed.

"That's that girl you tried to kidnap the other night?"

"The reporter. And it wasn't kidnapping!"

"I don't know what kind of shit you've gotten yourself into, Vita, and know what? I don't even wanna know."

"Just bring me to the senior center and take the rest of the day."

"You're the boss."

FIFTEEN

Cyrus Amos flipped the OPEN sign over.

"Mr. Amos?" Gretchen held a to-go cup of coffee in one hand, her notebook in another. She had been waiting for thirty minutes already.

Cyrus Amos had a spray of freckles across his cheekbones and nose that made him look younger than his sixty-seven years. Reddish hair crept out of a worn leather flat cap. As he unlocked the door to his shop, he turned toward Gretchen, raised his eyebrows, and smiled. "Yes, I'm Mr. Amos."

"I'm Gretchen Sparks. With *The Metropolitan*? Marty Mitnik's reporter. I spoke to you during Sandy for the *Crier*?"

He opened the door, stepped in halfway, and pressed the buttons on the alarm system. Then he peered out at Gretchen. His smile faded. "How can I help you, Miss Sparks?"

"I wanted to speak with you." She looked around. A few people waited for the bus close by. Some cars sat idling at the light. "Can we go inside?"

Cyrus Amos nodded and stepped away, holding the door. "After you."

Sunlight filtered in through the sale signs on the windows. Cyrus led Gretchen back through an aisle filled with hardware. Even in the dim light, she could tell the store was exceptionally neat, each bolt and nut sorted, each shelf dusted and occupied.

He unlocked a door off to the side of the aisle and switched on a light. It was a clean room with a sink, a refrigerator, and a big table with a blue-and-white checkered tablecloth. It was about the size of Gretchen's apartment. Cyrus went over to the counter and filled the coffee pot with water. He didn't tell Gretchen to take a seat, so she stayed standing. As he busied himself with the coffee, she examined the snapshots that formed a collage on the wall: people embracing, posing, smiling on the beach, the board-walk, in the hardware store, at the Mermaid Parade. One even outside the Leaning Tower of Pisa.

"Do you take cream and sugar?" Cyrus finally said.

"Yes. I mean both."

"Splenda? Sweet'N Low?"

"Sugar is fine."

He got a little sugar bowl out of the cabinet and a carton of half-and-half from the fridge. "Please," he said, bringing them to the table. "Make yourself comfortable." The coffee started to perk.

"That's just my employees, their families." He gestured at the photos. "We're one big family here." He sat and folded his hands on the table. The light coming through the break room window made a stripe across the table, and it extended right up onto Cy-rus's face. He wasn't smiling, and Gretchen felt like she was in-truding. She hadn't done a proper interview in ages, not one that required any finesse anyway. She glanced at her notes, at the wall again, noting some people who populated many photographs: a thin, tall boy with a light brown complexion and sleepy eyes, from adolescence to graduation from college; a woman with freckles and reddish hair, often in braids, getting married, hold-ing a baby in the hospital, smiling in hospital scrubs.

"How lovely," she said. "Looks like these two just about grow up on this wall. Are they your kids?"

"Sure are," he said. "Those are my babies." He chuckled. "Well, not babies anymore. They've got babies of their own."

"I hope I'm not breaking the news to you that Marty is in the hospital."

"No, sadly. I've heard."

"Really?" she hadn't expected this. "Who told you?"

"Marty and I, we're old friends. Roberta called midweek. Any news?"

"Nothing new, I'm afraid." She pushed her glasses up her nose with her knuckle, a rare self-conscious gesture. "Marty had asked me, before the . . . incident . . . to get in touch with you about a quote."

He nodded.

"There's a woman in the neighborhood, a Darlene Dabrowski. She says she has a seagull who is intervening in some crimes."

A smile spread across Cyrus's face. Not the calm, obligatory smile of just seconds ago. A smile that spread from his lips to his eyes. His entire face changed. She realized that he had a gap in his front teeth and his eyes were almost gold. He chuckled. It started small but seemed to fuel itself because soon he was holding his belly and rocking his head back. Here, she understood why Marty loved him.

He wiped a tear from his eye and sighed. "That Marty is one to watch." He stood and went to the counter, opened a cabinet, and retrieved two mugs. "So you're telling me you came all the way out here to ask my opinion about some gossip? Why not just call?"

Gretchen fixed her coffee. It smelled about five hundred times better than the brown water she had gotten across the street. But she felt a sense of dread. She had a feeling that Cyrus Amos did not like being played the fool. This was it. She had Marty's source right in front of her. Why did she feel like she was about to blow it?

"I know we reporters are only as good as our sources, Mr. Amos—"

"Call me Cyrus, Miss Sparks." He sipped his coffee.

"Then I'll ask you to call me Gretchen."

He nodded. "Gretchen it is."

"I heard you may have spent some time with Marty the day before his heart attack."

Cyrus's eyes caught the light, and flecks of gold appeared again. "I did."

"Were you aware that he had a line on a story?"

"Marty's got lines all across the five boroughs and halfway through Jersey."

"But something new. Something he was keeping quiet."

"I can't say."

Gretchen paused.

He said, "I understand you have been with Marty for some years."

"Twelve years," she said, surprised by how quickly she summoned the fact.

"And I'm sure he trusted you very much."

"He does. Mr. Amos—"

"Now, Gretchen."

"Cyrus. Sorry. If you don't mind my asking. What did you talk about that morning at Cowboy's?" The refrigerator clicked on and began to hum. "I'm just trying to piece together something he mentioned to me just before he—"

Cyrus stood up, looking taller than ever. "We just caught up that morning. Nothing to say about it. Now if you don't mind, it's time for me to open up the store."

"Did he say anything to you about a lead or a source? Did he mention anything about something maybe happening around here?"

"Around here?" He knit his brows.

"Well, yeah, in Coney Island." She tapped her pen on the table.

"There's nothing happening around here. If you'll be so kind—"

"Anything about a woman named Dominica Padilla?"

"Never heard of her."

Gretchen stood. "Cyrus, I'm gonna be frank with you. I think Marty sent me to see about the seagull as a ruse—to set the groundwork for a big investigation. I think he had been down there talking to a neighbor boy about some kind of a wrongful death suit. And I think a state senator is involved."

"And I said I don't know nothing about it."

"It's in the public interest to know if there's something going on in that hospital. It's in your community's interest."

Cyrus turned, his eyes flat now. "You don't know nothing about my community."

"Marty would want you to tell me."

"There is nothing to tell." He picked up his coffee cup, turned, and walked away.

Gretchen brought her own cup to the sink. She washed it out and put it on the rack to dry. Then she left a business card on the refrigerator under a magnet that said in bubble letters LIFE IS GOOD! Outside the break room, the shop was still dim, and Cyrus was nowhere in sight.

When she made her way outside, the sky was dark and it had begun to rain, not heavily, but enough. She had blown it the moment she stepped foot in the store, and she knew it. Marty was their common ground. Breaking the ice with an anecdote would have been easy. And Cyrus was right. He's in the phone book. She should have called. It had been too long and she was too rusty. She shook a cigarette out of her pack, lit it against the brick of a building.

But why would he have contacted Marty in the first place? He didn't seem like the socially conscious type, nor did he appear to be affiliated with the hospital or Dana Quinn. He's not even in Quinn's district and is unlikely to be a Republican. Her early-morning certainty that he was the source faded away.

She had two options. She could run down the boy, Jaime, for more information and try to talk to the mother. She could probably shake an extra hour free before making it back to *Metro* to check the databases and make a dozen inquiries with Medicare, accreditation agencies, and the department of health, and spend hours looking into civil lawsuits . . . and for what?

What was she looking for? Why should she care? A million injustices in the world. What was one more?

Her second option: she could go back to Manhattan and proofread Zaiden the intern's listicle about Bronx Zoo babies born since 2000, maybe stop on the way for a cup of tea, maybe put a little whiskey in the tea.

She turned toward the subway steps. Her phone rang.

"I got something you might find . . . interesting," someone said, her voice like a wisp of smoke coming out of a tar pit.

"Who is this?"

"I've been waiting to hear from you . . . Gretchen Sparks."

"I'm going to hang up now—"

"You media people are only interested in the rich and famous. Never the average Joe Schmo. It's Darlene Dabrowski. And I have something very special for you."

Gretchen looked at her watch. Every time she tried to break free from this nonsense, something happened.

She thought about the whiskey in the tea, about Marty up at the hospital. She took a drag of her cigarette and let out a moan.

"Hello? Gretchen Sparks?"

"I'll be there in ten minutes." She hung up.

Dabrowski was waiting on her porch, the rain pooling in her yard. She wore a roomy pair of black slacks that tapered at the ankles and a voluminous pink blouse with tiny Eiffel Towers scattered like seeds on a watermelon.

Gretchen jogged to the house, but Dabrowski blocked her way onto the porch. "You got a lot of nerve," Dabrowski said from under the awning.

"What is it you have?" Gretchen yelled over the rain. "Can I come in?"

Dabrowski flashed a toothy smile. Then she turned and went inside. Gretchen followed.

The house had the same Febreze-and-cigarettes odor as before, but it appeared empty, at least downstairs. There was no Mr.

Dabrowski—or whomever—with the set turned up. Dabrowski sat down in an orange easy chair and folded her hands. She had painted her fingernails since Gretchen last saw her. They were the same turquoise as her eye shadow.

"Why did you call me?" Gretchen said.

The woman rubbed her palms together.

"You said on the phone you have something for me? Is it about Leonard?"

She sat there, smiling.

"Mrs. Dabrowski, have I done something to upset you?"

The woman laughed. "You media people."

Gretchen knew full well that they were adding the bird story to her clips of fluff pieces on local weirdos, but she sensed that Dabrowski was in a bargaining mood. "I apologize for coming all the way out here Friday without more knowledge of the story. But we couldn't corroborate it."

"Couldn't corroborate it," Dabrowski repeated, nodding her head. "Is that why you chased him, Leonard, down the block?"

"Listen," she said. "I thought it was a nice story, and for all I know"—she shrugged her shoulders—"it could be one hundred percent true. But it's like I said. If the sources don't check out—"

Dabrowski felt in her pocket for something. "What if I made it worth your while to believe me?"

Gretchen almost laughed. Here she was, in this shitty duplex with this lonely woman who was now trying to bribe her with what little money she had to print an asinine story about her imaginary friend, all while Gretchen's mentor hung on to life miles away. But it wasn't Dabrowski she felt sorry for. It was herself.

"Please don't do that."

"Don't do what?" she lifted her hand from her pocket. She was holding an outdated smartphone, the screen cracked.

SIXTEEN
Author's Note

I puzzled for quite some time over what Gretchen was thinking when she walked out of Dabrowski's house. Maybe it was the old lady's longing to be plucked from the annals of obscurity and elevated, for one day, in four hundred words, to the realm of the known, the noticed, the important.

Back at NYU, during one of those noontime lunches in the park, I had told Gretchen of my minor crisis. My parents had issued me an ultimatum: I could change my major from poetry to something that would make me employable, or I could transfer to a state school. My parents are immigrants, and the myth of upward mobility burns bright in their hearts. I asked Gretchen, "Why journalism?"

She looked at me as if stunned. "Why journalism?" she said, lowering her sandwich. "Because I am curious. Because I care about how the world works and whom it works for. Because I have a responsibility, Raj, to bring it to light. Why journalism?" She gave a thin laugh. "Because it's the only institution protected by name in the Constitution. That's why." And she went back to reading her paper.

Though she wouldn't admit to it, that flame never died, not with Dominic's death, not with Borough Features, not with the drinking. Never. I think that's why she walked out of Dabrowski's house and knocked on the Padillas' door, though Gretchen never said so.

SEVENTEEN

"**H**ey, kid."

Jaime held a skateboard, as if he was just about to go out. He smiled, showing two dimples. "You're back."

"Is your mother home?"

"She's at work. And she wouldn't talk to you anyway."

"Why is that?"

"She doesn't speak English."

"You said your mother argued with the doctor. Did the doctor speak Spanish, too?"

Jaime smiled again. "You got me."

"I just have a couple questions. Then I'll get out of your hair."

The apartment was a mirror of Dabrowski's, but it could have existed in another time zone. The tile floor was scrubbed clean to the point of shining. A modest couch sat against the wall, a cushioned folding chair next to it. A TV/DVD set sat on a stack of hard-shell suitcases. On an end table, a bright yellow coffee can held cut flowers. Sunlight flooded the room from the window, the shade drawn up.

This time, she would attempt to connect. She began with a softball. "What was your grandmother like?"

"Just like any grandma, I guess."

"Was she from here?"

"Nah. She came up from Puerto Rico before I was born." He rolled the skateboard back and forth with one foot. "She got all the documents in order. She didn't know anybody but had some friends write to some friends from the island and got a place to live with them, a job at a factory. She did it all for my mom, who was just a baby."

"It must have been devastating to lose her."

He let the skateboard go, and it rolled gently down the hallway. He gestured to a framed, black-and-white photograph. A young woman—pretty—with big, penetrating eyes crouched on a dirt road, her hands on the waist of a little girl who was just barely standing up. "That's the two of them before they came to New York."

"The doctor who argued with your mom—what was his name?"

"I don't know. White guy. Not fat and not thin."

"That narrows it down." Gretchen scratched the description down in her pad. "Was there anyone else who talked to you?"

"Yeah. The nurse. But she couldn't do anything either."

"Did you get her name?"

"She barely said anything to us. It was the morning after we admitted her, and security had just hustled us out. It was so hot I could see the air moving over the pavement, you know? Like waving? Mom was crying. Then this nurse comes out the doors with this concerned look on her face. She asks if we're Dominica's family. She asks if we knew what part of the hospital grandma was in. We said no. Then she asks for Mom's number. She has her write it down on a little pad of paper."

Gretchen was quiet, listening and writing. "What'd she look like?"

"Black lady, pretty young . . . oh, and glasses. Like those nerdy kind of glasses that are in style now?"

"Thick frames?"

"Yeah."

"Did she call?"

"Nah. Mom thought about going to find her, but then those men started coming by."

"What men?"

Jaime scratched a pimple on his cheek. "I shouldn't say any more about that."

"What men?"

He sighed. "A couple men came by not long after Grandma died. I wasn't here. They scared her."

"What did they say?"

"They tried to give her money to stop calling the hospital—what do they call it on *CSI?*"

"Hush money?"

"Exactly! They offered her a couple grand. Mom slammed the door in their faces. *Gringos* was all she said. She's not too descriptive, but she was scared shitless. Then they came back. And then the calls started from bill collectors."

"Anything else you can tell me about the nurse?"

"Tall, average weight. I think she had a weave or long hair or whatever. And freckles."

"Freckles?"

"Yeah."

"Black woman with freckles."

"Yeah. It happens."

"I'm gonna ask you something. I want you to think hard about it. Have you ever heard of a woman named Vita Pozi or Vita Quinn?"

Jaime squinted his eyes again. He shook his head slowly.

"How about Dana Quinn?"

"No," he said. "Do these people work at the hospital?"

"Did anybody else from a newspaper come by here to talk to your mother? Any other reporters?"

"Well yeah, of course. Isn't that why you came in the first place?"

She tried to hide her disbelief. Who was it? Gunderson? Stewart? And then she remembered something Marty had said: *I need to work with someone I can trust to do the things I can't do.*

"White guy, older than you." A smile cracked across Jaime's face. "He had these pointy eyebrows, like Dracula."

"When did he come here, Jaime?"

He thought back. "A month ago?" He rubbed the back of his neck.

She pulled up the calendar on her phone.

"I answered the door. Mom was scared but let him in. I still can't figure out why. She's been shaken up ever since all this happened. But she made him coffee."

"What did he ask you?"

"Same questions you're asking me, which is another thing I can't figure out. Don't you reporters talk to each other? You've been looking at me like you never heard a word of this in your life. And Friday you pretended you hadn't wanted to hear a thing either."

"It's how we corroborate sources." It wasn't a lie, but it wasn't true either.

"So you gonna write about it or not?"

"Do you have any hospital records about her stay?"

"Just bills. They've been coming for months."

"Can I see them?"

Jaime shrugged. "Sure. It's all back in the kitchen." They passed an end table with a tall votive candle burning—the kind Gretchen would buy at the bodega for when the power goes out—and a statue of the Virgin Mary, some prayer cards, a small paperback Bible. A crucifix was affixed to the wall. The kitchen was bright and clean. A round red wooden table sat in the corner with four chairs pushed in. Chili peppers were strung between the cabinets above the sink, the lemons on the wallpaper were plump and ripe, and a big clock showed the time: twelve-thirty.

Jaime sorted through mail on the counter. "Check it out. Bills and bills and bills. All for the same shit. She calls Medicare every week to figure it out, and they just say, 'If that's what the doctor billed, that's what you have to pay.'" He cringed. "She should have taken the money to pay all this."

Gretchen snapped some photos of the statements. Just glancing, she saw the Padillas owed close to $30,000.

"Is there anything that other reporter asked your mom that I don't know about yet?"

"Yeah," Jaime said, smiling. "He asked her how she was feeling. She wasn't feeling good."

She took a card out of her wallet. "Try to convince your mother to talk to me on the record. Let me know how it goes."

EIGHTEEN

At six-fifteen, she walked up the old steps, still of chipped tile and worn-away treading, the railing shiny from so many hands polishing it. The *Crier* printed Thursday nights. Mondays were busy because every day was busy, but people could usually leave the office by six o'clock. The person Gretchen needed, she knew, would be there.

She had spent the day hemming and hawing, managing to stay under the radar at work despite her inexplicable tardiness— inexplicable because she did not want to tell anyone about Dominica Padilla, Dana and Vita Quinn, Cyrus Amos, or Darlene Dabrowski. Not yet anyway. Not while she could still walk away from it and go fill her travel mug with whiskey down the street. But she didn't. Instead, she had edited the listicles and moderated the comments and typed up her Bird Lady piece in a flash.

At the top of the steps, Gretchen stood and listened. A printer whirred, low voices murmured, and off to the left, WFMU's jazz hour played. Misty Phelps was present.

Checks were cut, so to speak, on Tuesdays, an old holdback from when it took more than a few days to get them printed before everything went digital. Misty Phelps did the books back then and she did the books still, and she wasn't ever too excited about adjusting to the twenty-first century. She could memorize codes and names and numbers, and once she had one in her mind, it never left.

The tradition had always been to frame the covers of the best stories and hang them in reception—but eventually, they ran out of room. The farther in you went, the better the graphics got. Gretchen looked at her reflection in one from before her time, but she knew the story well. In December 1994, when the other small presses were hanging an elementary school teacher who had revealed in an op-ed somewhere that she had been a stripper, Marty was investigating voter fraud in the November midterm election. His story found a Staten Island precinct had been fudging votes of Black voters who had been turned away under the guise of a botched registration. The cover was a simple graphic of a ballot set over the shape of the island with FRAUD printed in big, block letters. It was the story that showed New York that Marty was a force. Gretchen combed her bangs, licked her finger and brought it under each eye, trying to smear away the circles. She had to get some rest tonight.

She all but tiptoed into the office. A few people remained at their desks, bent over copy or with their eyes on their monitors.

Misty Phelps was practically an institution at the *Crier*. She loved jazz, always brought a ham sandwich and salt-and-vinegar potato chips for lunch, and hated coffee. This evening, she wore a lavender cardigan over a cream blouse with a Peter Pan collar. Her gray skirt just covered her knobby knees. Her little black pilgrim shoes sat together beneath her desk to the right of her stockinged feet. Her big monitor showed a list of figures, and she, wearing a thick pair of glasses with tortoiseshell frames, traced her finger along a line and jotted something down on a notepad. Marty had moved money around in the budget to buy her the huge monitor. It was the only way they could convince her to adopt the slightest bit of a digital system.

Misty didn't acknowledge Gretchen when she sat down. She kept tracing her finger across the screen and jotting down information in her notepad. Gretchen knew better than to interrupt. She quietly took out the pictures she printed of Dominica Padilla's hospital bills. It was all gibberish to her: $6,290 for TR908 PROCEDURE, whatever that was, $3,000 for resuscitation.

Can they really charge that much just to keep someone from dying? Especially if the person dies anyway?

Then there were other fees: the biggest just listed as HOSPITAL STAY 7/4/16–7/6/16 at almost $25,000. From what she could tell, Medicare chipped in for just half the bill. And it wasn't even Medicare. It was called Medicare PURE, whatever that meant.

She pulled out the paperback book she had gone home to retrieve, a trade romance novel with a damsel in distress on the cover, her bosom straining against a corset as she fell into the arms of a topless buck with shining pectorals. Misty had tried to get Gretchen into romance novels years before, but it didn't stick.

Finally, Misty removed her finger from the monitor and began adding figures on her adding machine. Without ever looking up at Gretchen, she tabulated the figures and wrote something down on the notepad. Then she started all over again at the monitor.

"I thought you'd be here." She placed the novel on Misty's desk.

The older woman didn't take her eyes of the figures. "It's two years late."

"But better late than never?"

"Your borrowing privileges have been revoked."

"Damn."

"It is Monday at six-thirty. What could possibly be more important on a Monday at six-thirty than me getting our freelancers paid?"

"It won't take a minute."

Misty wrote one last thing in her notepad and swiveled her chair around to face Gretchen. Her lovely gray hair was swept back in a French twist that she performed every morning. She had a small chin and heart-shaped lips, and the same sense of self-possession that Gretchen had always admired in her.

She smiled thinly and raised her eyebrows above her glasses. She put down her pencil. "She returns."

"It's good to see you, Misty."

"And you. Glad to see you're still inhabiting planet earth."

"Just barely."

"How's my long-lost son? Has he woken up yet to make me a cup of tea?"

Misty had that rare gift of making the deadly serious commonplace, casual, hardly of note. She spoke out of the corner of her mouth, which was incongruous to her pretty, librarian-like face.

"He woke up for a few minutes Saturday. But no. He's not there yet."

"And you, prodigal daughter? What's that you have there?"

"I'm not sure it's anything. Just a lead I got. Thought you would take a look?"

Misty gestured for the papers and spread them out on her desk. "What am I looking at?"

"Hospital bills."

"I know it's hospital bills. Obviously it's hospital bills. But what am I looking for?"

"Just tell me if anything stands out to you."

The radio announcer's plaintive voice said it was Thelonious Monk's birthday; then Gretchen recognized the first few bars of a song.

"They've changed so much since I worked at Mount Sinai in the eighties," Misty said, "but if I'm not mistaken—see this?" She turned one of the pictures around and pointed one mauve, oval nail. "That's a psych code. And this? That's a chest x-ray."

"A psych code? Are you sure?"

Misty raised one eyebrow.

"OK, so it's psych. But what? Like, is it for a medication or for a doctor or—"

"It's probably an observation."

"So it's possible the patient was kept in a psych ward?"

"Could be." Misty scanned the other bills. "It's hard to tell off the top of my head. It would help if you could give me a little bit to work with here."

"I know someone trying to settle some debts."

"For a story?"

"Maybe for a story. But it's probably not worth getting into."

Misty sat back in her chair and crossed her arms. "I see."

"OK." Gretchen glanced over her shoulder. The office was quiet. No one was likely to walk by at this time of night. "The patient died. Her daughter doesn't know what the hell happened. Marty had been talking to the daughter before he . . ."

Misty pursed her lips. "I see. Well I feel her pain. Medicare is hardly kicking in anything."

"Why would that be? And what is Medicare PURE?"

"No idea. Medicare is a tough nut to crack." Misty opened her bottom drawer and retrieved her purse—a no-nonsense beige leather handbag—and, taking a quick look around, slid out a smartphone. It was a better phone than Gretchen had herself. The latest update.

"Misty!" she whispered.

"Shhh!"

"When did you?"

Misty blushed and turned it on. "It was just a little birthday present to myself. Don't you dare tell a soul or I'll let the whole newsroom know that you've got a story for them."

"You wouldn't!"

"I would." She pursed her lips and scrolled through the many colorful icons on the big flat screen. "I have a reputation to up-hold around here." She turned the phone around to face Gretchen and put it on her desk. "There. This is all you need."

"An app?"

Misty winked.

"You use apps."

"What can I say?" She shrugged. "You can't stop progress."

"I guess not."

The six o'clock AA meeting had just gotten out below her apartment. Gretchen darted through the crowd of people, hoping to avoid Danny. A man stood against her door.

"Excuse me," she said without looking up. She fished in her bag for her keys. He didn't move. "Sir, trying to get by here."

She looked up at him. He was tall and pale. He wore black jeans and a white V-neck T-shirt, an undershirt really. His neck was long and his Adam's apple was a hard knot in its center. He had red lips—not just pink or whatever, but actually red. They curled in a smile that made Gretchen clear her throat and lock her jaw.

"Buddy," she said, "I don't have all day."

"My apologies," the man said, stepping aside. "Please, be my guest." His voice was overly formal in a way that made her skin crawl. As she turned the key in the lock, she snapped her head his way and narrowed her eyes. "Have a lovely evening," the man said.

"Creep." She slammed the door.

Her apartment was stifling.

Already with the heat?

She opened her one window and stepped outside on the fire escape. One young woman stood in the center of a group of men who looked like they wanted to eat her alive. A big man in a leather vest with long flowing hair swept up the cigarette butts. A woman in a pantsuit typed into her phone. The tall creep wasn't anywhere. He must have stalked off to spook someone else.

She felt punchy, irritated. She went inside and poured herself a whiskey, just a shot, and to assuage her guilt, she dumped some soda water into the glass. Then a finger more of whiskey. The first sip loosened the ball of anxiety that had been building in her chest since she stood outside Cyrus Amos's hardware store.

She took down the paper that she had pinned above her desk the night before, and next to Cyrus's name wrote "NURSE?" She drew a line from that word to Dominica's name, and next to that she wrote, "PSYCH WARD." She bit her lower lip and pulled up the photos that Dabrowski had texted her. One showed Vita on her ass in the yard, her long legs kicked out from under her. In another, she scrambled to the black Benz.

In no time Gretchen found the year's campaign contribution database. The internet made everything so easy, so much so that she almost wished she had been a reporter during the days when she would have had to go down to city hall or wherever and ask some old lady to look up the information she needed, and then to have to stand up at a counter reading it because she wasn't allowed to take it home. She almost wished it in the vague, nostalgic way she missed Times Square peep shows—both things she had never actually seen but heard about as some kind of mythical old New York she was too late to see. She had told this to Marty once, and he had laughed. "Trust me," he had said, "you don't want to be needing anything from city hall. Reporters go in there and never come out."

Dana Quinn had run for state senate twice before, in 2012 and 2014. She printed out three years of Quinn's campaign contributions. In 2012, they totaled just over $550,000, which was low, even for a working-class district. In 2014, they climbed upward of $800,000—not unusual for a second-term candidate. But this year, Gretchen noted, her eyes wide, in just mid-October, the contributions totaled $1.3 million already. She circled that number and sat back in her chair. She took a gulp of whiskey and savored the burning.

South Brooklyn Hospital, she learned, went for-profit in 2014, just a year and half before. Owned now by United Hospitals Alliance out of Nashville, it must be seeing some changes. She jotted down a list of questions she'd have to answer to find a place to focus. Was the hospital accredited? Had the standards of care changed since the buyout? Was there a link between it and Quinn—or had she and Vita been at the same residence for completely different reasons?

She measured what she had: a stack of psych bills, pictures of an aging beauty queen scrambling away from a crazy woman's seagull, a state senator with cash flowing in faster than a snow cone melting on a boardwalk in July, a flatulent boss in a coma who would likely die any day now. Her phone rang. It was a Queens number she didn't recognize. A man said, "I got an Otto Sparks here with me."

The cab got her to the 43rd precinct within thirty minutes. The waiting room was a zoo. An old Latina woman held a baby who was screaming bloody murder, as Carla would always say. An unwell guy stood in the back, walking up two steps and back two steps and shouting out, "Thunder!" and "Cunt!" and "42nd Street!" A couple of adolescents sat in orange chairs against the wall, looking terrified. A guy slept with his arms folded. A woman stood in the back putting on deodorant, two heavy bags stuffed with all her junk at her feet. An officer led a woman in a skimpy dress through the door to the jail.

In their pictures of her father as a boy, he had a stub nose that would grow to be less like that of a pug. He had straw-brown hair and hazel eyes that caught the light and looked like amber. In her parents' wedding pictures, he wore a full beard, a handlebar mustache, and long golden hair.

"Sparks!" Another officer now held the arm of her father. He looked like a withered spray of Saint Anne's Lace. His thin white hair stuck out sideways, completely surrendered to a cowlick and Marta's efficient clippers. His body drowned in the beige jumpsuit they had given him. His back was so hunched, his shoulders so curved in, that he appeared almost Gretchen's height.

Columbus Day. She had told Marta to take an extra day off and forgotten about it.

He shuffled toward the center of the room, a vacancy about him that crushed her. She almost didn't rise. And then she did.

"Come on, Papa," she said, moving toward him slowly. He faced her and stood very still, blinking his eyes.

"Hi," she said, fighting the urge she had these days to speak to him like he were a baby. She held her breath while he looked at her. The day would come where he wouldn't recognize her at all—where instead he'd see a stranger. But it wasn't today.

"Hi," he said and smiled. His lips were chapped and the skin on his face was flaking. He wore his own shoes and socks, the blue Velcro Adidas she had bought him for his last birthday. She guided him over to the chair and sat him down.

A cop gave Gretchen some paperwork to sign. "Somebody thought he had to go to work at seven this evening," he said.

"Oh, I'm sure he'd love to do that."

"My old man never wanted to retire. They had to fire him!" He laughed, and she joined him in laughing. It was sweet of him to pretend like Gretchen's father's problem was simply that he wanted to go to work and was too old to do it.

"Does he have a caretaker?" he said.

"She was off today. For the holiday."

He nodded. "Your father was walking around in his shorts, disoriented. We're obviously not going to charge him with anything. But I do have to give you a warning. And I need a couple more numbers for him. The one he gave me was disconnected. Luckily, you're known well around these parts." He slid another form across the desk. "I'll need three more contacts."

Of all the things her father had forgotten, he remembered Dominic's phone number. She jotted down Carla's landline, Aunt Jana's cell, and who else? Nicola? What would Nico possibly be able to do in this situation? She hoped it would never come to that and scribbled her number.

"Let's get you home," she said, and put her father's arm around her shoulders to lead him outside. He smelled like urine.

"Carla?" he said as they climbed in a cab.

"No, Papa. It's me. It's Gretchen."

"Gretchen?" he looked around.

"Yep, that's me."

He waved a hand. "She died."

"I didn't die, Papa. I'm right here."

"She died crossing the Atlantic." He laughed then, a sudden burst of air that led to coughing. Then he said, "I never knew her." That much was true. Oma Ada had had a small picture of the baby, not even a year old when they boarded a freight ship and hid in the engine room. There was another Gretchen too— well, Grete, his father's sister. She had died of tuberculosis during World War I.

"Come on, Papa," Gretchen said. "That was a long time ago. The war is over! We missed it!"

"The war," he said waving his hand, "it took them all." He meant his brother, who was killed in Vietnam. And his son too, although Gretchen wondered if he would remember that tonight.

She managed to get him out of the car, into his building, and up the elevator to the fourth floor. The apartment was two rooms and a bath. In the kitchen, she reached into the cabinet over the stove and pulled out a bottle of rye. She poured a shot of it and drank. Then another. Then she poured a glass of water.

"Here you go, Papa." She put it to his lips, but he ducked away.

"No!" He scowled.

"Papa, you gotta drink. You're dehydrated."

"No!"

"Come on and do it for me, please?"

His lips found the glass, and she held it as he drank. "See? That wasn't so bad, was it?"

He shook his head. Then he put his arms around her waist and hugged her. She looked in the mirror. His eyes were closed and his head bowed. She smoothed his hair. "What are we gonna do with you?" She felt one of his hands grab her butt. She gently took his wrists and stepped away. The sexual stuff was new too. It had started in the summer. She felt the rye blossom in her chest.

"Papa, what were you doing in your shorts out in the street?"

He blushed and brought his hands up to his face. She tried to think back to the last time she had been here. She had been to the doctor with him at the end of September.

In the bathroom, Gretchen started filling the tub. On the sink, Marta had laid out his medicine in two small bowls. One was yellow, like the sun. One was white, like the moon. That had worked in the past. It didn't work today. She scooped them into her hand and sorted them out. The orange one was once a day, so she'd give him that. The big white ones twice a day, so she'd give him one. She wasn't sure about the small white ones or the blue ones, but he probably needed them all. She knew it wasn't perfect, but it was her best shot. And he took them gladly.

"I almost forgot!" she said, smiling. "I have a present for you!" She went to her bag and came back with the mug. "Ma said you wouldn't remember, but I thought you would." She held it up in front of him, and his eyes lit up. "You remember?"

Then he scowled. "No." He put his finger in his ear and shook his head. "Where's Nicky? That boy's staying out too late." He looked around the bathroom and started to get up.

She felt herself recede a little, as if on a small boat that was drifting from shore. Gretchen eased him back down and then checked the water. "Papa, you know we buried Nicky," she said, using the nickname to avoid any more confusion.

"No," he said, swatting the suggestion away with the hand that had been in his ear.

"Papa. Nicky died. We loved him, and he died."

He shook his head, as if the idea were impossible to accept, as if Nicky were sitting in the next room.

Her father had been the one to give her the news three years before. Almost to the day. She had been at the office late when he'd called. He had wanted her to go home first, but she made him tell her on the phone. He had cried then.

He looked up at her and reached his arms out. His eyes were a deep, watery blue-green now, and he searched her face as if waiting for her to laugh and say it was a bad joke.

"Papa," she said.

He shook his head. "No, not Nicky." He snapped his fingers dryly several times, trying to reach into his past for a word. "Henry!"

"Not Henry. Henry died in Vietnam."

"Put your shoes on," he said. "We're going to the store. Your mother needs tomatoes."

So she told him—just like she had a dozen times before. And she envied his forgetting. The bath was full. She turned off the water. "Nicky was a doctor. Do you remember that? He didn't want to be a regular doctor though. He didn't want to fix people here in New York. He wanted to fix people on the other side of the world." She made him reach his arms up and pulled the shirt off him. His chest was white and hairless. Then she turned around, and steadying himself by holding her shoulder with one hand, he pulled off his pants. She heard him step into the tub and sit down.

"So he went to Afghanistan to work in a civilian hospital. Nicky liked helping people, remember? He did. He wanted to help the little Afghan children who were blown to bits by bombs." Her father splashed around, and she reached behind her back to hand him a washcloth. He took it. "Squirt the soap on it," she said, and he did. He was good at bathing when someone was there to remind him to do it.

"And he was only at that hospital for two weeks when he had to go out in a jeep to find some soldiers who got blown up. And Nicky, Dr. Sparks actually, went for a ride with his bag of medicine." She sat down and leaned her head against the tile wall. "Put the soap in your hair, Papa."

He grunted with satisfaction.

She could imagine Nicky still, his hair pulled back in a bandanna maybe, and his brown eyes searching the dunes for fallen men and rubble as the jeep tore around the terrain. She imagined that he held on to the door with one hand. In the other, he held his bag. In his eyes, he held fear and love and purpose.

After her father had told her about Nicky that afternoon in October, she had sat at her desk at the *Crier*, staring at her screen saver until her computer went to sleep. Then people started to say good night, one at a time, and as was often the case, she was alone on the floor. Marty was in his office, door slightly ajar, doing his final read of the paper before sending it to press. A part of her was suddenly missing, the part that knew what to say and when to drink and when to eat. A lot like the part that was missing from her father now.

She reached behind her with the plastic cup. "Take this, Papa. Fill it up and pour it on your head. And can you believe it? We don't even know if he had any time to help anybody," she said, "because he got blown up trying to find those soldiers, and then they sent what was left of him, and we buried him in Queensbridge."

She reached her empty hand back now, and her father took it in his.

"Gretchen," he said.

She closed her eyes and felt the world swirling outside of her. "Yeah, Papa?"

"I'm sorry."

"It's OK."

She thought of Marty shaking her by the shoulders, saying, *Gretchen, it's me. Let's go home.*

"Papa?"

"Hmm?"

"Why did you name me for the dead Gretes?"

He began to hum.

NINETEEN
Author's Note

But let me tell you about our first date.

I had been at the *Crier* for an agonizing three months when I finally worked up the nerve to ask one morning. We had fallen into the habit of catching up in the break room during the buzzy mid-morning rush. Or rather, I had gotten in the habit of finding a reason to be there when Gretchen ducked in to get a cup of coffee. The words flew out of my mouth before fear gripped me. "What's the plan Friday night?" She had paused mid-sip and looked at me quizzically.

"Raajen," she said. "Are you asking me out on a date?"

After I recovered from the shock of her saying yes, I set about planning. I knew Gretchen better than to take her someplace pretentious. Had I suggested Momofuku Ko downtown, or Le Bibli-oquet uptown, she would have been completely justified in swatting me across the nose.

I was doubly challenged because Gretchen is a New Yorker. When friends came up from New Jersey to visit, I impressed them with the easy places: Chelsea Market, Eataly, some $18 tapas, or just let them eat off the food carts for authenticity's sake. But I neither could try too hard or not hard at all. Like in college, Gretchen's desires eluded me.

The day arrived. Gretchen asked over the watercooler, "Where we going later?" And I said geekily, "I'll surprise you!" As the clock inched toward lunchtime, I began to sweat.

135

As if feeling my utter panic, Marty Mitnik, God bless his old heart, patted me on the shoulder at noon and said, "Lunch?"

I had never been to lunch with Marty. Others had—he was the type who extended an open invitation to all. But I had come from another line of work where people ate sad ham sandwiches alone. We tucked into a pizza joint on Broadway, and over a big anchovy and onion pie—"whatever you like," I had squeaked, "I'll eat it"—he asked me questions. Where was I from? Where were my parents from? How did they meet? Did they fall in love? Do most people in arranged marriages fall in love? When did they move to the United States? Did I have siblings? Where did I go to school? Why did I want to write? *What* did I want to write? How was I getting along generally? Specifically?

I barely ate. I just . . . talked. And he listened, nodding, eating, chugging Diet Coke, only interrupting to say, "You gonna eat that?"

And perhaps because he seemed to take such an interest in me, because he seemed so genuinely curious about my small life, I cleared my throat as he polished off the last slice, and I said, "I'm taking Gretchen Sparks out tonight. I think I may be terrified."

Those devilish eyebrows wobbled, and he chuckled. I wiped my mouth with my napkin. The way he laughed made everyone in the restaurant look over at us. He kept right on laughing until it became clear that he was in fact laughing *at* me, not *with* me, and I began to laugh at myself, too.

Then he said, "You *should* be terrified!"

Our laughter emboldened me. "Please tell me where to take her."

He managed to stop laughing long enough to say, "Gretchen isn't the type of girl you take anywhere. She takes you."

He picked up the check and walked across the street to the Strand. I followed and watched him poke around for some twenty minutes, totally engrossed in each selection, only to leave the store empty-handed. He ambled with me back to the office. "Take her somewhere you feel comfortable," he said at last, holding the door open for me.

Later, as casually as I could muster, I stopped at Gretchen's desk on my way out and said, "Shall we meet at the fountain, like old times?"

She scowled at the sentiment, but then smiled and said, "Sure. Seven o'clock?"

S he had gone home to change her clothes and shower. I half thought she wouldn't bother and nearly didn't myself, so worried about appearing too eager.

She had brushed her hair to a shine, wore a tight kelly-green blouse with a boatneck (collarbones for miles) and an A-line denim skirt (legs for miles). But what I was worried about were the shoes.

Gretchen is tall like her father, and I am short, like mine. Barefoot, she stands two inches taller than me, and in those big, chunky boots, or God forbid, high heels, I must tilt my head to kiss her. But she was, for once, merciful. On that first date, and most dates thereafter, she wore two-tone perforated Oxfords. Flats.

We walked around for an hour with no destination in mind. She told me about her years at the *Crier*, the stories she'd written—I managed not to let on that I had read them all—people she'd met, how her parents were proud of her despite themselves. She caught me up on her family. Her sister, that little butterball I'd met a few times over the years, was in high school. Her brother was in med school—no surprise there.

Unlike years past, Gretchen wanted to hear from me, so much so that I thanked Marty silently for providing me with such an excellent lunchtime rehearsal, until I wondered if they'd conspired together all along. Why had I left my previous job? Had I had many girlfriends? Was I still writing poetry? She was especially interested in my parents, having become interested in her own immigrant grandparents at the end of their lives.

This was a softer, kinder Gretchen Sparks than I had known back in college. Was she still spunky? Yes. Still fiery? Definitely.

Still hot-headed? I didn't know it yet, but yes. What was different was an awareness with which she moved through the world, a sense of self-possession, of integrity.

We ate peanut butter and banana sandwiches at a sandwich shop and stopped off at a bar. I had two beers, she two glasses of wine. I did an impression of a history professor we shared freshman year, and she slid her hand onto my forearm and laughed. She left it there for eight minutes.

I walked her home, and she kissed me good night. You read it right. *She* kissed *me* good night. This may be a softer Gretchen, but I was relieved to find her still very much in charge.

TWENTY

One's whole outlook can shift just by driving thirty minutes north of Harlem or west to New Jersey. From the back of the car, Dana chatted with Maurice about basketball, something Vita had no interest in.

Vita did not like leaving the city, not anymore. It made her feel inhibited, naked. Dana, on the other hand, loved the suburbs, being a suburbanite himself. Visits to Connecticut brought out the best in him, and once they settled into Howard and Cindy's colossal home, even Vita felt the tension tame between them. But today, they weren't going to Connecticut. They were going to Rye.

Twenty-one days stood between Vita and the election.

The day before, after Maurice had brought her home from the whole Coney Island debacle, Dana had brought takeout from Portofino's—her favorite eggplant parmesan and garlic knots—and a bottle of good wine. He'd set the table with a candle lit in the center, next to a dozen red roses. She stood there in her leggings and socks and T-shirt and decided she didn't want to fight any more, and they ate together.

As they ate, he explained that he didn't recognize the name the day before—that Dominica Padilla was no one to him, but he knew Vita wouldn't bring it up if she weren't legitimately concerned. So he had the interns look back through the old database from 2012 that hadn't even been properly merged with the 2014 one, let alone the 2016, and they found that Dominica Padilla of

86th Street was a registered Republican and a senior citizen interested in volunteering with the campaign. But why would she want to volunteer for a campaign in another district? Dana shrugged his shoulders. And why would he have her name and address in his planner? He had names scribbled down in every inch of his life, he claimed. He reached across the table and took her hands.

"I know what's really bothering you, Vita." He had gotten a haircut, she realized when she looked up at him. It was barely perceptible, just a trim, but she knew it. She raised an eyebrow. "It's my speech the other night. I had no right—no right—to do that without asking you first. I had been worried. I meant to tell you in the car, but I was so damn nervous that I decided against making the speech at all. I knew it wasn't the right thing to do, dammit."

Vita strained to remember what he had looked like that January night twenty years before when he stepped out the window and introduced himself by first and last name. But that night had fallen away in an avalanche when Alexander died, and there was no getting it back.

"And then my fucking father—I'm sorry. I know you love him. I love him, too. But what I'm trying to say, Vita, is that I feel terrible for doing that to you, for putting you through that. You have been through enough." He came to her side, kneeled on the floor, and put his head in her lap, tears in his eyes. "I understand if you can't forgive me. I don't deserve it. I can't forgive myself for any of it."

Later, in bed, Dana had asked her to join at the Vittleses' dinner party.

He had said she could say no, that he would understand. But that this money was important, and it would be important for his US Senate run in two years—the big one—and that after he was in Washington, she could do whatever she wanted. She could live in Brooklyn, or she could live down in the Keys for most of the year, or she could live with him in a D.C. apartment and he'd take care of her. There would be no more parades or fundraisers or public displays. He'd manage without her. But in Brooklyn, he needed her. He couldn't win the 22nd unless she were by his side.

He traced his fingers around her belly button and kissed her skin till it glowed, stroked her mound over her cotton panties, and even though she said *no, not now, later, I swear*, he put his mouth on cotton and stubble grazed her thigh, and by the time he entered her, she was fighting not to see the thin wisps of clouds moving overhead, or to feel the beach towel riding up her thighs, or to smell salt and suntan oil, and fighting also the sound of the waves in her ears. He flipped onto his back and brought her with him. Her body bucked on top of him, and gulls screamed in her ears.

She lay awake for a long time after, thinking about brushing the sand out of Alexander's hair and about him diving into a wave just before it broke and about the way he smelled when he was no bigger than a bundle of bedsheets, like powder and birthday cake. She didn't fall asleep until nearly dawn.

In the morning before her nine o'clock class, she was running on the treadmill when she heard the women behind her laughing and whispering. With a jolt, she remembered the woman at the Padillas', the pictures. She slowed the treadmill and pulled up the *Metro* website. Nothing. The old lady had lied.

Or had she? Maybe it would take another day. Maybe they just got the photos. She knew how to find out. She'd left the gym without showering and dialed the number for *Metro* while standing in the alley. The receptionist transferred her three times before Gretchen Sparks picked up the phone.

"Sparks," she said.

"Gretchen," Vita said. "So good to hear your voice. It's Vita. Vita Quinn. We met the other day."

"Really? I must have misunderstood. You kidnapped me and left me on Flatbush at rush hour."

"Kidnapped is such a strong word."

"But alas, it fits."

"I had the wrong idea."

"Calling me on the phone might have worked, too."

"I said I was sorry."

"Did you?"

Did she? Vita sighed. "I apologize."

"Is that why you called?"

"Partly."

"Ah. Partly."

"I happened to be down at the Padillas' yesterday."

"Gone slumming?"

She ignored that dig. "A neighbor may have taken some . . . compromising pictures of me and mentioned the name of your paper."

"Ah," Gretchen said. "The truth comes out. Don't worry, princess. We don't publish gossip. If Dabrowski ever read the paper, she'd know that. I sent the pictures to myself and deleted them off her phone. And I'm about to delete them off mine."

"Meet me. I want to see you do it."

"You always get your own way, don't you?"

"You may not know this, but my husband is a very important person—"

"Oh, I know it. State senator. A big cheese. Nobody cares, Vita. I gotta get off the phone now."

"Wait! Meet me today. I'll come to you."

"Goodbye."

"Please!"

And the little wretch hung up.

As Dana and Maurice discussed college football, Vita tried to put all of it out of her mind—Dominica Padilla, the fat lady next door, and Gretchen Sparks. She tried to think of what she would do after the campaign was over. In the past, they had celebrated with a vacation. Disney the first year with Alexander, Rome the second year without him. She wanted to go someplace new this time—and alone.

Harlan and Linnie Vittles lived in a stately home in Rye—white with shutters and a wraparound porch that Linnie had installed to give it a Southern feel, she had told Vita each and every time they visited, which was more frequent than Vita had liked.

Dana took a fifty-dollar bill out of his wallet and slipped it up through the window to Maurice. "There's a steakhouse on Main. Go down the road and take the second left. Then a right. There've got a beautiful mahogany bar. Tell Rutherford I sent you. We'll text in a few hours."

A few hours? Vita cleared her throat.

Maurice thanked him brightly and said, "Rutherford. Got it, Senator Quinn. You have a nice time tonight." She knew Dana liked it when Maurice called him Senator Quinn, but he rarely did. Vita figured he wanted a cigarette and was anxious to get them out of the car.

Linnie waited on her porch in a yellow dress with a crocheted collar and crinoline. Her hair, singed with a curling iron, hung limp around her face, the ends crinkly. She had put too much blush on her pinched cheeks, and her eyelashes were like tarantula legs. Dana had come around to open the door, and he helped Vita out like she were a Southern belle herself.

"Harlan!" Linnie sang though the screen door. "They're he-er!"

Dana took Vita's hand, and they walked toward the house just as Harlan came out, followed by Harry Shears and his moth-like wife, whose name escaped Vita. She remembered a trick her father had told her once. When in sales, if a guy is giving you guff and being evasive, focus on making the wife comfortable. If you get the wife, you've made the sale. Vita wasn't selling anything, but if she was here to help Dana, she might as well try.

Harlan blamed the insurance companies for his suffering practice, but his house and Cadillac told a different story. He shook Dana's hand and drew Vita in for another papery kiss on the cheek. She laughed so she wouldn't cringe.

Linnie handed her a spritzer. Although they had all been to visit before, Linnie subjected them to the grand tour. The decor was a mix of what Vita imagined was called "tasteful" in *Southern Living* magazine. It had a Southern country theme of reclaimed barnwood tables and mason jar vases, a stained and polished picnic table in the breakfast nook, and a kitchen mosaic of a plantation, complete with two dark brown "workers" shoveling a bale of hay into a cart. ("Isn't it just bucolic?" Linnie said.) Vita caught Harry Shears's wife staring at it with her mouth open. The kitchen was a trip. Baskets hung from the ceiling and lined the walls. A big island stood in the center of the room, adjacent to a hutch filled with salt and pepper shakers. ("I've got hundreds in storage because, as Harlan says, 'Modesty is a virtue.'") Off the kitchen was the "maid's bed and bath" that Linnie kept tidy, although their maid wasn't allowed to rest in it or do anything in it but clean.

They climbed the stairs to tour Harlan's billiard room, a rec room, and five bedrooms, all but one unoccupied. ("I keep our sweet Bo's room—Bo is short for Beaufort—just as he left it.") She did—complete with wrestling trophies and a poster of a girl striding from the ocean in a two piece, nipples pressing against Lycra.) And then there was Harlan's office, which he kept locked. ("We all know a man needs his space!" Linnie winked at Vita.)

"Speaking of which," Harlan said, "shall we retreat to the parlor, gentlemen?"

The Shears wife reached desperately for Harry's hand as Linnie led her and Vita away to the sitting room with its straight-backed velvet couches and grand piano that no one played, at least now that their darling son Bo (short for Beaufort) was in college down at Vanderbilt in ole Tennessee.

Vita was used to the routine. The men played pool and threw darts and talked about God knows what. As Linnie darted off to refresh their spritzers, Vita whispered to—it came to her suddenly, Patricia!—"Let's get fucking shit-faced."

Patricia laughed dryly, and her shoulders relaxed.

"Linnie!" Vita called. "You got anything stronger?"

It wouldn't be proper for them to drink straight whiskey, but Linnie brought out some sour mix, and Vita made her sit down as she fixed the drinks. Before long, Patricia's words slurred together, and Linnie's cheeks had a bright blush to them.

Like a doll found in an abandoned orphanage.

She turned to Patricia. "So what's it like being Mrs. Shears?"

"It's Summers," she said. "I kept my last name."

"Of course you did." Vita never considered it, but it privately pleased her that many in the borough still referred to her in passing by her maiden name.

Linnie wanted none of it. "I would never have dreamed of insulting Harlan in such a manner. Why it's simply devastating for a man to endure."

Patricia rolled her eyes. "It's 2015. And trust me. Harry's masculinity is very much intact."

Linnie blushed.

"How'd you and Harlan meet?" Vita said.

The woman's mind was easily diverted. Linnie now squealed. "Vita! You know I simply *hate* to be the center of attention."

"Indulge us." Vita got up to mix another round of drinks, going easy on herself and Patricia and hard on Linnie.

"Well it was such an awfully long time ago." Linnie received her fresh drink and took a gulp. "I can hardly remember the spring day when my class visited Vanderbilt for a concert. I was at Lipscomb University, you see, studying home ec, and Harlan—who has the brains—was at Vanderbilt Medical School."

"Get to the good part," Patricia said.

"Well, I didn't see it coming. Father said I was to find a husband in Tennessee. Why else would he send me to college? But he did not mean that I should marry a scholarship boy! Imagine!"

"Scandalous," Vita said.

"What with father—who is a descendant of General Jubal Early, I'll have you know, and the best dang banker in the state of Virginia! And mother, why, she herself was descended from Martha Washington!" Linnie's face darkened a bit. "No, father wasn't happy when I brought home Harlan. But try telling that to a girl in love."

"Linnie," Vita said, grinning, "are you saying that Harlan was poor?"

Linnie polished off the drink—number four already. "You must understand, father only wanted what was best for me. He didn't know about Harlan's talent in surgery. We married in 1980, just after graduation, and he went right on in his studies, straight through for nine more years. Folks don't know just how long schooling takes to be a surgeon!"

"I met Harry long after that, thank God," said Patricia. "I missed his starving resident era."

Vita's mind drifted, revisiting the events of the day prior, the woman's ratty brown robe, her pudgy fingers, that damn crazy bird coming out of nowhere.

"Father kept us afloat, of course. I knew he would. I got lonely at times." Linnie looked off, her fingers worrying her glass. "And I suffered his hanger-on mother with nary a word of complaint. Bore a beautiful baby boy in 1990. Why, the only dark spot on those first ten years came with Vestal Vittles III—out of the penitentiary."

"What?" Vita and Patricia said in unison.

Linnie, her face flushed, chuckled. "Harlan's big brother came home, bearded and filthy looking. Hooked on the drugs. He'd be in and out of the commode all evening." She put one finger on the side of her nose and sniffed; then she waved a hand and frowned, as if batting away his memory. "I wish they'd have let him rot in there."

Vita felt something leave the room—the liveliness that accompanied Linnie everywhere.

"What was he in for?" Patricia asked.

Linnie leaned forward, the three of them now in a huddle. She whispered, "Vestal murdered their daddy when he was but fourteen years old!"

"Well, look at this pretty henhouse," Harlan boomed from the bottom of the stairs. Linnie jumped and hid her empty glass behind her back. "Please forgive my interruption," he said, "but we've eaten the pimento cheese and are liable to start on Harry's arm next." Linnie laughed too loudly and headed to the kitchen.

"We should help," Patricia said, and they followed her.

Linnie fussed around the room, opening the ovens and closing them, rocking back and forth. Vita steered the little woman to a chair. On the way, Linnie reached for a drawer and knocked over a big mason jar full of serving spoons.

"Let us do that for you," Vita said.

"Oh! Of course, little darling," she said. Her voice was not a song but a slur.

Vita had figured out months ago that Linnie didn't actually cook. Vita didn't care about that—she could cook only a handful of dishes herself. But what bothered her was that Linnie pretended to cook. Somebody came to her house and slaved away all day making a roast and mashed potatoes and biscuits and green beans and bacon and three to four other side dishes, plus a cherry pie!—and then Linnie took all the credit. The same person probably came to clean it all up too.

But pour a little liquor down her gullet, and Linnie Vittles was all right. As she talked, she drank white wine without Sprite in it. Harlan cut his meat in small pieces and drank from a glass of ice water, and Linnie regaled them with stories of her old plantation house in Virginia. Vita was a little light-headed, but more so from the sugar in the sour mix than the whiskey. She hadn't had much to drink herself.

At some point she noticed Harlan slip his hand around the stem of Linnie's wine glass, and in flash, move it next to his own. Linnie noticed too and abruptly stopped speaking. Then the doorbell rang.

"Oh dear," Linnie said, rising from her chair, "who could that be?"

Harlan made to rise.

"Sit down, sit down—Linnie will see what's the matter," Linnie said as she swaggered to the foyer, her toes turning in.

"You girls certainly had fun this evening," Harlan said, staring at Vita. His smile was false, and she was glad she had gotten to him. But Dana's look of disappointment was clear too.

"Harry," Vita said, ignoring them both, "tell me about yourself. Sunday I think we nearly got through fishing."

Harry Shears smiled, his white teeth shining unnaturally.

"There's not much to tell," Patricia said dryly, and she and Vita burst out laughing.

Then Linnie appeared again. Her face was pale, stricken, her mouth open in an O. She made her way toward them like a sleepwalker, saying softly, "Harlan, Harlan." He got up, wiping his mouth with his napkin, and rushed past her. Then Dana was up, holding her hand like he was leading her into a horse-drawn carriage.

"Harry," Dana said, "would you get some ice water for Mrs. Vittles?" He led her into the sitting room.

Vita had a funny feeling. She left Patricia alone with the feast and went to the hall. As she opened the door to the half bath, she looked at the front of the house. Harlan was out on the porch. He was arguing with someone, his face red with rage. She squinted her eyes and stepped just a foot to the right. Dana was talking to Linnie in low, soothing tones. She stepped another foot to the right and saw the other person: a man, much older than Harlan, skinny and with red hair sticking out beneath a yellow baseball cap. He wore a short-sleeved, beige dress shirt and pale yellow tie, like someone dressed up for court in an outfit the public defender bought at T.J.Maxx. He didn't look like he was arguing though. His pained face looked away from Harlan, at the porch floor.

He looked familiar to her, but she couldn't place him.

Then Harlan turned toward the house, and Vita scrambled into the bathroom and shut the door. She heard the front door open and shut. She heard footsteps coming down the hall and then Dana's voice. "Everything OK? Harlan?"

She tried not to breathe. What she heard next scared her.

TWENTY—ONE

Gretchen's cup was filled with ice. She poked it with a stirring straw, as if trying to uncover more whiskey. They sat in the back of Cowboy's. Some drunks crooned along to "Ring of Fire" a few booths down.

Dana Quinn's campaign finance reports were spread across the table, a rainbow of highlighter and pen marks. "If only I knew what to look for, maybe I could make some sense out of this."

Misty Phelps punched her calculator, lighted magnifying glass in hand. "You have to be patient. Numbers aren't words. They don't reveal themselves as easily to you."

Gretchen rubbed her eyes. "I've been looking at this shit for hours, Misty. What am I missing?"

The woman put the magnifying glass down and crossed her arms.

"What?" Gretchen said.

"I can't help you without more information."

"I don't have any more information. I've told you everything."

"There's a senator, this Quinn," Misty said. "He's running for his third term. His wife picks you up in her car because you were down at the Bird Lady's."

"Right."

"She knows you were down at the Bird Lady's because she saw you talking to a boy on the block."

"Right, Jaime Padilla."

"And this Jaime Padilla tells you that his grandma died in the hospital under suspicious circumstances. And later he tells you that Marty was down there to see him too."

"Yes."

"And how did Marty find out about him?"

"Cyrus Amos, I think."

"The hardware store owner?"

Gretchen laughed. "How do you know that?"

"We ran a feature on him. Don't ask me stupid questions. So Cyrus. He's a do-gooder. Have you spoken with him?"

"I tried. He stonewalled me."

"What's his connection to the dead grandma?"

"I don't know. Maybe he knows the family or someone at the hospital."

Misty tapped her pen on the table. "What does your gut tell you?"

"Cowboy!" Gretchen called. The old man was up at the bar, sitting behind the counter on a stool, asleep. "I need another one." She got up. "You?"

"No. I didn't need the second one either." Misty went back to the magnifying glass and the numbers. "Ring of Fire" ended, and nothing else came on.

"Cowboy!" she said, knocking on the bar.

"Meh!" He shook awake. "Gretchen! Where's that old man?"

"Home," she said.

"You tell him to come see me?"

"I forgot."

"You tell him, eh?" He got off the stool and ran his hand over his head.

"Give me another and one for her," Gretchen said. "Please and thank you." She put a ten on the bar.

"That's twelve dollars," Cowboy said. "Prices have gone up." He laughed, and the laugh turned into a hacking cough. He put the liquor on the bar and bent over the ice bin.

"Jesus," Gretchen said, "we'll hold the ice." She filled up two cups with Johnny Walker.

She put another five on the bar and made her way back to Misty.

"Look here," the woman said, turning a report around so Gretchen could see. "What's this?"

"A&S Photos?" Gretchen said. "It's a photo shop."

"A photo shop."

"So?" Gretchen shook her head.

"And here," Misty pushed another piece of paper toward her and pointed. "Another one." They were both on Ocean Parkway.

Misty thumbed through the papers, producing another. "What's this?"

"T&Y Copies? What year are all reports?"

"They're 2016. I'm betting that if you ran down some of these, you wouldn't find much."

"They're dummies?"

Misty smoothed her hair with both hands and sat up straight. "The contributions from the 2011 and '13 are substantial, and the donations are small. Look: $250 from the Dollar Store on 5th Avenue in Brooklyn, $100 from Mahmood's Party Supply Store, $500 from A1 Barber. These are real places. Maybe he promised them something—better trash pickup or a change in parking regulations. Maybe something more substantial, like a rezoning or a new tax bill. Or they just agree with his values."

"And those are all in '11 and '13."

"No, they're all here, too." She pointed to the 2015. But along with them . . ." She tapped the list.

"There's these dummy businesses." Gretchen scanned the list. "So where is the FEC?"

"For all you know, they got him by the balls already. Maybe they don't." She peered into her purse, at her secret phone no doubt, and grinned. "That's all I can tell you now. I want to look into some of these PACs and get a second opinion on those medical bills. You"—she gestured at Gretchen—"see what you can find out about the hospital. Accreditation, investors, political links."

Gretchen gathered the papers. "To be honest, I'm not sure I even want to look into it any further."

Misty narrowed her eyes. "It's time, Gretchen."

"Time for what?"

"It's time to get your life back." Before Gretchen could object, Misty stood and walked in tight, quick steps toward the exit. Gretchen finished her drink. A headache was starting behind her eyes.

She had woken up resolved to forget the whole thing. Got to work on time for a change, spoke to Roberta for the obit, and started a decent draft. She might have finished the draft if Conway hadn't commissioned her to check facts on yet another story about the missing girls.

No new news, but the city was obsessed. And who was assigned to cover it? Gunderson, Stewart, Dreyfus. Gretchen knocked back the rest of Misty's drink, felt it harder than the rest, but warm. She nestled down in the booth and crossed her arms. Patsy Cline came on the jukebox.

Just that afternoon, Stewart had been calling the fourth girl's parents in Iowa nonstop. The poor people couldn't shut off their phones in case their daughter called. They'd have to answer every single New York number.

Stewart—what a bastard.

So many girls in New York. The city was full of them, from Ohio and Florida, from Illinois and Louisiana. Mexican girls, Panamanian girls, Russian girls, Filipino girls.

She gulped down a lump in her throat. Who was looking out for them all? Not the NYPD. Not Gunderson and Stewart. They were practically itching for another girl to disappear. Marty was dying blocks away. How many times would she tell her father the story of his dead son? She wondered if maybe hearing it was like re-reading *Romeo and Juliet* for him, knowing the ending but hoping it would change. She tried to circle back to the original thought. She got lost in it all.

Her phone vibrated in her jacket pocket.

"Listen, lady. I don't want to play any games with you." Vita Quinn's panicked voice snapped Gretchen out of her trance.

"How did you get this number?"

"No more games, Gretchen Sparks. I need those pictures."

"Games?" Gretchen snorted. "Like pushing a reporter into a moving car?"

"The car wasn't moving, and Maurice is the most responsible driver in New York City."

She tried to fetch another thought, but it tumbled away from her. She stood, but the room wobbled. She thought of something Marty said to her way back, when she had first started her internship.

We have a great responsibility, Gretchen. We decide each and every day whom we will give a voice.

How do we know who?

We read and we listen and we find the people we don't already hear.

"Hello?" Vita said.

More people had appeared in the bar, people Gretchen didn't recognize, their voices loud and demanding.

"I've got a proposition," Vita said. "If you show me that you've deleted the pictures and promise on your mother's life that you have no other copies, I'll owe you a favor."

A favor. Gretchen tried to focus on the invitation. She thought of Vita's tan skin and manicured nails, her sickening, sweet smell.

"What kind of favor?"

"Honey. I've got all the gossip in the borough."

Would Vita Quinn make for a passable source in the future? Quite possibly. "Let's be clear," Gretchen said. "I have no intention of ever publishing your photos or showing them to another sorry soul. But if you insist on wasting my time, I'll keep you in mind as a source in the future." Gretchen swept the stack of papers into her bag but missed, sending them scattering across the sticky barroom floor.

"And you deleted the photos from that woman's phone?"

"That's what I said. Dabrowski's not so bad, you know. Just lonely." She heard another call coming in.

"How do I know you're telling the truth?"

"I gotta go now, your highness. Call me tomorrow."

She switched to the incoming call, leaving the Bay Ridge Beauty with her mouth surely ajar. The room spun a little, but she righted her ship and started walking.

"Hi, Gretch-EN!" The way Nico talked, you could always tell when she was smiling.

"What's up?"

"Ma wants us over there at nine o'clock *in the morning*. Can you believe that shit? I'm gonna have to get on the subway at like, seven-thirty—"

"Tomorrow?"

"And I have a date tonight. Ma has been up my ass all week." She paused. "Gretch-EN. Do not tell me that you forgot."

Gretchen stepped outside onto the sidewalk, and the realization smacked her whole body. It was the anniversary already. Another one. "Oh shit."

"You forgot."

"I've been under some stress."

"Ma has been calling me all week about it. She wants us to take the subway together."

"But that doesn't make sense."

"Of course it doesn't make sense. Please tell me you took the day off."

"I did. Months ago." Actually, Marty had arranged for the personal day when she didn't turn in her requests for the quarter. Remembering that gave her a dizzying pain in her chest.

"Do you have inside information about these girls? My roommate had chemistry with the Hamm girl. No relation to John Hamm. I checked. Girls are getting seriously freaked out around here."

She couldn't follow Nico's celebrity shit right now. Cars zoomed past her on 6th Avenue, their lights shooting pain into her eyes. "Are we picking up Papa on the way?"

"Oh my God, Gretchen. Have you even spoken to Ma? She doesn't want Papa there. I figured she told you all of this."

Gretchen jumped aside as a bicycle nearly sped right into her. "Have you ever wondered why Papa can't remember that

Dominic's dead?"

"No. He has dementia, Gretchen. De-MEN-cha."

"But maybe he makes himself forget. Is that possible?"

"What, like you forgot about the anniversary? What is with you? You forget my birthday every year, so, like, whatever. But this is Dominic. You can't forget shit like this."

She crossed the street on a red with the slow, confident strides of someone very drunk. "What'd you do for your birth-day?"

"Nothing. I got drunk and slept in your bed. And the next day this guy bought me lunch. He's, like, Goth or something. I know what's happening here. You're practicing avoidance. You need to move out of this stage of grief."

"I'm sorry I missed it."

"Just be there tomorrow morning, OK? Don't make me do this alone."

"I promise. Enjoy your date."

"OK. Love you, bye!"

She was almost home. The whiskey made everything swirl around in her mind. She needed to lie down. She struggled with her keys outside the building and dropped them. The door to the AA meeting was open, a curtain keeping everyone's anonymity safe. She stepped toward it. She heard laughter, as she often did, and she imagined some smug story that ended in one revelation or another. She heard clapping. If it was the eight o'clock meet-ing, Danny would probably be there. The thought of seeing him repelled her. She reached down for the keys.

First, her knees hit the pavement. Then her hands. Her bag was so heavy. Her ancient laptop weighed a ton. A plump woman with green hair came out of the AA meeting. She rushed to Gretchen's side, took her hand, and draped Gretchen's arm across her own shoulders. "You all right?" Her voice and face were unfathomably perky.

"I got it." She attempted to stand.

"No, you clearly don't," the woman said and sniffed her. "Jesus. You've come to the right place!" Under the streetlight,

Gretchen could make out her black dress with little cat faces all over it and opaque pink leggings. More people came out and gathered close by.

"No," Gretchen said. "I live here."

"Where do you live, friend?"

"Friend?" Gretchen nodded to the door.

"Over here? Let's get those keys." Holding Gretchen up with one arm, she reached down with the other to grab her bag.

"How'd you do that?" Gretchen asked.

"Easy," she said. I'm not loaded. "Nothing to see here, people! Go back to your business. Just a couple ladies with arms entwined!" The herd moved toward the door. "Which key?"

Gretchen pointed. She saw Danny over her shoulder, and before she knew it, Cat Faces had her inside. She was glad. The other time he saw her wasted, he brought some AA woman up to the apartment to talk to her. It hadn't gone well.

Cat Faces sighed. "Of course it's a walk-up."

"I can take it from here."

"Maybe so, but if I leave you, I'll be up all night wondering if you split your head open and died." Her pillowy bosom held Gretchen's head as they lurched up the stairs.

"You smell good," Gretchen said.

The woman laughed. "You smell terrible."

By the time they got to the fourth floor, Cat Faces and Gretchen both were sweating. "You do this every day?" Cat Faces said.

"Yeah," Gretchen managed, coming around the corner. She stopped short.

"If you're all set then—"

Her door was slightly ajar.

"Looks like somebody got home first?"

Gretchen walked in the apartment. Cereal was dumped on the floor with milk. Her desk drawers were flipped onto the floor, folders and papers scattered everywhere. Her cabinets hung open on their hinges. Her bed was stripped, her clothes tossed onto the kitchen table. Every book she owned was on the floor with every bowl and fork and magazine. Her *Crier* cover stories, which she kept in the closet in a special box her father had made for her, were torn up, the pages littering her bedroom and even the fire escape. The pages of a photo album were under water in the kitchen sink.

"So my first thought is that you live in a closet," Cat Faces said.

Gretchen ran to the bathroom, got down on her knees, and puked.

"We're gonna need reinforcements," Cat Faces added.

Gretchen couldn't imagine why the woman was still in her apartment, but she didn't have the energy to tell her to leave. Her puke was red and chunky and smelled awful. She flushed and then eased her face down onto the floor.

"Yeah, it's me." The woman was still talking.

Why is she still talking?

"I'm gonna need some help up here. This lady, she's loaded, and I think somebody robbed her. No, don't call them. They're nothing but trouble. Ring the buzzer. OK. I'll be right down." She stepped one foot into the bathroom. "You stay right there, friend."

Gretchen heard the woman barrel down the stairs. At least they had left the window open so the heat could get out. Her head was full of lead. How had this happened? She had eaten at the Italian place on Spring Street, and there was wine, and she had taken a cab to . . . Cowboy's, where she waited an hour and half for Misty to come down and help her with this godforsaken story.

Cat Faces was standing over her. "I can't tell," she was saying. "I think she's asleep? Oh! Hello."

Gretchen's mouth felt like the inside of a gym sock. "Danny, bring this lady some water!"

"Danny?"

Cat Faces went out of view and then came back. "Here. You gotta sit up. What's her name?"

"Gretchen," Danny said. "What the hell happened here?

157

Your apartment is trashed."

"Thank you for stating the obvious." She shielded her eyes from the bathroom light. "Go on home."

"So you think you've got it from here, Danny?" Cat Faces said from the kitchen. "Or do you need me to stick around?"

"I got it," he called. "And Raven?"

"Yeah?"

"Thank you."

"Just"—she stuck her head in—"just take care of yourself, Danny."

The cold floor felt good on Gretchen's face.

L ater, she woke in her bed on the bare mattress. She heard a familiar voice.

Danny sat back in a chair with his legs stretched out in front of him and his arms crossed, watching *Seinfeld* on her laptop. He laughed quietly. In the glow of the computer screen, his face looked boyish and kind. A mop was propped up against the closet next to a big garbage bag. The floor was cleaner than it had been when Gretchen had left in the morning, the cabinets closed, her books put away. Everything in its place. She slid down from the bed.

"Oh, hey, sleepyhead." He got up, stretched his arms out wide, and yawned.

TWENTY—TWO

The Queensbridge cemetery reminded Gretchen of an orphanage in a way: the graves were set in perfect rows, all evenly spaced apart, with very few trees. American flags and plastic flowers dotted some of the headstones. Dominic's was in the center of a small plot, all alone, with space for graves on each side and for three more below it. The grass had come in this year but would be dry soon. It was already turning yellow. When they had first come to the site, the earth had been reddish brown, a pile of it on either side. "That's where the girls will go," Carla had said, as if Gretchen and Nicola were not standing right there. Then she had made the sign of the cross, and the sisters followed. Gretchen fought the habit whenever she visited home on these occasions.

So many people had said, "It's a terrible thing for a parent to survive a child." But Gretchen had always imagined Dominic would outlive her, too. For one, he was younger by twenty months. He was healthier—drank socially, never did drugs or smoked, and ran every morning. Gretchen treated her body as if when she used it up another would be waiting.

At the wakes—Carla had insisted on three, and each created a line around the block—Gretchen sat off to the side away from the receiving line. All the sympathy buoyed Carla through those terrible days. Not to say she wasn't devastated. It extinguished the last of her light. And Nico, poor optimistic Nico, said through her tears, "It's moving, isn't it? To see all these people come out for Nicky?"

159

No folded flag, no military salute. Nicky had gone to Afghanistan with a nonprofit, not with the military, and his parents paid the US government to have his remains shipped home.

When Gretchen hadn't cried publicly by the funeral mass, Oma Ada whispered, "You must grieve. You must let it out, Grete! Do like your mother."

Three years later, Oma Ada was gone—cancer—and Gretchen still hadn't let it out.

Now Gretchen darted out of the subway at Queensboro Plaza and puked all over the covered trash can.

When her mother opened the door, she said, "This is how you show your brother your respect?"

"Don't start with me, Ma. I got a splitting headache."

Carla put her hands on her tiny hips. "Where's Nicola?"

"She's meeting me." Gretchen kissed her on the cheek.

"I told you to come together!"

"She's not a child, Ma. She rides the subway all on her own every day. Would you stop being so controlling?"

"What, with all these girls going missing!"

"Can it, Ma. I got a headache."

But Nico didn't show up, and since Carla could only focus her animosity on one person at a time, Gretchen got a pass.

Brunch at Rosalina's seemed inappropriately lavish: eggs benedict, ham, french toast, smoked salmon. But Italians grieve by eating. Otto tried to sit next to Carla, called her sweetheart, tried to put his arm around her. Each time, Aunt Julia—Carla's sister—had steered him toward Marta, all while joking and laughing and calling him her boyfriend. Julia wore a purple silk scarf around her neck and a low-cut black blouse, a spray tan streaking her chest. She may have looked Jersey Shore, but she read Gogol and Balzac cover to cover and never, ever missed one of Gretchen's stories, not even a Borough Feature.

"Vito!" Carla said when the waitress plunked down her brother's manicotti and veal parmesan. "It's hardly ten in the morning. Your cholesterol! Think of your nephew, huh?" She made the sign of the cross. "Please don't take him, too, Lord. I couldn't bear it."

"Please," Vito said, New Jersey in his voice. "The Lord makes me lose my appetite." He laughed.

But every infraction was "I can't lose you, too" and "Think of your sister" and "Everything you are doing to your body you are doing to mine." Carla mastered guilt, shame, and denunciations of every kind, especially on holidays, birthdays, weddings, and death anniversaries.

Vito lifted a fork, only to have it slapped out of his hand. "Grace!" Carla said. The family made the sign of the cross and folded their hands in their laps. Carla closed her eyes and cleared her throat.

"Lord, we come to you on the day of our dear Dominic's death," Carla intoned, louder than was appropriate. Other diners hushed each other and put their silverware down. As Carla was known to say, parts of Kew Gardens still knew the Lord's Prayer.

"You took him, Lord. We know we don't get to know the reason, but we're confident that you in your wisdom had better plans for our Dominic." Gretchen let a sigh escape. "And even the least grateful among us"—Carla shot Gretchen a look— "trust in our hearts your plan."

"Dominic?" Otto said. "Where *is* Dominic?"

"Hush, Otto," his sister Jana said, taking his hands and squeezing hard.

"Lord, in your wisdom," Carla continued, "you have taken my husband's mind in punishment for our separation. I don't know what to tell you—he was insufferable."

If Dominic had been there, he would have kicked Gretchen gently under the table now to keep from laughing. She closed her eyes and pictured him across from her: his deep-set eyes and curly brown hair were all Carla, but his big cheeks, short nose, and broad smile were Otto through and through. He had a mole on his neck and curly hair on his chest that somehow stuffed itself through the buttons of his shirts. He was always sweaty, no matter the season, and many of his shirts were stained under the arms. During his residency, he'd sweat right through his scrubs and have to run and change a few times a shift. He had been middling height and stocky but slimmed down once he started med school. In the last years of his life, he grew a short curly beard and mustache. Gretchen made a note of all these details, like checking off a list.

But a pang of irritation interrupted her reverie. Who the hell had tossed her apartment?

Vita Quinn? She had kidnapped her once. Wouldn't be surprised.

Gretchen tried to remember her brother's voice, a voice that managed to sound friendly even when he felt otherwise. He had an ease with others. He called teachers "Teach" and doctors, even those above him, "Doc." If a bodega owner was always reading a book, Dominic called him "Professor." The cheesiest names came about when he indulged his fondness for musicals. The woman who had done Carla's hair for decades was Frenchie, bankers were Daddy Warbucks, Nico's friends all Tracy Turnblad and Peggy Pingleton. He managed to pull it all off without appearing disrespectful. She closed her eyes tighter, trying to summon the voice.

"Amen," everyone said, and Carla finally sat down.

"Finally!" Uncle Vito said. "Pop always said, 'God rewards brevity.'"

Aunt Julia reached over to swat him.

"I kid. I kid. Thank you for taking us out, Carla. You know I love you."

Carla pinched his cheek and smiled. Then, remembering herself, said, "It's a shame Nicola didn't see fit to join us."

"Nicola?" Otto said, alarmed. He tried to rise, but Marta gently pressed on his shoulders.

"She just overslept, Papa, don't worry." Gretchen signaled for more coffee.

"My eggs are cold," Carla said.

"That's because you prayed for twenty minutes," Vito said.

"I have a good idea." Aunt Julia was always one to have good ideas. "Let's all say something happy we remember about Dominic."

162

Uncle Vito put down his fork and took a big slurp of coffee. "I love it. Lemme start."

"Finish chewing, please," Carla said.

"Remember back when he assisted at Ma's funeral mass? Just a little tyke swimming in this big robe. It must of been a man's-size robe. Carrying that huge candle? The flame got bigger and bigger as he walked to and fro lighting the other candles." Vito's eyes followed an imagined little Nicky back and forth across the restaurant. "And every time the flame got close to his robe, Carla would yell, 'Dominic! Your undies!'"

Gretchen chuckled.

"I was bereft!" Carla said in defense. She laughed. It was like everyone had been holding their breath and they all let it out at once. "Ma hated laughter in church."

Gretchen watched her father, wondering what was sinking in. What was his favorite memory of his son? Did he have any left?

"Not that I'm one to upstage my brother—" Julia said.

"Oh really?" Vito said.

"But my favorite memory of Nicky is this. Picture it: Disney World, 1988. Otto made him one of those flattened quarters in the machine. It had, I don't know, a Donald Duck on it or what-ever. Nicky was so proud, especially because his big sister didn't have one." Julia chucked a smile at Gretchen. "He carried it around all week. The last day, we're at the airport when some-one"—she kicked Vito under the table—"decides to take one last photograph with his new camera."

Vito laughed, his mouth full of veal.

"We're all smiling for the picture, and Gretchen yells, 'Ma! Ma!' and points up at the escalator." Julia paused here to get hold of herself. "Nicky is holding on to the railing for dear life scream-ing, 'My quarta! My quarta!' as the escalator takes him up to the second floor."

Even Aunt Jana laughed at that one, and Carla shook her head in her way that meant she felt happy, sort of. It meant, *I am not angry in this moment.*

Gretchen's father slammed a hand on the table so suddenly

that Gretchen jumped in her chair and gasped. "Now I'm serious, Carla!" His face was red with alarm. "Where *is* Dominic?"

Gretchen felt tired, so tired, not because of her hangover, but because she realized then that she would never stop telling the story of her brother's death—reliving the story—until her father died. And now, she wanted him to die.

"Let's go for a walk, Mister Otto," Marta said merrily, removing the napkin from his collar.

"Don't you touch me!" Otto said.

"Otto!" Jana said. "Don't talk to Miss Marta that way! All the things she does for you! Please, Marta, allow me to care for him, and take the rest of the day off."

"No!" Carla said. "If she's on the clock, she'll be at his side. End of story."

"Like you pay for it!" Jana said.

"Please, if you will just let me—" Marta tried.

Carla stood, glowering at her husband. "Dominic. Is. Dead."

"Jesus," Julia said. "You don't have to announce it to the whole restaurant."

Otto pushed his chair back and scrambled to his feet.

"Mister Otto," Marta said.

"It's all right." He put a hand on Marta's shoulder. "It's all right. He's just with Nicola. They're on their way. Nicky and Nico." He smiled, looked around the restaurant for them.

"We'll get some air," Marta said, taking him by the arm. Aunt Jana took the other arm, and the women led him away.

"That poor woman," Gretchen said.

"Don't start," Carla said.

"You think she wants to be here?"

"Gretchen Binacci Sparks, do not test me today, I swear to—"

"Swear to what, Ma? The Lord you keep going on about? What's the plan, Ma? What's this secret, special plan the Lord had for Dominic?"

"Gretchen!" Vito scolded. "Don't talk to your mother that way. Today of all days."

"Oh shove it, Vito."

"Gretchen!" Julia this time.

"It's OK," Carla said, eerily calm. "Gretchen takes after her father, always has. He has a fit. She has a fit." She speared a chunk of cantaloupe with her fork.

Gretchen rubbed her eyes. She should have let it end there, let Carla have the last word, and she almost did. They rode in silence from the restaurant to the cemetery.

His headstone was small and rose colored. Gretchen had argued for musical notes and the First Aid symbol, but Dominic ended up with praying hands and a crucifix to commemorate his life. He had traveled to India and Sri Lanka to study Buddhism and Hinduism and animism and everything in between. He had been to Mecca, all while managing to finish med school. He thought Jesus was "a halfway decent community organizer but it pretty much ends there."

When they got to the plot, Gretchen took one look at it and said what she'd always thought: "This headstone is a joke."

Carla narrowed her eyes, turned, and slapped her across the face.

"Mercy!" Aunt Julia ran to her side and cupped her cheek. Uncle Vito grabbed his sister by her wrists.

"You disrespect me and you disrespect him!" Carla said. "You make a mockery of my life. You make a mockery of my son!"

"Carla, please! Get a hold of yourself!"

"Today isn't about Dominic," Gretchen said. "It's about you. Everything is about you."

"God will punish your insolence!"

Gretchen's face burned. She was so unaccustomed to crying that she didn't recognize the wetness on her cheeks to be tears. Carla looked so small struggling against her brother, but wiry and strong, and for a moment, Gretchen worried that she'd break free and come after her.

When she turned, she saw her father stepping away from the car, his hand on Jana's arm. Jana's mouth opened as if on a spring. She tried to turn Otto around but he walked toward them with Marta in tow. For a moment, he looked tall again, strong, like the pilot you wanted to fly you across the continent.

"Gretchen!" he said in the old way when he'd call her down from her room for a scolding. "What did you do to your mother?"

"I didn't do nothing, Papa."

"She is your mother."

"Oh, that's great!" Carla said. "Silent for thirty-five years and now you pipe up. Get away from me with your servant." Her voice was strained, and Gretchen could tell she was on the verge of tears.

Before her eyes, her father shrank again. "If only Dominic were here," he said, "he'd know what to do." He turned and walked back to the car, and Gretchen began to laugh.

"You torture them, Carla," Aunt Jana said through clenched teeth. "You tortured this man into forgetting his own children!"

"Shut up, Jana," Vito said.

Carla stopped struggling and put her arms around Vito, glaring over her shoulder at Gretchen. "You leave here right now."

Gretchen turned and started running, and she didn't stop until she was out of the cemetery on the street with her phone vibrating in her pocket.

TWENTY-THREE

She had no time for her usual Wednesday morning workout, but Vita wore spandex, a high-compression sports bra, and sneakers when she left the house. Dana barely looked up from his coffee and laptop when he said, "Don't forget. You're expected at the Amerigo Vespucci Lodge at two o'clock. And tonight's the banquet." She nodded and scooted out the door. Him thinking she was on her way to the gym was enough.

Vita Quinn jogging along Shore Road was not an unusual sight, so she took Bay Ridge Parkway to the bay front. She'd go see Julian and sniff around for trouble. Then she'd get on the phone with Cathy O'Rourke.

That morning while Vita was dressing, Gretchen Sparks had called her. The girl had some nerve, accusing Vita of tossing her shabby apartment. And she already wanted the favor before they met to exchange the photos! Gretchen Sparks wanted the name of a nurse at the hospital. A Black woman with glasses and freckles who worked in the ER or in psych, and that would take more than one morning's doing. Cathy O'Rourke had better come through, or she was out of the book club.

She focused on the burn in her legs, in her butt, with each stride along the bay and tried not to think about the night before. It had ended ominously. As Vita fanned Linnie with a throw pillow, she saw out of the corner of her eye Harlan catch Dana by the arm and whisper something sharp that made her husband's eye widen. She texted Maurice to come pick them up.

Just got my steak, he had replied.

GET A BOX.

Patricia and Harry had exited arm in arm, Patricia stopping to kiss Vita a little too close to her mouth. "Call me anytime," she whispered and handed Vita her business card. She worked at an upscale realty firm in Midtown. Figures.

The Benz rolled up ten minutes later. "Who was that at the door?" Vita asked once they were in the car, the divider to the front seat closed.

Dana had searched out the window, tapping his foot.

"Dana?"

"I can't believe you got her drunk."

"That woman has needed to get that drunk for her whole life."

He wouldn't look at her.

She scooted back across the seat. "What happened back there?"

"Shut up," he said. "I'm thinking." His fingers drummed his thighs. Then he slid open the divider. "Maurice. Tell me, where were you yesterday morning?"

Her stomach tightened. She could see Maurice's eyes in the rearview mirror, looking straight ahead at the road. "What's that?"

"It's a simple question. Where were you yesterday morning?"

"I was doing what you asked me to do," he said.

"Which was . . . ?"

Maurice looked in the mirror now. "You want me to say it?"

"Sure," Dana said. "Say it."

"I was driving that boy around town, like you said."

Dana turned to Vita. "And what were you doing?" It was getting dark. Headlights from another car flashed across Dana's face.

"I was home. I wasn't feeling well."

He reached forward and slid the window shut.

"If you're in trouble, I can help you," she said.

He'd looked away. "You've done enough."

Julian lived in the Towers on 65th, right at the top of Shore Road, but Vita cut west on a side street shaded by cottonwood trees, the sidewalk busted through with roots. She hopped over them as if she were on an obstacle course designed just for her. She could have done it in her sleep because this was the block where Vita Pozi had grown up, in the two-story colonial on the corner. The pool had gone years ago, and the owners planted junipers along the border. When Vita lived there, the house had been bright white with brick steps, neat hedges, black shutters, and a red door.

The place wasn't the biggest in the neighborhood, or the prettiest, but her father went all out for Christmas each year. Miles and miles of lights, a full team of lighted reindeer towing a sled overflowing with gifts that provided a photo-op for the entire neighborhood, a Santa clinging to the chimney. But every year, he also added something different: a family of snowmen, a choir of angels, a collection of nutcrackers. His nativity scene rivaled that at Our Lady of Perpetual Help, so much so that the monsignor beseeched him to tone it down. He never did.

The house looked different now, and she knew not to expect a great show of lights after Thanksgiving, but as Vita stood just at the gate, she felt calm for the first time in weeks.

Then she thought of Julian, and the words Harlan had said to Dana the night before.

Your brother-in-law . . . trouble . . . a girl taken.

She dragged her feet as she walked away, headed for the Towers.

She knocked for a few minutes before he answered the door, eyes bleary. He curled a lip, turned, and walked toward the bathroom, so she let herself in. She went to the kitchen and opened the cupboard. Garlic powder, hot sauce, a half bag of rice, salt and pepper, a ton of ketchup packets, and chop sticks. She found the coffee in the freezer and made a filter out of a paper towel. The kitchen was sparse—no table, hardly anything in the cabinets, the refrigerator bare.

169

The whole apartment was like that. As a teenager, he kept his room cluttered with posters and books, skateboards and VHS tapes. But now? If you were to walk in, you'd think no one lived there at all, that the last tenant had left behind a futon and a few sets of clothes.

Once, Vita thought that Julian would tell her if he knew what had happened to Sharon Draper. But he never did. And after the whole investigation finally petered out, after Sharon's brothers beat Julian within an inch of his life, after he came home to the house and convalesced . . . Well, of course he was never the same, but he wasn't normal to begin with.

She opened another cabinet, found some sugar packets and an expired powered creamer. Behind the creamer, a slim prescription bottle.

Back on the medication? Good.

But there was no label on the bottle, and inside she found only two very large white pills.

"Find what you're looking for?"

She slammed the cabinet door shut. "Cream and sugar." Vita washed out two mugs and set them on the counter. She turned and crossed her arms.

"I want to apologize," she said. "I was a world-class bitch the other day."

He smiled and looked down, as if trying to suppress laughter when being yelled at by a teacher.

She poured them each a cup of coffee. "You still take two sugars?"

"I don't drink coffee anymore."

She stifled a sigh. "We need to talk, honey."

He raised an eyebrow and cast a cold stare. "Yes, honey?"

"You been watching the news?"

He smiled then, and her insides turned to ice. He put on his Southern accent again. "I don't know what you speak of."

"That's another thing. What's with the accent?"

He drew his hands up to his face and giggled. "I made a new friend."

"Who?"

"A Mister Vittles."

"Harlan Vittles?"

"I may be acquainted with his brother."

Why, the only dark spot on those first ten years came with Vestal Vittles III, out of the penitentiary.

"What kind of trouble are you in?"

"I wouldn't know what you describe."

He's sick. He can't help it. Ask about the girls.

"I heard Harlan and Dana talking," she pressed on. "I heard Harlan saying you were mixed up with some girl. That you had taken a girl."

"You must mean my girlfriend."

"Your what?"

"My girlfriend. What's the matter, sister? Can't I have a little love in my life?"

"Please stop talking like that."

"I'd love for you to meet her. Sadly, she is indisposed at the moment."

Vita pushed past him and rushed to his bedroom. The futon lay against the wall, a comforter twisted up, the pillows on the floor. She opened the closet to a few shirts and pants, a vacuum cleaner, and a box of books.

"She's not here," Julian said from behind her. "She needed some rest. She's under observation. But I am confident she'll be back on her feet soon."

Vita did something stupid then—something she knew better than to do. She pushed him hard through the door and into the bathroom. He fell onto the open toilet. Once he recovered from the shock, he laughed.

Vita raced out the apartment door and down the steps of the Towers, taking them two at a time, and she didn't breathe until she got to the end of the block.

Walking home, her head spun. Julian was manipulative and unnerving, but Vita never actually thought him dangerous. And she still didn't, did she? She had mentioned the news early on, hadn't she? He wanted to give her a scare. And maybe what she had heard last night was just Harlan repeating the age-old Sharon Draper gossip. Still. Julian shouldn't joke about that shit, not after everything they had all been through.

She had almost calmed herself down when she stopped at the corner of 3rd Avenue and 89th Street and noticed a beige BMW double parked half a block away. Eighty-ninth was a one-way, and narrow, so the street was blocked, and another driver lay on her horn. Vita jogged across the street.

Vita's mother always said, "You never know who you're gonna meet once the liquor starts talking." Linnie Vittles must have the hangover of her life.

Why would Julian know Harlan's brother? Had she heard that right? She pushed the thought away. First things first. She'd call that numskull Cathy and see what she could find out about this nurse. Then she'd get those pictures from Gretchen Sparks and never have to deal with that little smartass again.

So confident she was in her plans, so assured that her problems were almost over, that she didn't notice the BMW pull up beside her until the driver's door opened and Harlan Vittles got out.

"Mrs. Quinn." He walked around the front of the vehicle and opened the passenger door. "Need a ride?"

She took a step back. "You following me?"

"I was just in the neighborhood." He gestured toward the car. "If you don't mind. I'd like to have a little chat, Vita."

"Fine. But I'm sweaty and hungry."

The BMW smelled like oiled leather. Harlan got in and started to drive. "We never get to talk, just the two of us, do we, Vita?"

"To be honest, I never saw a need to."

"That's what I like about you. You're always so honest, which is why I'll be honest with you."

She emitted a faint laugh. "OK . . ."

"Dana and I are working very hard to establish things so South Brooklyn Hospital can be of maximum benefit to the community—your community. I understand your poor mother had to go into Manhattan for all her treatments. We'd like to see Brooklynites get treated in Brooklyn for all of their needs."

"So I've heard." She felt his eyes on her, but she stared out the window at the passing houses on the residential streets.

"Then I'm sure you can understand that we don't want anything to get in the way of that. You and I share something in common. You may find that hard to believe. You haven't hid your disdain for me as well as you think, but I don't take it personally. And to be frank, your marriage perplexes me. But my wife—bless her heart—has a genuine soft spot for you."

"She was rather affectionate last night."

"Linnie's always had a loose tongue. She knows better than to have more than two or three wine spritzers. I can't fault her—the transition to city life wasn't easy, and even in all the years we've lived here, she hasn't made many friends. But once she gets talking . . ." He made a talking motion with his hand.

"Look. I don't want to know your business—"

"She mentioned my brother's checkered past. Much like your brother's."

She turned to him. "Neighborhood gossip, that's all."

"And you've done a fabulous job redeeming the family name."

"The family name has never suffered."

"Maybe so. Maybe so." He turned onto her block.

"What are you getting at, Harlan?"

"A little bird told me you'd been down around Coney Island—and not to visit my hospital." He passed her house without slowing. "Any particular reason you were down around 86th Street?"

"I can get out here. I have an engagement to keep."

"At two o'clock. There's plenty of time."

She'd had it now. "How the fuck do you know that?"

"Vita. Vita. Your husband and I are closer than you are aware. I know why you were in Coney Island, and I can tell you truly, your Dana is faithful." He turned right and went quiet for a block. "I just wouldn't want him to see any compromising photos of you."

Vittles, Dabrowski, Gretchen Sparks. They could all go to hell. Vita let a long moment pass before she said, "Harlan, if you're trying to blackmail me, get on with it."

"But blackmail is such a strong word!" He laughed. "Not to mention being illegal. I just want you to be wary, that's all. These media types can be very manipulative." He pulled up to her house. "And Vita. Let's just keep our brothers' secrets, well . . . secret, shall we?"

She opened the door.

"I hope you'll join us at the opening for the new cardiac wing on Friday. Don't disappoint me, Vita."

She got out of the car and turned to him.

"Stay away from my brother, Vittles," she said. "Or I'll fucking kill you." She slammed the door.

TWENTY-FOUR

Back in the Nexus and faced with a wall of craft beers, Gretchen scratched her head. Each name was wackier than the last: Blind Pig IPA, Great Big Kentucky Sausage Fest, Arrogant Bastard Ale, Brew Free! Or Die! Gretchen wanted none of it.

But she'd made the decision to only drink beer for the rest of the week. All the water in it would keep her hydrated and thus keep hangovers at bay. And she could work while drinking beer, and she had made the decision to work. Surely they had some Miller High Life stashed away.

At the counter, a tall, unshaven beast of a man explained hoppy-ness to a young couple.

His voice sounded like too many cigarettes and too much whiskey, like sawdust and rust. An octopus tentacle reached up from under his V-neck undershirt and wrapped around his neck. An elephant charged from his bicep. A woman's name— Clarice—stretched around his wrist.

Gretchen looked around. Didn't look like Clarice was present.

"Basically," he said, "with a beer like Wildfuck, the hops aren't bitter. They're floral because they're added at the end of the boil."

"Wait," the woman said, "beer is boiled?"

"We'll try Twisted Granddaddy then," the man said.

The guy rang them up, and Gretchen turned to examine the beer again. Her mind turned to work.

If you're gonna do this, you have to do it right.

And there was so much to do. Was Dominica's death a one-off fuck-up or a system failure? Who, if anyone, would go on the record about it? United Hospital Alliance was funneling money into the Quinn campaign. What was he giving them in return? Her headache hadn't abated. Just one shot of whiskey could fix that.

No. Focus. She could get a six-pack of High Life at the bodega.

"Something I can help you with?"

She turned. Gretchen was tall like her father, but the guy towered over her. "I don't think so." She looked at the door.

"Try me."

He smelled fruity, that alcoholic sweat that she knew so well. He smiled, showing crow's-feet around his eyes. Midforties, probably. Not born here but has lived many places. Was formerly in a band but now does solo stuff. The Beast, she thought, was in his last stretch where so many tattoos made him look younger. Red blossoms flushed her throat and chest.

"I think I'm better off at the bodega." She turned and headed toward the door.

"Well. Can't say I didn't try."

Focus.

"I'll be here till eleven if you change your mind." The bells jingled as she pushed out to Houston Street.

Her apartment was mercifully intact, counters clean and uncluttered, clothes stored in drawers and closets. She'd have to do something about Danny. She had been lucky he hadn't called the cops last night. All she needed was some code citation on the building to send her onto the street. He had argued in the morning that they might have checked surveillance footage from the surrounding buildings. "Probably just a wrong apartment. I'm not worried about it."

She was, in fact, worried about it, but the last thing Gretchen needed was someone breathing down her neck, protecting her.

She opened a High Life and sat at her desk.

If Dominica Padilla's death was a random accident, she needed to find out; otherwise, she'd waste precious hours digging around for nothing.

United Hospital Alliance, the parent company of South Brooklyn Hospital, employed three hundred thousand people at seventy hospitals around the country. Most were in the South and Midwest, but in the past four years, they'd bought South Brooklyn, one in Trenton, one in Philly.

Fine. They're expanding. So what?

Gretchen chewed on her lower lip. A story about UHA would be big, but she knew the loopholes the corporation's attorneys could create were bigger. She read article after article about them maneuvering out of skirmishes with Medicare. The company had been investigated and charged with seven felonies in the nineties and paid the government $400 billion—*$400 billion!*—but had been avoiding controversy since, it seemed.

The CEO was a guy named Jessup Landry, a former evangelical pastor with Hand of God, a megachurch south of Nashville. He ran for governor twice and lost. Came to UHA in 2008 and skyrocketed up to CEO by 2010.

"It's a documents game," Marty used to say. She requested Hand of God's Form-990 from the IRS and jotted down the names of the church's board members, including Jessup. Secondary sources turned up a lawsuit against the church: a volunteer with a sexual assault record had molested a child.

No rabbit holes!

But she searched the name of the reporter just in case. Reporter Avery Lane had a near obsession with UHA, Jessup Landry, and Hand of God. She had covered it in the city's altweekly and had a few op-eds in the daily. And then there was her blog *Cumberland Watchdog*. Her reporting was good, if her writing somewhat rambling. Gretchen jotted down her name.

Gretchen had never been to Nashville, nor had she ever considered going. Country music? Cowboy boots? And in a land-locked state? No thank you.

She pulled up the Centers for Medicare & Medicaid Services website. A thousand separate pages. She poked around the regulations for hospitals page, and her eyes glazed over a dizzying list of subtopics.

Her journalism textbooks were outdated. They could instruct her little in the way of online sources. She remembered some even elaborated on the importance of an organized rolodex, something Marty never gave up.

A few pages near the end of what one professor called the Reporter's Bible advised checking the Joint Commission, and listed a phone number and mailing address. The website had it all, except for an accreditation report for South Brooklyn Hospital. Gretchen remained skeptical. It was only two years old. Surely it takes time.

Gretchen looked away from the computer. She cleaned her glasses and remembered that Miller High Life loses its luster at room temperature. She'd need an expert for the Medicare stuff. And another beer.

With a start, she searched for the board members of the Joint Commission. Jessup Landry sat on the board.

She sat back in her chair and took the measure of what she knew. She had a CEO on the board of the commission meant to inspect his own business. She had a Southern reporter obsessed with both Landry, his church, and UHA. She had a state senator with a jealous wife and the name of a dead woman in his notebook.

Gretchen turned to Quinn's campaign finances. She was not surprised to find that many of his PACs were medical: medical instruments, pharmacology, physicians, surgeons . . . He was definitely in bed with these guys. But what was he giving them in return? She pulled up the New York State Senate page.

The bills he'd cosponsored over the years were typical: one against the infamous New York City soda tax, one requiring insurance agencies to cover hearing aids, another designating October Elder Appreciation Month. He wanted to raise pensions for cops, mandate tougher sentences for people who attacked cops, and divert SUNY Office of Diversity funding to create "In God We Trust" decals for police cars.

What an asshole.

But these were all from the 2015 legislative session. He had this whole second half of the year to scheme and plan, and January would herald a fresh crop of bills.

For over an hour, she sifted through his bills, scratching notes in a legal pad, discovering nothing that seemed relevant. What now? She cracked another beer.

Committees and subcommittees. He sat on Veterans; Homeland Security and Military Affairs; Judiciary; Insurance; Civil Service; and Pensions, Codes, and Health.

Quinn was quite active on Health, especially this past session. He sponsored a bill to add narcotics investigators all over the state, one for lupus research, two more to increase Medicaid and Medicare allocations for specific geriatric ailments. He knew his constituency. She kept digging, feeling a slight buzz from the beer. Nothing serious. Nothing that slowed her down. A fourth wouldn't hurt, but she'd stop there.

Finally, she found something that inched her closer. An agenda item from early 2015 featured a bill that would provide tax-incentive financing for for-profit hospitals.

Bingo.

It got out of the committee on a slim margin but died on the Assembly floor. But this was a favorite GOP tactic. Start with something big that's likely to be shot down. Then slowly erode the moral fiber of the legislative body. She jotted down the names of the bill's cosponsors, the yay and nay votes.

Coney Island wasn't in Quinn's district. The senator for district 23 was a woman named Diane Lupinacci. The Italians really had Brooklyn by the balls.

Lupinacci, however, was a Democrat, and voted opposite Quinn on many measures in Codes, Judiciary, and Civil Service and Pensions, the committees they shared. How might Diane Lupinacci feel about South Brooklyn Hospital? She had voted against it on the floor. It seemed Lupinacci would want a say in what's happening in her own backyard.

Gretchen read the agenda of the final Health meeting in the 2015 session, in which members voted on new appointments.

"Hello, Diane Lupinacci," Gretchen said. She rechecked the Health Committee members, but Diane was voted down.

This—this is something I can work with.

The discovery rang all through her body. Her toes tingled. Her throat flushed. She overturned the dead potted plant on her balcony and retrieved the doubloon and the key, pocketed them, and ran down to the street. She stood on the corner of Christopher and 6th Avenue. The rumbling of the subway shook the grate below her feet.

It had been so long, so miserably long since she'd felt the high of work, of digging up dirt, of wanting justice where the system had failed.

She wanted to keep that feeling, to stretch it out as far as it could go. The sheer thrill of public information made her lightheaded. She took off west past her apartment and into the dear, well-trodden maze of the West Village, its narrow streets and tiny storefronts, its darkened brownstones and bright bodegas. Before she knew it, she had taken enough left turns to end up at Christopher Street Pier. She ran across West Street and through the park, wind whipping at her hair, lungs burning from the chilly air and the week of smoking and the unexpected exercise. Summers filled the park with lollygaggers and lovers, but in mid-October, few remained. Her boots made a hollow thud on the pier's wooden floorboards.

She stopped at the end of the pier. Had it not been for the railing, she might have kept going. Blood pulsed in her ears and sweat wet her back. She let out a cry, a howl, a barbaric yawp to let the river and the Statue of Liberty and city know that she, Gretchen Sparks, was back.

She looked at her watch. It was ten-fifty.

She retreated across the pier and turned south toward Houston Street.

TWENTY–FIVE
Author's Note

D espite Gretchen's passionate argument for journalism, I changed my major from poetry to healthcare administration. What can I say? I have a knack for bureaucracy, for rules and regulations, for board meetings and policy and typing up memos. I got a graduate degree in Nursing Home Administration.

I kept attending open mics, depressing as they were. I kept sending my poems out to literary magazines far beyond my reach—*Harper's, The New Yorker, Ploughshares.* Aim high, my father always said, not about poetry.

I landed a job in a midtown nursing home almost immediately, managing billing. Before long, I managed purchasing, too, and then all of finances. I requested an hour a day to be on the floor, poking around with the residents. The director, a rich old bastard who seemed amused by the request, allowed it provided I could stay on top of my duties.

I kept dreaming.

Four years in, the director called me into his office to tell me he was to retire and would like to recommend me to the board.

Me? Quiet, daydreaming, eats-lunch-alone-to-read-John-Ashbury-poems me? "Yes you, Raj. You've got a mind for administration, both big-picture vision and detail orientation that makes you a reputable candidate. I never cared for the minutiae of the work. There are so many things I still want to do." He gazed out the window of his corner office at the East River and over to Queens, his skin so pale that it appeared translucent beneath his eyes. "I still have a few good years left to travel, write my memoirs, get back to nature. Life is short. You've done good for us here. The residents and staff respect and like you, but you've managed to keep yourself detached enough that there's no worry on that front." He picked up a marble paperweight from his neat desk and set it down again. "What do you say?"

I turned around and walked out of the room, went to my desk, and drafted a short letter of resignation.

Τhe night that Gretchen declared herself at the Christopher Street Pier, the doorbell rang at my SoHo apartment just after eleven o'clock.

I opened the door and jumped back in alarm. Gretchen Sparks, sweating and wild-eyed, leaned against the building, panting.

You didn't really think she'd gone back to the beer barn to shag that beast, did you?

Well, she didn't.

I stepped outside.

"What are you doing here? Is it Marty?" My words must have sounded so harsh, so accusatory. We stood face to face for the first time in over two years since she'd crammed the last of her things into a cab and said to me from the curb, "I'm sorry."

And what had I said? "No, you're not."

"Raj," she said now, "I'm sorry to show up like this."

So full of apologies.

She looked down at the ground. "I thought if I called, you'd hang up on me."

The truth was, she had been on my mind all week, it being the anniversary of her brother's death.

She looked pretty terrible. Her face was puffy. She had dark shadows under her eyes. Some mascara smeared from her eye to her ear, and her rectangular glasses, smudged with fingerprints, were a step in the wrong direction from the cat eyes that she wore for a decade. She had changed her hair, of course.

Don't they always change their hair before they show up late in the evening?

She wore it short, all the length that she had braided day in and day out, gone and replaced by a cute but unkempt shag the color of mice.

"Can I come in?"

"Who is it, baby?" Vidya said from the bedroom. The air left my chest.

"Oh," Gretchen said. "Never mind coming in. I wanted to ask you a couple things about Medicare. I'm doing some research and just can't wrap my head around it all. Could we meet sometime? Tomorrow?"

Had she come two years ago, I would have kicked whatever trollop lay in my bed out onto the street and took her by the hand.

"Is it for Otto?"

"Raj?" Vidya called.

"Gretchen. It's late. You showing up like this—it's not fair to me. If you don't have any news about Marty, I can't imagine what we might discuss." I went back in the house and began to close the door, but she caught it with her boot.

"But it is for Marty. I mean, it's a story that Marty started before—"

"Gretchen." I said her dear name again and nodded at her foot. "Good night."

I don't know what I would have done if she'd refused to remove the boot. I might have lunged at her and knocked her into the street. I might have cowered before her and offered myself to be sacrificed. But Gretchen Sparks removed her foot, said good night, and watched me shut the door.

I hardly slept.

TWENTY–SIX

Suite 4D was in its usual state of disorder. It opened up into a living room with a blow-up armchair half deflated, a zebra-print area rug, and a standard university dorm loveseat with wood frame and maroon cushions. The coffee table was covered with an incense tray overflowing with wormlike ashes, magazines, an open bottle of nail polish remover, and four bottles of candy-colored polish. On the walls hung black-and-white street scenes of Paris and Rome and Madrid—places Nico Sparks had never been. The bass of a rap song faintly pouted from another suite.

"Hello?" Gretchen peeked into the kitchen—sink full of dishes, an overflowing trash can with a pizza box crammed halfway inside, an open window. The door to Nico's room was open. Gretchen knocked and went in. The roommate lay on her bed, flipping through an issue of *Cosmo* with her usual bored and contemptuous expression. She didn't look up.

"Hey, Gabby."

"What do you want?"

"I'm looking for Nico."

Gabby stopped on a page smattered with handbags and yawned. "As you might have noticed, she's not home."

"She didn't show up yesterday for our brother's anniversary either."

Gabby shrugged.

"Did you notice if she overslept?"

"Nope."

185

"Nope you didn't notice, or nope she didn't oversleep?"

Gabby looked up. She had vacant, bovine eyes. Her mouth worked a wad of gum. "It's like I told the officer. She didn't come home Tuesday night. Had a date."

Gretchen's stomach did a flip. "Wait, what officer?"

"Detective Something-or-other. Came by last night." She turned the page of the magazine as if exhausted by the task.

"Has Nico called you or texted?"

"Maybe. Once or twice."

"She's been out of pocket for almost twenty-four hours. Aren't you worried?"

The girl sighed and put her magazine down with a splat. "She stays out sometimes. No big deal."

"Who's the guy?"

Gabby rolled her eyes and reached to her nightstand for a hairbrush. She pulled it through her molasses brown hair. "Maybe if you took a bit more of an interest in her life, you'd know that she met him in the park the day after her birthday, which you forgot."

"Is he a student?"

"Why don't you find one of her friends who is not quote-unquote an asshole and ask her?"

"You said she texted you. What did she say?"

Gabby flipped over and faced the wall.

Gretchen darted to her nightstand and grabbed Gabby's iPhone. "Hey! You can't—"

"Shut up." At 11:20 p.m. Nico had written, *omg we are totes connecting i think I'm gonna get some 2nite!!!* with three heart-eyes emoji.

Gabby hadn't responded.

Then, at 1:23 a.m., *now somewhere in the bk not sure where can u talk????*

"This one at one-thirty—did you call her?"

Gabby yawned and turned on her side. She started doing some kind of Pilates move with her leg. "I was sleeping."

"And did you respond in the morning?"

"Are we done with the interrogation? I don't know anything.

Now, I'd thank you to put down my phone and get out."

Gretchen left her business card on the nightstand with the phone. She turned and assessed Nico's side of the room. The bed was unmade, leopard print sheets balled up at the foot, a flat pillow without a pillowcase. Clothes spilled out of crooked, open drawers. Perfume, makeup, cheap jewelry, and a lighted magnifying mirror cluttered the top of the dresser. She picked up a strappy marine blue dress crumpled on the floor, folded it neatly, and put it on top of some other clothes.

Nico's desk was just as messy with psychology textbooks, more nail polish, and random odds and ends scattered about. She picked up a dusty picture of the three of them standing outside the church on Easter, Gretchen in a black dress, pale and unsmiling; Nicky in a navy suit and mustard tie, his messy mop of light brown hair sticking up everywhere; and Nico, just six years old, in a pink-and-white ruffled frock, holding an Easter basket and smiling, her already long hair in a tumble of curls. Another dusty frame held Nicky's high school photo. He wore a crisp white shirt and the same mustard tie, his hair cut a bit shorter and parted on one side, his smile the most natural thing in the world. She sifted through Nico's textbooks and notebooks, some of them as dusty as the glass of the picture frames.

It was just like Nico to call up Gretchen and put on a big guilt trip about her birthday and the family, only to shack up with some douchebag for a few days and turn her phone off.

Then she saw it: Nico's glittered notebook. She slipped it into her bag and turned. Gabby was on the floor now doing crunches. Gretchen stepped over her and out the door.

The mid-morning sun glinted off the cars and the buildings and caught her off guard. It was nine-thirty already. She took out her phone.

"What do you mean she wouldn't talk to you?" Carla said.

"Did you call the police?" Gretchen had to get to the office.

"What do you think, *stunod?* Of course I called the police! There's two more girls missing! Possibly more!"

"That's because every coed in Manhattan's mother is calling

the police at the first provocation. If you'd back off, maybe they could do their job."

"I can feel it in me, Gretchen. Like I did when your brother died."

"Jesus, can you not—"

"Lord, she takes your name in—"

"She's just out with some guy. You're gonna give yourself a heart attack over nothing. I'm going to work now."

"While you're downtown, go over to Parisi and get me a loaf of Italian bread and a mortadella. I'll pay you back."

"Goodbye, Ma."

Typical.

The sausage comes second to the missing daughter, but not by far.

On the subway, she read the most recent diary entry, almost against her will. The last thing she wanted was more details about her sister's life. And besides, their mother never respected their privacy. No matter where the Sparks kids hid their journals, Carla rooted them out.

> *Welcome to age 23, here's some alcohol, here's some shitty friends, here's a toilet to puke in. One for the books. I don't care so much that she forgot my birthday. Know why? I woke up when she climbed into the little bed. She put her arms around me and she snuggled me like a big spoon. It was a long time before I heard her breathing change and she fell asleep and even though I had to pee so bad I didn't move until it was time to make it to class. She'd be so mad at me if she knew I used her toothbrush but my mouth was so foul. I miss Nicky so much, and I can't help but wonder if it would be easier if Gretchen and I had a better relationship or something. Or something. Or something.*

That was it. The end of the entry. The subway screeched into Union Square.

She made it to her desk undetected. It was Thursday. She'd been putting the obituary off for over a week. And now, she knew she would do Marty's memory better by taking a little time for research before lunch.

Before she learned Medicaid, she had to learn hospitals. She read Senate bills and the minutes of House hearings. She read articles about New York hospitals, about Tennessee hospitals, about California hospitals if it seemed relevant—anything to give her a picture of that bright white landscape. She scanned medical journals for quantitative data and read personal accounts by nurses and doctors who had defected from the for-profit sector. She read and read and read.

NYU had required her to choose a second major. "Are you sure I can't just take the journalism classes twice?" Gretchen had asked. She'd had a series of arguments with the department chair who advised Economics of Statistics. Finally, the woman invited her to an event.

"A faculty lecture?" Gretchen scrunched up her nose.

"Yes, Ms. Sparks," the Chair said. "If it means you'll stop waiting outside my office, you can come as my guest. Maybe you'll be inspired by our speaker." She nodded toward her other students waiting in the hallway, handed Gretchen a flier, and scooted her out the door.

The lecture was titled, "Wild Over the Web: Training the Next Generation of Print Journalists." How was this going to get her out of an econ major? She got to the hall early and sat in front.

From the moment Marty Mitnik opened his mouth, she was transfixed. It wasn't one lecture, but a hundred. He talked about the "open unwillingness of veteran journalists and indeed some journalism professors to groom this generation for print." He said it wasn't the obligation of kids to embrace print journalism; it was the responsibility of faculty and investigators to make print as exciting as anything online. He told of a story for the *Metropolitan*—which Gretchen read just about every day—about the corporate lobbyists and legislators who cavorted to form the for-profit prison industry.

Wait! Gretchen nearly jumped out of her chair. She had read that story! Sure, she hadn't understood all of the public sector/private sector stuff—maybe that econ major would come in handy—but she had read it front to back and remembered best the people he described. The woman who said she was only given five tampons per month, the laborer denied treatment for a hernia until he had to undergo a costly surgery and lost part of his large intestine—Gretchen may not have understood every word of the economics and legislation, but she understood *them*.

He said that when he'd investigated that story he felt like he was re-discovering the reasons he had wanted to pursue the news to begin with: the honesty of it, the sheer heft and brawl of the facts that are always available somewhere if you're "crazy enough to start looking."

Gretchen scribbled notes as fast as she could. She didn't want to miss a word.

"It is nearly impossible," he said, "to keep that feeling up front day in and day out. I know most of you. We have to relearn the reasons we set out on this path and share that with these young kids, or else they'll be scattering across the web to regurgitate what's already been written, and before you know it, we'll be stuck in an endless circle jerk with no allegiance to facts or capital-T truth.

"Journalism," he reminded the group, "is the only institution named and protected in the Constitution." Gretchen's eyes widened.

He spoke passionately—red-faced, those pointy eyebrows rising and falling with every other word, sweat wetting the ends of his hair and making it curl in the over-heated lecture hall—often spitting right onto the front row. But in all the excitement, Gretchen became confused.

She *was* excited about print journalism. She *wanted* to make the world a better, freer place by reporting the hell out of it! Were there people who didn't? People in her very own program? She looked around for dissenters. The faculty members sat in varying states of engagement. Several had their own favorite papers on their tiny auditorium seating desks, bemused expressions on their faces. Some were taking notes. The Chair sat beside Gretchen, arms crossed over her chest, her head doing that dip when you're trying not to fall asleep. These were leaders?

By the time he stopped to take questions, half the faculty members had snuck out of the hall. Gretchen shot her hand up.

"Yes!" Marty Mitnik of the *Metropolitan* said, uncapping a bottle of water. "NYU's youngest faculty member!"

"If I understand you, Mr. Mitnik, you're worried because *other* journalists are worried that the next generation of journalists won't be passionate about print media? Isn't that kind of a circle jerk of fear?"

The Chair sat up in her seat, awake. Marty took another swig of water, as if considering her point.

Gretchen bowed her head but drove on. "I don't mean any disrespect, Mr. Mitnik. I just don't think journalism students are as doomed as you all might think. We're not all obsessed with tech fads. I don't even own a cell phone—though it would be easier to conduct interviews without my mother tying up the line." She looked up. Marty Mitnik wore a smile on his face.

Later, they sat at a table in the corner of the cafeteria, Gretchen in her trench coat and cat-eye glasses, her long hair in two braids, Marty in his button-down shirt with the sleeves rolled up. He must be tired from the presentation, Gretchen thought, because he let her go on for ages about what major to choose and what kind of work she hoped to do and what she thought of the department. He also must be hungry, she thought. He ate two Italian subs.

"What do you think I should do?"

"Do?" Marty said, wiping his mouth.

"About the double major."

"Oh. Well it's pretty simple. If you want to do investigative work, you have to understand everything you can about the society you wish to investigate."

"So . . . econ?"

He shrugged. "If I could go back and do it again, I'd study sociology." He threw back his third Diet Coke. "But what do I know?" He stood up. "I've gotta run, Gretchen Sparks. When it's time for your internship, I'd love to have you at the *Crier*."

"The *Crier*?"

"The *Village Crier*. That's my paper, these days." He smiled and handed her a business card.

Why would anyone in their right mind go from writing for the *Metropolitan* to the *Village*-freaking-*Crier*?

He'd taken her hand in both of his. "It's been illuminating."

"You have no idea," she'd said.

Three years later, opening Marty's mail at the *Crier*, she'd found the letter from the Riker's prisoner and got to watch Marty work. It was like her education had jumped off the page of a textbook and came to life with an endless commentary of expletives and self-debasing taunts that Marty delivered from his office.

Gretchen indulged some of these now as she picked through the hospital stuff, wishing Jaime Padilla's grandmother had died in any other type of institution on earth. But the previous night's exhilaration hadn't worn off, and for the first time in months, Gretchen did not have a hangover. Her mind was sharp and clean.

Critics of for-profit hospitals often claimed that administrators put money in pet projects at the expense of regular operations, like emergency services and dialysis machines. She went back to the hospital's website. A cardiac center would open Friday. So that was a start. But how would she find out where they allocate money?

It's a documents game.

But documents ran dry a lot faster when it came to private businesses. She checked Uniform Commercial Codes.

"The UCC," Marty would say, "is the wet dream of the insurance stooge. And the investigator."

The hospital's listing seemed uncompromising. It showed

bulk sales from medical equipment wholesalers, a lease with a telecommunications firm, banking transfers and loans . . . She couldn't possibly write it all down. She began to print.

On nearly all of the filings, the filer's name had been redacted, which was permissible by law. But in just two, it wasn't. *Patricia Summers*. She highlighted that name and cross-referenced it with the hospital board and physician list, UHA's board, Hand of God, and the Joint Commission. No match.

She made a note to find a contact at NYC Health + Hospitals; she needed to talk to someone in charge of South Brooklyn before it went for-profit. Should she check in with the state medical board? Did the hospital dump patients unable to pay? What agency would track that? Should she check civil lawsuit records? And what other private agencies might do business with South Brooklyn? Utilities, collections, ambulances? She remembered reading a story about a hospital out in the Midwest that got caught burning medical waste. What agency licensed incinerators?

How far had Marty gone? What had he already known? Who had tossed her apartment, and why?

But we have to be careful, Marty had said. *I don't know what these people will do.*

"Fuck me," she said. She took off her glasses and rubbed her eyes.

Stewart's head appeared above her cube. "Your comment queue is backed up. Last I checked, seven trolls awaited your moderation."

"Don't talk to me." She put her glasses back on and logged off her computer.

"You must be on a really hot tip to ignore HonestPatriot54."

"You don't see *me* memorizing their screen names."

"What's cooking, Sparks? This doesn't appear to be the usual fluffy goodness of Borough Features." She imagined herself ripping his Adam's apple out of his throat. "Turns out those two new missing girls were just skipping class."

"You sound disappointed."

"Do I?"

It was past lunchtime.

"Maybe I am disappointed. The idea hadn't occurred to me. If I am, do you think that makes me a bad person?"

"Shut up, Stewart," Gunderson said from within his cube.

She retrieved her printouts from the copier, got some chips and a Coke out of the vending machine, and sat in the break room just long enough for Stewart to complete the short search of his conscience. She thought about Vita. She was vain, condescending, and superfluous. But if Gretchen could endear herself to Vita . . . things might start looking up.

When she opened her email, she found a wonderful gift: scanned copies of a long list of names written in the unmistakable cursive of Misty Phelps. After each name, Misty listed the person's affiliated organizations. Physicians of New York Political Action Committee, Brooklyn Doctors PAC, New York OB/GYN PAC, Pediatricians PAC; there was a PAC for pathology and a few for cardiology, a PAC for ophthalmologists and one for pediatricians. There was a PAC for every part of the human body and more.

"I thought you might need another set of eyes," Misty wrote in the email. Gretchen could have kissed her.

She printed out the list and went about looking up those names for connections to UHA and South Brooklyn Hospital. A shocking number of the people were not doctors at all. They were investors, business people, the owners of hedge funds, executives. And about half of them lived in the great state of Tennessee.

The interns Zaiden and Brooklyn arrived at her desk arm in arm, one of them scrolling left-handed on a phone, the other right-handed, like some absurd take on a three-legged race.

"Conway wants to see you," Zaiden said, hair in his eyes.

"Now," Brooklyn said.

Conway's office was neat, hardly a stray sweater on a chair back, and always felt a few degrees cooler than the rest of the building. Gretchen knocked on the half-open door.

The woman sat in her large, leather chair, her glasses scooted down on her nose.

"Conway?"

"Gretchen. Close the door."

She sat down. "Is it about Marty?"

"No. His condition hasn't changed. And I haven't gotten an obituary from you yet. I'm handing it off. You're very close to him. It's normal that it would be difficult."

"But Roberta wants—"

"I can only be so sensitive to what Roberta wants. We're giving it to Timmins."

Gretchen didn't have room in her head to object. "Fair enough."

"But that's not the only thing we need to talk about. Your behavior the past two weeks has been unacceptable. Given the circumstances, I have let it slide." Her phone vibrated; she held up one finger and read a text.

"Conway . . ." Gretchen sat up straight. "Did Marty tell you about a story he was working before his heart attack?"

"What story? He didn't mention anything to me." She typed away on her phone.

"If this is a bad time, we can pick it up—"

"Tomorrow, yes. Clean up your act, Gretchen. Close the door on your way out."

Roberta would be disappointed, but Gretchen did a little twirl once she got down the hall.

Her investigation demanded her undivided attention, and it's what Marty would want. For once, a fresh pot of coffee awaited her in the break room, and someone's half-and-half wasn't yet expired. She was in for a long night.

As she rounded the corner into her cube, she stopped short, spilling her just-acquired beverage on her hand and shirt. "Dammit!"

A man swiveled around in her chair to face her. "Allow me." He stood and removed a folded paper towel from the pocket of his jacket and extended it to her.

Gretchen frowned and maneuvered around him to her desk. "I think you're in the wrong place."

195

"You Gretchen Sparks?"

"Yeah."

Gunderson's and Stewart's heads appeared above the cubicle walls.

"Detective Rudder. Missing Persons Squad."

"Oh, fuck me."

TWENTY–SEVEN

Everyone knew that Our Lady of Perpetual Help was the crown jewel of Bay Ridge. A few recognized it to be the crown jewel of Brooklyn. Every time Vita paused outside its inner doors to anoint her forehead with holy water, something stirred inside. "That's the Holy Ghost," her father had told her when she was a child, poking her in the collarbone. "It's within you. Don't let anybody tell you otherwise. Hear me? Now get outta here. Go play."

The morning meetings, first with Julian, then with Vittles, had nearly upended her whole day. She barely managed to get to the Amerigo Vespucci Lodge on time. Dana would not be happy to hear how it went. They were leaning heavily toward his opponent.

Despite the frantic afternoon, she'd managed to slip into church before the banquet. She wore a sage-green sheath with a boatneck and pair of d'orsays. Dana had sent her two texts reminding her to be at the Manor at seven.

She waited in line under the Stations of the Cross.

No palate cleanser like the Sacrament of Confession.

Dana had warned her about sharing private information with the priests, but she had nowhere else to turn. "Not during a campaign," he had repeated over and over.

Vita hadn't ever told him about the Holy Ghost within her. That wasn't something you shared with just anybody. Aside from her father, the only other person she had told about it was Alexander on the morning of his First Communion there at Our Lady of Perpetual Help.

It took a year after his death for her to feel it again. And still she sinned.

She sinned so often and came back to ask forgiveness so regularly that Father Robert, who was too old now to do much more than hear confessions, knew it was her before she opened her mouth.

He slid open the confessional window. They exchanged the usual formalities, and he asked how she had sinned. She poured it all out to him: Dana's secrets, his temperament, what he had said to her after the parade. She told him about staking out Dominica Padilla, about forcing Gretchen Sparks into the car, about Julian nearly getting arrested. She told him that she hadn't treated her chauffer right and now he was quitting. She confessed to wanting a divorce, to wanting to run away that very night, to meeting with the reporter to trade information. She admitted to being afraid of what Dana had gotten into, of what Julian had gotten into. She could see Father Robert in shadow, nodding his head. When she finished, she took a deep breath.

"Vita," he said, his voice barely audible. "I've known you your whole life. You were my first baptism, and I gave you your first communion. How long since you first sat in this box with me? Thirty years? Forty? I'm old." He coughed as if on cue. "I sat beside the Cardinal when you were confirmed. I married you and Dana here in this church. You were such a beautiful bride, and your mother, she was so happy."

Vita put her hand to her chest.

"My child, I buried your sweet boy. Jesus sees your failings. He sees them and he forgives them."

"Yes, Father."

"But His forgiveness is in vain if you do not forgive yourself."

"I feel like I've made too many mistakes."

"There are no mistakes too big for the Lord."

"But I'm in this mess now, and I don't know where to turn."

"You're thinking of it all wrong. Your journey is a spiritual one. James 1 tells us to ask of God in faith, with no doubt, for the one who doubts is like a wave that is driven and tossed by the wind."

"That's exactly how I feel."

"Ask how you can serve Him, and he will tell you. Go now, my child. Read James 1 and say ten Hail Marys. Ask the Mother for forgiveness, the Father for guidance. And do it without doubt in the power of His name."

So she went. She took a seat in a pew and read James 1. She asked in faith not to be "double-minded," not to "fade away in the midst of her pursuits." She lit three candles: one for each of her parents and one for Alexander.

Maurice was waiting outside in the car.

Vita watched Gretchen Sparks approach the Chinese restaurant in Sunset Park where they had agreed to meet. Maurice got out of the car and gave a nod.

Here we go.

"And here I thought we were having dinner," Gretchen slid into the back seat.

She wore that awful trench coat again but looked more . . . What? Alert? Alive?

"Drive us to Green-Wood, would you, Maurice?" She turned to Gretchen. "Just so we're clear, you are going to hand me your phone and I will delete the photos. No one will ever see them again. Then, I'll give you the information."

"Only if you're clear that I am not exchanging information for these photos. I don't want these photos."

"Yeah, yeah, yeah. You're not blackmailing me. I get it." Gretchen handed over her phone.

There were only three blurry photos, and Vita's face was barely recognizable. "This is it? Are you shitting me?"

"Would you have believed me if I told you?"

She certainly would not have believed Gretchen Sparks about anything.

"I won't tell you the name of the nurse unless you assure me that she has nothing to do with Dominica Padilla."

Gretchen laughed weakly. "Look, I'm sorry I've been such a

bitch. I have not been at my best lately. Or the past three years. Anyway, I can't promise you that. If that means you won't tell me the nurse's name, that's fine."

Vita hadn't listened to Cathy O'Rourke's forty-minute-long monologue about her bunion removal for nothing. "You're just gonna what? Let it go?"

Gretchen shrugged. "That's just how it goes sometimes. You have to put your faith in the process, I guess."

What is this shit? Faith in the process?

Heat rose in her face, and the inner calm she'd found in the rectory vanished. It seemed all her troubles started with Gretchen Sparks, and here she was, shrugging meekly and giving up. Vita thought of Vittles in the car, his beady eyes, his onion breath.

"You call me this morning and accuse me of breaking and entering, and then you want to wax poetic? You got some nerve, sister."

"Hold on." Gretchen put both hands up. "I didn't accuse you. I simply asked."

"Well, it wasn't me. You must hang out with the wrong crowd."

"I don't hang out with any crowd."

"Really? Hard to believe."

Gretchen sighed. She put her phone in her pocket and looked out the window.

Where are the insults? The mockery?

Maurice pulled onto 25th Street toward the cemetery.

"You must have more friends than you can count," Gretchen said. "Busy time of year for you. Must be exciting."

"Please. I'd rather let fish eat my eyeballs."

"What? You don't like being courted by tech companies and executives and doctors?"

"There are no friends in politics. Everyone wants something. Especially doctors." The car pulled up to the curb outside the cemetery's gates.

"I always thought doctors were the good ones."

"You are willfully naive. Doctors want to be millionaires. It's

200

the only reason they're doctors. I mean half of them are in real estate. Come on now."

"My brother was a doctor, and he did not want to be a millionaire."

"Oh yeah? Did he flunk out like you flunked journalism?"

"No, actually. Although I can't argue with your logic. He died treating patients in Afghanistan."

Vita winced. *Now who's the asshole?*

"I'm"—she put her face in her hands—"I'm sorry."

"It's OK—"

"It's this campaign. The endless speaking engagements, the constant attention. It's lonely. And the Shearses and the Vittleses and the press—I could scream." Vita laughed. "Maybe I should scream. Maybe that would do some good."

She felt at sea again, the wind knocking her tiny paper ship. Then she remembered Father Robert and James 1.

Do not be double-minded. Do not fade away in the midst of your pursuits.

"Well, thanks anyway," Gretchen said. "I can walk to the subway from here."

"Wait." Vita looked at her. "I don't know who tossed your apartment, Gretchen Sparks. But your nurse is named Cora Carter. She usually works the early morning shift, five to three." She opened her purse and retrieved the note with Carter's phone number. "Here."

Gretchen paused and seemed to be turning something over in her mind. Her eyes glimmered. "Dominica Padilla is dead, Vita. She went to South Brooklyn Hospital for a common flu and died a couple days later. The hospital won't give her family the body." She looked at the note. "Cora Carter—hopefully, she can make sense of this. Thank you. Vita, you won't regret this."

So that was it. The name in the planner was that of an old woman. Vita opened the car door and stepped out. "I already do. Tell Maurice what subway stop you need." She slammed the door and began the walk up the hill to the place where her son was buried.

"Wait!"

She turned. Gretchen stood at the base of the hill, car door open, wind blowing her coat. "What?" Vita said.

Gretchen looked up at her and said nothing.

"Go home, Gretchen Sparks!"

TWENTY-EIGHT

Vittles. *What a name.* Gretchen had scratched it down on a scrap of paper in her purse after Vita slammed the door. Vittleses. Shearses. Vittleses.

The name was almost not to be believed. Back at home, she brought the hospital's website up once again. Vittles looked like the forgotten member of a barber shop quartet. The thin hair parted on the side, the bulbous nose and cavernous face, the thin lips and fleshy jowls, Harlan Vittles, Chief of Surgery, hailed from Nashville, Tennessee.

Educated at Vanderbilt, he had a private practice on the Upper East and came on at South Brooklyn when it went for-profit. According to DoctorGrades.com, Vittles was an A-plus physician and surgeon. A true lifesaver. He was "quintessential and elegant," "handles angioplasties with aplomb and professionalism." He had published in medical journals, spoke at conferences, had admitting privileges to New York Presbyterian, and seemed widely regarded as a leading cardiologist in the city. So what was his connection to a rinky-dink hospital in South Brooklyn? She sipped her drink and thought about Marty. She tried to remember the last time he's given her one of his famous, massive hugs.

Someone good with documents.

Vittles's Upper East Side office was a private practice in a townhouse shared by two other cardiologists—a Connie Robinson and a Harry Shears. She thought back to a story they did back in the late aughts about a Bushwick slumlord who was mass-evicting his tenants, setting them up in another slum he owned for a higher rent, and evicting them again when the neighborhood got hot. The guy was what Gretchen's ma would call a real prince. Gretchen was a junior reporter at the time, had just done the fact-checking and spent a ton of time on the city register website. "Oh, the joys of public information," she said.

Back then, she had to study a few maps just to figure out the lot number. Now, she hummed, entering the address in the search bar. Harlan Vittles bought the lot for a tidy sum of $1.1 million in 2001. He refinanced in 2010, putting one of the other doctors—Harold Shears—on the bill.

The Shearses.

There were plenty of reasons to refinance, but the rate had actually increased with the second note, which smelled a lot like Vittles was going broke and needed this Harold Shears to foot the bill.

Another deed showed that something called Avia Development Group bought the lot for $5 million in 2014.

Doctors want to be millionaires.

Avia Development Group didn't seem to own any other property in New York City, not any she could find anyway. But Avia had many properties outside the city—in the South. The company had property in Atlanta, Savannah, Asheville, New Orleans. She found a few pieces published by a Nashville alt-weekly about the company, claiming they tour working-class Black neighborhoods looking for code violations and that they advertised a property as being previously owned by "bad-news people." And who had penned it?

Avery Lane, a reporter after Gretchen's own heart.

Avery Lane.

Gretchen arranged her notes. This whole thing was becoming eerie. Avery Lane was interested in UHA. Avery Lane was interested in Hand of God Church. Avery Lane was interested in Jessup Landry. And now, Avery Lane was also interested in Avia Development Group.

"Who are you?" Gretchen said.

What was the connection between Avia and United Hospital Alliance? Avia was one place where Jessup Landry hadn't made his association clear, at least not online.

It was a question for another day. She tried giving Nico a call once more.

Keep calling, Detective Rudder had said. *The sooner we can cross her off our list of people to worry about, the better.*

She washed up and brushed her teeth, and not until she was nearly asleep did she realized she had gone the entire day without a single drink.

The Brooklyn Heart Institute took over an entire wing of South Brooklyn Hospital—the only center of its kind in the boroughs. It seemed more like a hotel lobby than a hospital—all marble countertops and shiny tile floors, grass-green walls and leather sofas in the waiting rooms. The wing took up three floors on the west side of the building. A crowd gathered in the atrium.

"You wanna tell me why we're here?" Gunderson said. Conway had sent him along to babysit. She seemed more pissed off than usual that morning when Gretchen had told her about the opening.

"Sparks," she had said, exasperated by something Gretchen wasn't sure she had done. "I can't have you traipsing back and forth to Brooklyn every waking minute. I'm sending Gunderson along to see if the story is worthy of your time."

"Then won't it have to be worthy of both our time?" Gretchen had asked.

A big red ribbon stretched from a wall to a long reception desk. In front of it stood several dressed-up men and women, no one Gretchen recognized, but when one turned, she noted the beady eyes and pitted complexion of the man she had stared at on her laptop the night before. He wore an expensive-looking navy suit and a maroon tie, had his blond hair combed with a side part, and smiled as he greeted everyone.

"We could get a break in the girls story any minute," Gunderson said.

She scanned the room for Quinn. A small older woman in a yellow frock poured champagne into the little, clear plastic cups. Another woman, younger, rail thin with a black bob and pencil skirt, made her way around the room with a tray, a bored expression on her face. It was a quarter after ten, and Dr. Harlan Vittles consulted his watch.

"Here he is!" one of the champagne women cried. Gretchen turned to see Senator Dana Quinn walk through the automatic doors.

Jackpot.

"Who is he?" Gunderson asked. "If you don't tell me what we're doing here, so help me—"

"Sorry I'm late, everybody!" Quinn said, extending a hand up in a wave. The crowd parted, and he strode across the room to the ribbon. Vita's husband was even more attractive up close.

"Excuse me," someone said, putting a hand on Gretchen's shoulder. It was a young man, clean shaven. "Excuse me, if you're press, you have to move to the left." He herded her in that direction.

"Ladies and gentleman!" Dr. Vittles said, tapping on his champagne cup with a pen. "Allow us to get started." Gretchen turned on her recorder and sidled up toward the front. There was only one other press person, wearing a lanyard of the *Brooklyn Rail*.

"Thank you for being here on this beautiful morning," Vittles said. His accent was so thick that it couldn't be real, she thought, but she didn't know much about Southern accents except that they made people sound folksy. "We are all here together today because we believe in one common goal: bringing the standards of care found in Manhattan out to the boroughs. That's what South Brooklyn Hospital is all about!"

Applause.

"This," Dr. Vittles continued, "is the new crown jewel of medical research in New York City, and it is right here in Bensonhurst."

Gunderson scrolled through Facebook.

"You wanna hold this so I can, I dunno, take notes?" she said, shoving the tiny recorder on him. He grumbled but took it anyway.

Dr. Vittles was certainly excited about the new cardiac wing, but he was even more excited that State Senator Dana Quinn had made time to christen the new facility.

When Dana moved to speak, Gretchen inched closer. The man who had herded her to the left now shot her a look and shook his head like a bouncer. She scrunched her shoulders and stepped back.

"When I heard about United Hospitals Alliance wanting to build a state-of-the-art cardiac wing in my home of Brooklyn, New York, I said, 'Well, sign me up as a supporter!' Because the good people of South Brooklyn don't always have the time or the means to drive to Upper Manhattan for the best care. The men and women of Brooklyn—our seniors, our teachers, our service members—they deserve to get the very best care right in their own backyard!" Polite applause.

Quinn wasn't a big deal to this crowd, not like he was at the Columbus Day Parade. These were doctors and business people. They wore pearls and gold cufflinks and reeked of wealth. These people weren't from South Brooklyn, and they didn't care about a lousy state senator. But Marty did.

"Why don't you go get some coffee," Gretchen whispered to Gunderson. "Walk along the boardwalk."

"But this is just getting good."

"That's why," Quinn said, "I'm going to make it my business to introduce into legislation a bill that will loosen the chokehold Albany has put on hospitals in New York City!"

Real applause now, and lots of it.

"I will pay you to leave," Gretchen whispered.

Gunderson snorted and rolled his eyes.

"There is absolutely no reason why the people of Brooklyn can't have access to the same cutting-edge technology, world re-nowned physicians, and expectations of care as their Manhattan and Connecticut and Long Island counterparts," Quinn said. One of the champagne women handed him a pair of scissors. "This is hopefully the very first of many red ribbons I cut in Brooklyn hospitals." He smiled at Dr. Vittles.

"Ladies and gentlemen, the Brooklyn Heart Institute!"

The shorter woman in the frock held a tray out to Gretchen and Gunderson, one cup in her hand. Gretchen flinched. Gunderson looked around, shrugged his shoulders, and took a glass from the tray. The woman was older than Gretchen had thought, her face pinched. She seemed out of place among the suited doctors, her yellow dress like a dandelion. She raised her eyebrows and held out the cup. One tiny cup of champagne never hurt anyone.

"Bottoms up," Gunderson said.

The tour began. Instead of rooms, there were suites, including a big unveiling of the Hybrid Congenital Operating Cardiac Suite that Gretchen peered into from the back of the throng. A different doctor, handsome, a real silver fox, described each piece of equipment with enthusiasm, throwing in a dumb joke here or there. Gretchen glanced around the dwindling crowd for Quinn. She didn't see him—or Vittles.

"Can we get out of here now?" Gunderson said.

Gretchen handed him her empty cup. "You go. I'll be right behind you."

"And down this hall," the silver fox said, "are more of our luxury suites." Their doors were all slightly ajar, as if ready to welcome patients. "I'm sure you all have a lot of questions. I can take some now if you'll accompany me to the second floor. That's where the real magic happens." Gretchen hung back from the crowd. She peeked into the rooms. Each was alike: spacious with leather loveseats and chairs, large beds stacked with pillows, soft lighting and flat-screen TVs. They even had desks with Wi-Fi cables springing from them like little bouquets.

She heard footsteps, ducked into one of the rooms, and backed against the wall.

She thought of the photo on the shelf by the small altar at

Gloria Padilla's, of the young woman in the high-waisted shorts and camp shirt, crouching down on a road, holding a girl by the hips. Her smile was one of such hope, of such a sense of beginnings. In Puerto Rico, Dominica Padilla would have watched her young daughter sleep, her hand damp, her easy dreams spinning above her. What did she want out of the world then? How did Dominica Padilla want to live her life? How did she imagine she might someday die?

And how do I?

Would she die unconscious in a hospital bed like Marty would, her brain shut off, not a flicker of the person she had been? Or would it be sudden and violent—an explosion beneath her, her torso torn from her legs as if to escape the flames they had become.

She closed her eyes. Her head was light on her body and her bag heavy enough to drag her to the ground. She saw spots and strained to focus on the bed across the room. Steadying herself against the wall, she crept toward the bathroom. It was dimly lit and clean. She reached for a towel monogrammed with something or other. She turned on the water. Then she fell.

Gretchen woke up in a bright room and flinched. She covered her face with her hands. Balls of lead pushed out against her eyes. A migraine? Again? And this time without a hangover? She forced herself to sit up, cracked a slit in her fingers, and peered out.

"Well, looks like someone woke up." She knew him before she saw his face. "You took quite a fall, Miss Sparks. But I have to say," and he chuckled, "if you're gonna pass out, this might be the very best place to do it!"

She moved to bring her legs to the side of the bed, but they were trapped in the tucked-in white sheets.

"Now tell me," Vittles said, "what do you think of our new bed? It's not too firm, is it? We recommend some firmness for support, but, you know, everyone has their preference. I like a medium-firm, but my wife, she could sleep on a board."

Panic rose in her chest. She took a few shallow breaths as she struggled in the sheets.

"Now, now," he said, putting his hands on her thighs. "You mustn't get up yet, Gretchen. We're going to need to observe you for at least a couple of hours." He sounded friendly, charming even. But his grip on her legs was tight. "Try to relax."

"I'm fine," she said, her voice a whisper. "I feel fine. Just got a little overheated, that's all. Please." She pulled at the sheets around her legs.

"I know just the thing to help you to relax." He released her legs and moved away from her to the counter. There was a knock—two sharp taps—and the doctor who'd led the tour poked his head in.

He flashed a smile at Gretchen. "Good to see you've woken up. If you don't mind, I'd like to borrow your doctor. We'll be just a minute."

"Now Harry," Vittles said, "our patient is our first priority."

But Harry—*Harold Shears?*—said in an entirely different voice, "It is urgent, Dr. Vittles."

Gretchen noticed, even in her blinding pain, the dynamic of the names. Harry and Dr. Vittles.

Not Harry and Harlan. Not Dr. Vittles and Dr. Shears.

"We'll be but a moment, Miss Sparks," Vittles said.

The door closed behind them. Gretchen yanked herself free from the swaddling sheets and hopped off the bed. Her boots were beneath a chair, but her bag? She opened the closet—an ironing board and iron, hangers, a garment bag—and looked in the bathroom. It was gone.

She tiptoed to the door and could barely hear them, the one high-pitched voice of Vittles talking fast, the lower voice of Harry Shears rose. "I won't stand for it, Harlan. I won't!" Then quiet.

She felt in her back pocket. No phone, but in her front pocket, she had the small MP3 recorder. She turned it on before the door opened.

Vittles was still smiling, but Harry Shears wasn't. His square jaw was fixed in a grimace, his so-white teeth bared. Vittles held a folder.

"Miss Sparks, I hope you'll give us a lovely write-up in the *Metropolitan*. Harry here has been nice enough to put together a press kit for you."

She snatched the folder. "I'll be needing my bag."

"Of course," he said. "Harry, would you be so kind?"

Harry's eyes darted between them. He brought a hand across his forehead and then reluctantly retreated.

Vittles smiled. "What kind of story are you writing, Miss Sparks?"

"Just your normal write-up."

"Nothing too controversial, I hope."

Harry Shears entered the room again with her bag. "My card is in the folder," he said, "if you have any questions about the facility."

She checked for her laptop, her notebook, her phone. All there.

Vittles took her hand and pumped it lustily. "And please," he added, "give Mrs. Mitnik our condolences."

She stepped between them and out the door, exited the room, and ran for the atrium.

"It stops now," Conway said.

"I can explain."

"I'm getting real tired of excuses, Sparks. You've been gone for hours."

"I know," Gretchen said. "I am a loser employee."

"That's one way of putting it."

"An intern could do what I do."

"An intern *does* do what you do. An intern has been doing it all week." Conway looked exhausted. For the first time, Gretchen wondered whether the added workload was taking a toll.

"Have you had a day off since Marty's heart attack?" Gretchen ventured.

Conway crossed her arms. "I have not."

Gretchen looked down at the floor and took a deep breath. "I have been digging up documents about this hospital."

"You've been what?"

"I think it's something Marty was looking into when he collapsed."

"What makes you think that?"

"Because he told me he wanted my help on a story. Maybe something big, he said."

"I assure you I'd have known about it."

"Just listen. It all started on Friday. I'm down interviewing someone for a Borough Feature when this neighbor kid starts telling me about his grandmother's death. Marty had been down there to talk to his mom."

Conway looked at Gretchen over her glasses.

"Should I keep going?"

"Have I kicked you out of my office yet?"

"The grandmother died at South Brooklyn Hospital under suspicious circumstances, so I started reading up on it."

"South Brooklyn. It went for-profit a few years back."

"Yeah. It's owned by United Hospital Alliance out of Nashville. Accreditation is still pending, which wouldn't be fishy if the CEO weren't on the Joint Commission."

Conway drummed the desk with her fingers and looked behind Gretchen at the wall. "How much do you have?"

"Enough to make a start, at least. I'm sorry for being dead weight. I want to follow this thing. I think if we do it right—"

"Enough. You've made your case. I'm writing you a formal warning, Gretchen. No more coming in at ten-thirty. No more late lunches. No more dashing out early. I want you to sign in with me morning, noon, night. If you have a story, you attend a news meeting like everyone else and pitch it." She turned to her computer.

Gretchen lurched to her feet and toward the door.

"Prepare a proper pitch for Monday morning. That means a lede, documentation, a list of sources, and a timeline."

Gretchen let out all her breath and smiled. "Thank you."

"Sparks, do not make me regret giving you a chance."

"I won't. I mean, I'll try not to make you regret, or regret anything myself, um—"

"Close the door."

TWENTY-NINE

"**H**old up, Mr. Notelli." Cora Carter caught up to the man shuffling down the hall. She tied the strings of his hospital gown. When patients wore their own clothing, it gave them a sense of dignity in a place where it often lapsed. The morning had been hectic, and she hadn't had a chance to look in on him to get him dressed.

"Thank you, Juanita. Thank you." Mr. Notelli had undergone his third round of electroshock therapy Friday evening and was more forgetful than usual. It was something she didn't think she'd ever get used to: violent patients made docile, brilliant minds made spacey.

"Get down to art therapy now."

He waved at her.

Saturday mornings were a favorite on the ward for patients and nurses alike. They set a tone.

And after the shit that happened when she came in at five, she needed to breathe.

It was the usual. Two new patients came in back-to-back, one returning and a new one who threw a fit when Cora asked her to surrender her phone. Added to that, Natalie kept the ward up half the night by screaming in pain over her hemorrhoids. The overnight staff hadn't given her a thing to numb the pain, and by the time Cora came in, Natalie was crying quietly, blood on her sheets.

They'd each stay on for a few days until they met their insurance limits. Then they'd go home. South Brooklyn wasn't a place people came for long-term psychiatric treatment. It was for people in crisis. The staff was charged with getting them out of crisis and sending them on their way.

But now they all were in art therapy, and Cora finally had an hour to catch up on her records. She sat down for the first time since five o'clock, cracked open a bottle of water, and opened a file.

She had been too busy to think about that reporter—that Gretchen—but faced with a moment's rest, Cora worried. She'd gone over their conversation all night.

"Are you out of your damn mind?" her husband Jamal had said, back when Cora first presented the opportunity to him. Her father had been more open at first. He trusted the man from the paper; they were friends. But something had happened—Cora didn't know what—that changed her father's mind.

Going against the men in her life wasn't something Cora relished doing. But they hadn't seen what happened back in July. They hadn't taken the temperature of the sick old lady who mumbled in half-Spanish gibberish and hallucinated for two days, her throat so dry that Cora could practically feel her trachea scraping against her larynx.

Her chart said she had smoked synthetic marijuana. She'd had a kidney transplant in March, high blood pressure, asthma. She was on three inhalers. Cora's mother had been on two, four times a day, with a nebulizer treatment before bed. That's why she knew to test for *Candida auris*. Her mother had gotten to nearly the same state once, hallucinating and yelling, even cursing at Cora and her father. They took her to United Methodist on 7th Avenue—they had a car, which made all the difference—and the ER doc tested for it right away. She lived seven more years, long enough to know her grandson, before heart disease took her.

Imagine. Synthetic marijuana. An old lady like that. Cora's own mother had lived in Trinidad until they'd sent her, at eleven years old, to work as a maid in Brooklyn. To send money home. To await the rest of her family who would never arrive.

Cora's husband and her father all but forbade her to talk to the reporter. Buy they hadn't been made to feel small and stupid by a white male doctor ten years their junior. They hadn't had all their expertise discounted in a second, and before their own colleagues, when they spoke truth to power. Cora had, and it didn't make a bit of difference.

She was so preoccupied that she didn't hear Osha's sneakers squeaking on the floor. "You eat yet?"

Osha was one of those annoying friends, rail thin with the metabolism of a bumblebee. Always hungry. Always eating. Cora still hadn't lost the pregnancy weight from six years ago.

"Haven't had time."

"Come on," bossy Osha said.

"I'm behind. I haven't even updated my records yet."

"Girl, what time did you come in?"

"Five."

"Here it is eleven o'clock. Put that folder down and come on to the cafeteria. That turkey chili you like is on special."

The staff side of the cafeteria was never as busy as it used to be. People didn't have time to eat. They grabbed a piece of fruit or a granola bar, or at best a tuna sandwich, and scarfed it down in the elevator or at their desks. Even in a supply room closet. But Osha was good about taking a lunch, and she made Cora do it too.

They clocked out at the kiosk, making a careful note of the time.

Cora did like the turkey chili. At only 350 calories without cheese, it made for a tidy lunch.

"Give her that cheese," Osha told the cafeteria worker. "And some sour cream." Cora was too tired to protest.

"Let me tell you about my date last night," Osha said as they sat down.

When Gretchen Sparks first called, Cora had lied and said she didn't remember anything about a Padilla. ("I see a lot of patients.") The second time, she said she remembered a Padilla but couldn't speak on her treatment. ("HIPAA laws and all.") The third time, Gretchen asked if Cora could just look over a billing statement and help decipher it. ("I guess there'd be no harm in that. Can you meet me at the Dunkin' Donuts on Ocean Avenue?")

"And after going to the bathroom five times in an hour," Osha said, "he didn't even pay for dinner! Can you believe that? Cora?"

"Huh?"

"Am I talking to myself?"

"I got a lot on my mind." She scraped the last of the turkey chili from the paper bowl. "Sounds like you need to stop that online dating."

"I told you. I didn't meet him online. My cousin set it up." Osha smoothed her short straight hair. "What's on your mind?"

"How long have we been working here?"

"I don't know. Seven years?"

"Eight years. When was your last vacation?"

"You know I went to Atlantic City last month."

"For two days. When was your last real vacation? I'm talking a week or more."

Osha sipped her Sprite. "I know what it is. It's that psych ward. It's wearing you out."

"Maybe you're right."

"I know I'm right. We gotta get you back in the regular rotation where you belong. How much longer you got over there?"

"They said six months a year ago."

"Damn."

"I know."

"Well, better you than me. You know I can't be dealing with crazy people. I had enough of that in my life."

It was Osha's way of saying thank you, she knew, but still. The only reason Cora was in psych was because she'd switched assignments with her friend when UHA had taken over. Osha's mother had lost her battle with bipolar disorder the year before, and the new administration was reassigning half the nursing staff. It wouldn't hurt to show a little more gratitude. Osha at least owed her that.

"Soon you'll be in that bougie heart institute," Osha said.

"I doubt that."

"Assignments coming down the pike soon."

Cora checked the time. They had only nine minutes. "O, I need you to keep something between us."

"Ooooh, gossip! Is it about that orderly with the tight butt—Conrad?"

"I talked to that reporter yesterday."

Osha pushed her chair away from the table and slapped her hands on her thighs. "We talked about this."

"I didn't say anything on the record."

"Yet. Then she's gonna come back and say, 'Can't I just write this one lil thing?' Before you know it, you're out of a job."

"Will you lower your voice? It's not like that, Osha."

"What's it like then?"

"How many patients have you had to send home sick and in pain? How many times have you heard folks crying and wanted to help them but you're running around with nobody else to help out?"

"Time to clock in."

"How many times have you gone home worried about some old lady, wondering if the specialist got down to see her in time?"

"Plenty. But you have to watch your back."

"That's the problem these days. Everybody looks out for their own selves."

Osha got up, leaned toward Cora, and put her hands on the table.

"I'm looking out for *you*. Your problems with this place are valid. But this reporter, she's going to use you to get famous and you'll be out of a job."

"O, it's not like that."

Osha snatched her tray from the table and stormed off.

She thought about that hot July morning, eight o'clock and the heat coming off the pavement burned through her shoes as she called out to Padilla's daughter. She had looked to be Cora's own age, and like Cora, she had a son. And like Cora, she had lost her mother.

Cora didn't need Osha's approval, or Jamal's, or her daddy's. For once in her life, Cora would not play it safe.

THIRTY
Author's Note

S he called for the third time on Saturday. Vidya was at a retreat for the weekend. I didn't want to answer, but I felt drawn as if to a lighthouse in a storm. I wanted to anchor my ship to her port, if only for a phone call to see what it was all about.

I couldn't get a word out, and we sat in silence for a long moment.

"Raajen? Are you there?"

"Yes. I'm here."

"Thank you for picking up. I wouldn't blame you if you hadn't." Her voice sounded bright and warm. I hadn't heard it like that in a long, long time.

"Would you have given up if I had let it go to voicemail again?" I said.

"Probably not."

"How's Marty?"

"His brain activity has taken a plunge. I guess it's only a matter of time."

"Roberta?"

"Hanging in there."

I put water on for tea, an anxious habit I picked up from my mother. She still leaves steeping cups around the house, untouched. "What do you need, Gretchen?"

"I'd like to tell you about the story I'm working. I could use some help deciphering some Medicare bills and looking into hospital spending."

"Generally?"

"No. Just one. South Brooklyn Hospital."

"Well that's for-profit, Gretchen. There's far less information available."

"But I read that someone with the right knowledge base might be able to interpret some Medicare data."

Medicare data. I had run from it, promising myself I'd never look back. "What you need is an RAC."

"A rack?"

"A Recovery Audit Contractor. They're sort of like software-wielding anti-fraud privateers for Medicare."

"Like pirates?"

"No, privateers. They're—"

"I'm kidding. Ha-ha."

"Oh." I smiled.

"Do you think you could maybe look it over and then see if I need one?"

I got to the café early on purpose. I wanted to establish myself, as if on a turf. I wanted to have the upper hand.

I had proposed Cowboy's. Old times' sake and whatnot. But she had paused, said, "Actually, I'm trying to lay off the sauce."

She arrived on time, for once. She wore the same jacket, worse for the wear, her hair damp from the drizzle outside, and a charcoal cowl neck sweater and blue jeans.

And whether by chance or intention, she wore those Oxford flats.

Hesitantly, she asked me about myself, complimented with explicit details a review I recently wrote about a MoMA exhibition and one I wrote a year ago about an obscure chapbook of poetry that seemed to drive traffic away from the *Crier*'s website.

And then she hefted a few thick folders from her bag and we got to work until evening came and her mother called.

"I'm sorry," she said. "I have to go. I forgot to tell you. Nico hasn't been back to her dorm since Tuesday night. The police are on their way to speak to us." The shock of either her sister's unknown whereabouts and her own abrupt departure must have registered on my face, because Gretchen reached over and touched my hand. "Don't worry. I'm sure she's just holed up with some guy, giddy with excitement about what she's putting everybody through. Thank you for this, Raj."

She put on her jacket and made her way around the tiny tables of the café. At the door, she paused and turned toward me, smiled, and headed out into the rain.

THIRTY-ONE

The chiming of bells during the Liturgy of the Eucharist filled Vita with dread. Three days ago she'd spoken to Gretchen Sparks and climbed the hill to sit beside Alexander to talk to him. She had started as she usually did, saying how she and Dana loved him so much, and Uncle Julian and Uncle Michael and Uncle Salvadore loved him so much. And Grandma Cindy and Grampa Howie loved him, and everyone missed him so much and said hello. She talked about the weather and the big, exciting campaign that Daddy would win. But as she'd neared the end of her speech, she thought about him lying there in the cold earth, just bones now. Just bones. And she'd cried.

She zoned out during the Gospel and couldn't follow the homily. She held her grandmother's rosary so tight it left a white stripe around her knuckles. She said the Nicene Creed almost mechanically, feeling nothing.

Julian was missing. He hadn't been home in at least three nights, the neighbor said. He left Wednesday afternoon, probably not long after Vita had shoved him and taken off.

He had left, and it was her fault.

At first, she wasn't worried. He was angry with her and wanted to hurt her, and maybe she deserved it. She'd called Michael in Jersey and asked him to keep an eye out for their bedraggled youngest brother.

She called the precinct and the hospitals.

"I'm sure he's fine," Dana had said on Thursday. "He probably is just, I don't know, blowing off steam about something."

Dana was in Connecticut visiting his parents. He needed a day off from the campaign. She needed a day off from him.

But now. Now. This was a very long time for Julian to be at large, and still, Dana was unconcerned.

Maybe he hoped Julian would never return.

She had managed to stay out of trouble for a few days at least. She had handed out campaign fliers at the PTA meeting and read to the students at Holy Cross. She thought she had made some headway with the wives of a couple of high-ranking police officers in the district over brunch on Saturday.

She asked God to keep Julian from harm, to not punish him for her own sins. She asked for understanding with Dana and for integrity in her public life. She asked the Holy Ghost within her to direct her toward the right action.

The face of Harlan Vittles came to her.

She stood and filed down the aisle to receive Communion, slipping into Father Robert's line. He smiled at her, warm and assuring. She closed her eyes, and he placed the host on her tongue. "This is the body of Christ," he said. She crossed herself but did not move aside. She wanted to be just for a moment in the glow of Christ, in His grace and love. Father Robert put his hand on her head and whispered a prayer.

THIRTY—TWO

W hen Gretchen decided at seventeen to major in journalism, she thought mostly of dashing around the metropolis, pencil in hand, interviewing everyone under the sun and then typing all night. She didn't envision herself scrunched into a desk, eyes dry from staring at a computer for so long, mouth feeling stuffed with cotton.

But here she was, doing the real work, poring over deeds and court filings. She had turned up some civil cases against the hospital that were still pending. The legal process, she knew, was designed to make people either run out of money or give up before they felt justice had been served. Once the pitch was accepted, Jackson—the old stalwart court reporter—could help her with his contacts.

She had a prospect in Diane Lupinacci's office. The district 23 senator's chatty errand girl had a blog called "Philosophy Gurrrl" that consisted of selfies and philosophical musings that all amounted to "there are no coincidences."

Gretchen followed the blog and signed up for updates. Then she commented on a post.

Hi gurrrl. Love the blog. Want2chat about NYClyfe?

The blogger messaged her right away.

Thanx!!!

Within minutes, the gurrrl was yammering on the phone about her own aspirations to get the fuck out of the borough and join Gretchen in the Nexus, a softball topic that Gretchen knocked out of the park.

After twenty minutes, the gurrrl said, "Wait, what are you writing about?"

Gretchen explained that she was putting a piece together about some legislation drafted by Senator Quinn. Nothing too serious.

"Are you kidding? Diane hates that guy. She calls him Mr. Douchebag. He's pretty hot though—for an old guy." She burst out laughing. "God. I should not have said that."

"Don't worry," Gretchen said. "I told you, it's all off the record. I'm just researching."

"Well, I really shouldn't be talking to you."

She had a feeling that Philosophy Gurrrl would be open to another convo, provided she didn't philosophize herself to death first.

She got off the phone and rubbed her eyes. She was tired. The night before, she had started out in bed with her mother, but Carla's snoring kept Gretchen awake. She took to the narrow couch in the living room and finally drifted off. Maybe a minute passed before Carla started screaming from the bedroom.

"What is it, Ma?"

"Where are you?"

"I'm out here!"

"Is Nicola with you?"

"No!"

This repeated itself until she dragged the pillow back to her mother's bed and smashed it over her own head.

It was now Sunday. She'd last spoken to Nico Tuesday. No matter how many times she told her ma not to worry, the dread filled her veins with ice water, and she could only keep it at bay by working.

She had given the diary to the police and contacted the few friends of Nico's she knew. She knew embarrassingly little about her sister's life, so little that Detective Rudder accused her of holding out on him.

Since the two false alarms that disappointed the newsroom boy squad Thursday, no other missing girls had been announced.

But they hadn't announced Nico either, so maybe the cops were keeping things quiet to make their own lives easier.

Stewart and Gunderson had been on her case about the detective's two visits to the office. Suddenly, they were bringing her coffee and asking her to lunch.

Nico would make five girls, and all of them had been last seen on a date with someone new. But something compelled Gretchen to believe Nico was not linked to the others. Maybe it was Carla's mounting hysteria that made Gretchen grow calmer, Carla's escalating certainty that made Gretchen cautious. Even Gabby had called Gretchen Saturday night.

She opened her email.

Finally! A reply from Avery Lane, that Nashville reporter.

Dear Ms. Sparks,

I'll call you at 10:30, CST.
Warmly, Avery Lane.

How formal. That wasn't too far away. Gretchen pulled out her Post-its and went about organizing her notes. What she knew still had a big hole. Why had Avia Development Group bought out Vittles and the Shears? How did they stand to benefit? Would Quinn do some creative rezoning? She went back to his long list of sponsored bills.

She now knew one of Quinn's enemies. Who were his allies? Who might be drafting sister legislation? New York City's senators were so heavy on the Democrats that she knew she'd have to look north, maybe even as close as Westchester.

One question kept pressing, overtaking the others and crowding them out. It was the thing Vittles had said to her, just before she fled.

Give Mrs. Mitnik our condolences.

He didn't know the family well enough to express his condolences directly. And he didn't seem to know that Roberta kept her own last name—Krom.

And anyway, condolences? Marty was still alive. His heart still faintly rendered a pulse. The fact alone that Vittles knew about his condition filled Gretchen with foreboding. Her phone rang from a number she didn't recognize.

"Nico?" she said, surprising herself.

"I'm calling for a Gretchen Sparks." Dogs barked in the background.

"Yes! This is Gretchen. Is this Avery? Avery Lane?"

"The one and only," Avery said. "Shut up! Sorry. Not you. I've got a few extra dogs this weekend."

"OK . . ." Gretchen tried to wade in slow, but Avery Lane was ready to talk. Had been ready since the day she was born. Gretchen could barely keep up.

Avery had worked on staff at the city's daily at one point, but it got bought out by a media conglomerate, and Lane resigned in protest. "I refuse to write for clicks," she said. Gretchen thought of Borough Features and hoped Lane hadn't looked into her. But of course she had. "You used to do some good work up in New York," Lane said. "What happened?"

Anxious to cut through the small talk, Gretchen said, "My brother died and I lost my mind. I have found it."

"Wow."

"Your work is pretty darn good, too."

"Oh. I just complain in public."

"What do you know about United Hospital Alliance? Have any patients sued UHA for malpractice down there?"

"Many have. Few have succeeded. They've got a rug this big."

"What do you know about Jessup Landry?"

"Rufus! Get the ball!" Lane paused. "Landry is the scourge of the earth."

"Whoa. I didn't find that in my research. What'd he do?"

"He," said Avery Lane, "is a virulent racist. And a misogynist. And an anti-Semite." So there was a bit of a personal vendetta involved.

"Know anything about Avia Development Group?"

"Avia. Have you been to Nashville recently? Have you seen the dozens of cranes dotting the skyline? They think they're building Rome, but it'll die like a fart in the wind by 2020. You heard it here."

"I'm mainly interested in any connection between Avia and

UHA or Landry or this guy . . . Harlan Vittles."

"Vittles? *The* Harlan Vittles?"

"I only know of one."

"Doctor, right? Yeah, his brother killed their father when I was a kid. Pretty much destroyed everyone's childhood."

"Everyone's?"

"Mine, everyone's."

"What happened?"

"His brother went away for a long time. Got out say . . . midnineties or so? Supreme court decided to hear evidence of abuse in cases where children killed their parents. Both Harlan and Vestal and the wife left the state not long after that."

"Holy shit."

"Holy shit is right."

"How about Avia? Tennessee's online records search is not exactly user friendly."

"Your best bet is go down to the Office of Records on Deaderick Street."

Fuck. Gretchen was not going to Deaderick Street.

"Or I could go for you."

"You'd do that?"

"For a fellow muckraker? Sure, I'd do that. Tell you what. Tomorrow's Monday. After I walk and feed the dogs—could you stop! Sorry. I'll go down to Records and see what I can turn up about Avia."

"Avery Lane," Gretchen said, "you're a stand-up gal, aren't you?"

"I try," she said.

The dogs were barking when Gretchen hung up.

THIRTY–THREE

Damn. Gretchen checked her mail. She knew Nashville was in Central Time, but Avery Lane must have been at the Office of Records on Deaderick Street at the break of dawn.

> *Dear Ms. Sparks,*
> *Coming up on quite a few Avia Development deeds. I searched for your Dana Quinn.*
> *Nothing there, but a Howard Quinn bought a chunk of land 40 miles south of Nashville last year and sold it a couple months back . . . for five times the original price. I will keep you abreast.*
> *This is probably a shot in the dark, but ever hear of a Patricia Summers? She's on the deed as the realtor.*
> *Very Truly Yours,*
> *Avery Lane.*

Patricia Summers . . . Gretchen dug through her paperwork. Summers had filed for South Brooklyn Hospital with Uniform Commercial Codes. And now she had closed a sale of Howard Quinn's land in Tennessee? Could the Connecticut Senator—darling of the Dems—be in on this racket, too? Her heart going like mad, Gretchen glanced at her watch. It was time.

They were all waiting in Conference Room C when she arrived. Well, waiting was not the exact word, because Gunderson was up at the whiteboard outlining Quinn's political history. When she stepped in, they barely turned.

"UHA," Gunderson was saying, "United Hospital Alliance is out of Nashville—big money there in medical. The CEO is Jessup Landry. He's got an interesting past. Former evangelical pastor, opened a mega church south of the city that has raked in millions. Ran for governor twice in '02 and '08. Lost the Republican ticket both times, but not by much. Came on at UHA as a board member in '08 after the election, skyrocketed up to CEO by 2010. He's grown the company exponentially since. Hospitals in twenty-six states."

Conway nodded. When she didn't ask any follow up questions, Gunderson took a seat. The managing editor turned slowly in her chair.

"Sparks," she said.

"You said the meeting was at nine. It's eight-fifty-five."

"I wanted to catch up with the guys first."

Gretchen seethed.

"You brought copies of your lede, I imagine?"

She had it all prepared and collated. She slid the stapled packets across the table and took a deep breath. This had been a weekly occurrence at the *Crier*. The little pitch room with the water-marked ceiling, the stained carpet, Marty looking over his glasses that sat on the edge of his nose. But that was then. Each picked up the packet and perused her lede.

"We're waiting," Conway said.

"Right. As you're reading, a seventy-six-year-old Puerto Rican woman—an immigrant who gained citizenship at forty—died at South Brooklyn Hospital, which as you know from Gunderson, is one of three bought by UHA in the Northeast since 2012."

She paused and looked around. Conway made a nearly imperceptible nod.

"The next pages of the packet are copies of Senator Dana Quinn's campaign finance report. The first is 2015—this year. Quinn is the state senator of District 22."

"Which is?" Stewart said.

"Brooklyn," said Jackson, the stalwart court reporter and life-long Brooklynite. "Dyker Heights, Gravesend, Sheepshead Bay, Bay Ridge—all those South Brooklyn neighborhoods. Very white, working class."

"Exactly," Gretchen said. "Quinn is a rich boy from Connect-icut. His father is Howard Quinn, the Connecticut senator."

"So how's this guy elected—what—three times to a working-class neighborhood in Brooklyn?" Stewart said.

"It's the wife." Jackson rolled his eyes. "What do I tell these knuckleheads every time? We cover the whole city! Learn it!"

"Enough," Conway said. "Go on."

"Jackson's correct. Quinn's been parading around his wife, a former beauty queen named Vita Quinn, née Pozi. She was sec-ond runner up to Miss America in '89."

"Who remembers the second runner up?" Gunderson said.

"South Brooklyn, I guess. They worship her. She's like Kim Kardashian to them. Or Jackie O."

"Working-class folks," Jackson said, turning to his young col-leagues, "they have alotta pride. Loyal to their own. For Miss New York to come outta Brooklyn—not Westchester or Nassau or Rockland. Not a debutant. She wasn't presented to the com-munity when she turned sixteen." He gestured wildly. "Working-class folks—they'll take what they can get."

Jackson's enthusiasm buoyed her. He wasn't on her side—not yet. But he was doing something invaluable—legitimizing the story's possible value. So far so good.

"The finance reports?" Conway was impatient.

"In 2011 and '13—final page of each is in your packet—you've got regular contributions. A couple hundred from a small business, maybe a thousand from an individual. Maybe $5,000 from a club. But this year, he triples what he made in 2012. Dou-bles 2014. PACs are highlighted in yellow. Most are medical. But the ones in pink—"

"Copy shops . . . beauty salons . . ." Jackson looked up at her. "They're straws?"

"I've looked into a few. They're store fronts with a disaffected kid working at a counter. There's a single copy machine in one. A send-away photo shop that takes up to two weeks and sells dusty picture frames and albums. An eyebrow waxing salon with a C sanitation rating and the highest prices in the city. No one in their right mind would go in there."

"You checked all these out yourself?" Conway said.

"I did."

"This is a big allegation, Gretchen." Conway took off her glasses. "You're suggesting that a state senator is taking money from a corporation illegally."

"I know."

"And from what Gunderson told us, Quinn's got a bill?" Conway asked.

"That's the link. Or one of them anyway. He claims he's going to loosen restrictions in Albany to pave the way for more for-profits, which means," she paused, "more buyouts for UHA."

"What about the old lady?" Jackson said. "Where's she fit in?"

"Getting there. You should see this cardiac wing. Embroidered towels. Flat-screen TVs in every room. Beds like in luxury hotels. They don't even call them rooms. They're suites. The best equipment money can buy."

"And let me guess," Conway said. "The other half doesn't see any of it."

"Exactly," Gunderson piped in.

Gretchen ignored him.

"I have a nurse who says since UHA bought in, they've seen drastic cuts. Nurses shuttled around to departments where they're untrained—she was moved from pediatrics to psych herself. Broken equipment. Layoffs. Doctors with so many patients they can't provide care. They send people home sick. Nursing errors are way up. Several cases are frozen in litigation right now. That's on page fifteen of your packet."

"You can hardly blame a state senator for a poorly run hospital," Jackson said, and Conway raised her eyebrows Gretchen's way.

"True," she said. "But you can look at where the money's going. I talked to a Medicare specialist who is trying dig into the CMS reports, but with a private hospital, there's a lot less information. The cardiac wing is run by the head of surgery, a doctor named Harlan Vittles. A Nashville man."

"What kind of a name is Vittles?" Stewart said under his breath. She ignored that, too.

"Isn't that a lot of responsibility?" Conway said. "Running a wing *and* acting as chief of surgery?"

"It is! Especially for someone with his own practice to boot."

"Go on."

"The same nurse claims she worked a double on the Fourth of July, and in early morning, a woman came into psych from the ER. They thought she had smoked some synthetic marijuana. But the nurse didn't think she smoked marijuana. She thought it was ridiculous. So she put in an order for a test for candida."

"Candida?" Stewart said.

"It's a yeast infection," Conway said.

"In the throat. Dominica had asthma and used inhalers. It can enter the digestive tract and the blood if it's not checked out."

"Jesus," Jackson said. "So wrongful death on top of campaign finance fraud? Will the nurse talk on the record?"

"Not yet. But I think she will. She needs a little time."

"Again," Stewart said, "you can't blame Quinn for an ER doc's malpractice."

"Let her finish," Conway said.

"The next page of your packet is the deed to a townhouse on 5th Avenue."

"From 2001," Stewart said. "Jesus, even then, at $1.1 mil."

"Right. Deed is in his name only. But turn the page. He refinances with his partner, Harry Shears. And then—"

"What's Avia Development Group?" Jackson said.

"A big developer in the Southeast. Atlanta, Nashville, Birmingham. So I looked into it, and guess who sits on the board?"

She hadn't put this in the packet, and she let the question hang for a moment, the way Marty would have.

"Jessup Landry."

"Damn," Gunderson said.

The team studied the packet. Gretchen realized she'd been holding her breath the entire time. And that wasn't even all of it. But she'd hold out. She thought of Marty, how if he were there he'd be flipping through the papers, sighing audibly and saying, "Goddamn these motherfuckers."

Conway closed the packet and put it down. She leaned back in her chair. "What else you got?"

"Gloria Padilla is going to speak to me on the record."

"And your other sources are?"

Gretchen swallowed. "I got some help from the wife. From Vita Quinn. But she's not likely to go further and needs to be treated delicately."

"How much she tell you?"

"She got me the nurse."

Conway looked up, raised her eyebrows. "How did Mrs. Quinn know about the dead woman?"

Gretchen froze. She knew the question would come and hadn't yet prepared an answer that didn't sound crazy.

"Sparks," Conway said. "Exactly what does she know?"

"She saw me down at the Padillas' house with the seagull lady. She was staking out Dominica. I mean, she thought she was. She didn't know she was dead. She thought her husband was cheating on her with Dominica Padilla. She found her name in his desk."

"So she sees you down there and calls you?"

"Not exactly."

"The senator knows about the dead woman?" Jackson said. "Why would the hospital tell him that information? Wouldn't it jeopardize the relationship?"

Gretchen shrugged. "I think it's all Vittles. I think Vittles put Quinn up to sending some people pretending to be immigration to the Padillas' to scare Gloria off of finding a lawyer."

"Why wouldn't Vittles just do that himself?"

"Simple. To have something to hang over Quinn's head."

"Wait, wait, wait," Conway said. "If Vita Quinn didn't call you, how did you hear from her?"

Gretchen swallowed. "We went for a drive."

"You what?"

"After work that Friday. She pulled up on 14th Street and wanted to talk."

"And you got in her car?"

"Well, not willingly . . ."

"Sparks!"

"It wasn't a big deal. I was fine."

"We have to report that to legal. That is a serious threat. It places you and the entire paper at risk."

"But there's nothing to report. We talked. She dropped me off. Then I went to Roberta's and found Quinn's campaign mailer on Marty's desk."

"I need the room," Conway said, not breaking her gaze. And the others cleared out.

Her face was a mask of efficiency and calm. "Sparks," she said. "Do you realize what you've done?"

"I guess I don't."

"You have built a story off of a crime committed against you. These papers," Conway held up a packet, "are worth nothing. How can I trust you with a story of this complexity if you can't follow basic protocol? Not to mention the potential for bias after the fact?"

Gretchen felt everything in her stomach twist. "What are you saying? I'm off my own story?"

"I don't think I have a choice!"

"I'll talk to legal. I'll tell them the truth. Maybe it's not so bad."

Conway stood up. "Stay out of it. I will talk to them. Is there anything else I should know?"

Better get it all out now.

"Vita told me about the nurse because she insisted on meeting with me for some photos."

"I am not hearing this."

"It's not what you think. A neighbor of the Padillas— Dabrowski with the seagull—she took some pictures of Vita down there and gave them to me. I was planning to delete them before Vita called me. But it was not a blackmail-type situation."

Conway stood. "We're done."

Gretchen sprung to Conway and took her by the hands. "Please. Don't take this away from me."

"Gretchen, I have tried with you. I have." She pulled her hands back. "I'll talk to legal and see what they say. In the meantime, keep looking into this Avia Development Group. But don't get your hopes up."

She'd written her first cover story at twenty-five. She still remembered that pitch. She had been with the *Crier* for just a year and half—and a year before that through an internship. Getting the job was a total fluke. She was a mail girl. Queries and crazy letters and CDs poured into the office each day, and Marty, being Marty, would leave no stone unturned. He was averse to anyone touching the mail—especially an intern—but his staff had begged him to relinquish some of the responsibility. So he trained her. Throw away the CDs. Open the letters. Don't worry about how professional the letter looks. First, check for a name. If it's anonymous, don't even read it. Look for the human story. When you find one, ask yourself why it matters. If you don't know, it doesn't. If it doesn't, throw it away. Be curious, but use discretion.

So three afternoons a week, she sorted through the mail. She was just twenty-one, a senior in college, full of herself and loving the sociology double major Marty had suggested.

She found a story in a letter from a guy at Riker's. The handwriting was almost illegible. It started out conversational, how he's such a big fan of the paper and would they listen to his rap CD his auntie could bring by and could they see about getting the warden to let them get the paper inside. *Bam!* After a couple scribbled paragraphs that the censors must have attempted to redact, she thought she saw the word *strychnine* and something about a fire.

Marty had been a Pulitzer finalist for that one.

237

He liked her. He asked to see some clips from the campus paper she edited. When her term was up, he said he wished they had an opening.

A few weeks later, she was pushing a mattress up a third-floor walk-up in Harlem—her first apartment—when he called. The calendar editor had quit. Would she work full time for $18,000 a year? "It's not much," he said. "But you have a good eye, kid." She always had remembered him saying that.

Now, she paced up and down the *Metro* stairwell. How had she been so naïve? She had practically gone in there with her pants down. What would she do now?

And there was Nico. The incompetent NYPD had turned up nothing. What if it was too late? What if Nico, dear, dumb Nico—what if she was gone?

Gretchen shot off a couple texts and then dialed Roberta's number.

"Gretchen, I've been trying to get ahold of you. Do you know your voicemail's full? I refuse to text."

"I've been running all over town. How is he?"

"He could go at any time. But they said that yesterday, and, well, here we are."

"You at the hospital?"

"Day three. My mother's at the house. You should really come down here."

"I want to." She went to the window and looked out at Union Square. She was six stories above it, and it looked . . . beautiful. Pumpkins dotted the square. The leaves were red-brown and yellow. But she knew trouble was waiting for her outside. "I'll come today."

"Slip out during lunch, OK? Come say goodbye."

She turned away from the window.

Roberta sat in a chair by the window, looking out at 3rd Avenue. Marty had been moved to a private room with a door that closed.

He looked so different than he had just Sunday. Older. Thinner. Not like Marty at all really, but like a husk of a small man of little consequence.

The ventilator bag inflated, deflated, hissing as it did the work of breathing.

"I'm so glad you came," Roberta said, still looking out the window, her hand under her chin, her elbow resting on the arm of the chair. "He would have wanted you here today."

How could he have wanted something he could never imagine? But she guessed that was something you knew after spending over half your life waking up next to the same person, day in and day out.

She said, "Of course." Then, "How do you feel?"

"Like I'm . . . watching everything, him, me, us sitting here. I feel like I'm observing myself from a distance."

Gretchen nodded. "It will feel that way more so after. You'll see yourself and be angry that you continue to move through the world without him. That you continue to exist."

Roberta turned to her. She looked lovely and sharp and intelligent. She always had this look of genius emerging.

"How long will it last?" she asked.

Gretchen looked beyond Roberta, into some dark place that Roberta didn't populate yet, but that she would. "I don't know."

They sat together among the machines.

Gretchen didn't know how much time had passed when Roberta said, "Are you really breaking a story he started."

"I think so." She flushed. "I hope so."

"If it's this story that kills him, at least it wasn't entirely in vain."

Roberta did not know how true her words actually were. And Gretchen felt—at least for now—that she shouldn't know the truth. It was time to get back. She had a string of texts from Danny that she didn't read. One from Aunt Julia. A missed call from Gunderson. Nothing from Nico. She put the phone away and crossed the room.

"I have to ask you something, and I'm sorry. It's selfish and it's cowardly, but . . ."

"Gretchen," Roberta said.

"It's embarrassing, really. I shouldn't even—"

"Gretchen," she said again and put her hands on her shoulders.

"I'm on the brink of something here. And I'm so afraid I'm gonna mess it up. And if Marty were here, he'd know what to say."

"Do you know why he brought you to *Metro*?"

"Because I was losing my shit?"

Roberta shook her head.

"I was useless and I couldn't stand it. And I went to the office every day and gave everybody shit because I couldn't write anymore." She choked on that last part, holding back the grief rising in her chest.

"No," Roberta said, still shaking her head. "No, you're wrong."

"I'm right. You don't have to pretend. It was good of him to do it. He might have saved my life."

"You think it was charity?" Roberta said, as if the idea offended her. "You think Marty Mitnik, my husband, this man right here, hired someone onto his team out of charity? You think that was his ethos?"

"You don't understand," she said. "The part of me that worked—the part of me that made me work . . ." She couldn't find the words.

"You think it died with your brother."

It had become as much a part of her as her own handwriting. But she had never said it.

She was fried. The machine that was doing the breathing for Marty kept breathing. She wished she had one for herself.

240

Roberta wrapped her in a hug. "You know what he said when you broke the NYPD story? His exact words were, 'Motherfucker. She's already surpassed me.'"

Gretchen laughed.

"I shit you not!"

"He didn't."

"Oh, Gretchen. You will never know what you meant to him. He was a hard man to love. Moody. Irritable. Never did what he was told. I hate him for working himself to death. But what can I do?"

Gretchen pulled away from the hug and looked at Roberta. Her face looked thin, ancient somehow. Her large, dark eyes regarded Marty. She bit her lower lip and creased her forehead in worry. Marty's chest rose and fell as the machine forced him to breathe.

"Up until yesterday, I could still feel him here. Not just here in the room, but when I was across town, at home. I could feel him every moment." Roberta pressed her fist to her chest. "But I don't anymore. And he's still alive." She looked at Gretchen with those big eyes Marty had loved.

The thing that haunted Gretchen most about Dominic was not knowing when, not feeling when it happened. Where was she at the exact moment, and how did such a cosmic upset occur without causing her pause? The exact time of death was unknown. He was found scattered among the rubble of a jeep just before nightfall. It would have been morning in New York. She would have been standing in line at Murray's bagels, or walking down 13th Street. Or maybe it was later, when she was on the phone calling up a source. She might have been in Marty's office updating him on the lack of progress on the story, the sources that wouldn't cooperate, who got scared off.

"I think it means," Gretchen said to Roberta, "that you're ready. You're ready to let him go."

THIRTY-FOUR

The office buzzed with a bevy of volunteers calling voters. Each turned and looked at Vita as she strode past. The campaign manager rose from his chair in protest, but with one look from Vita, he cowered back to his desk.

She had woken up still undecided, determined to find Julian but unsure where to look.

But in the late morning, she'd received a text from Gretchen Sparks.

If you could use your superpowers of gossip . . . My little sister hasn't turned up for several days. She's 23, brunette, big boobs. Goes by Nico. Looks nothing like me.

True to the events of the past week and a half, Gretchen Sparks seemed to be making decisions for her.

Vita slammed the door of her husband's office behind her. "I'm gonna give you one chance to come clean. And if you don't, I will burn you to the fucking ground."

Dana Quinn stood behind the desk. "Listen, Burt," he said into his phone. "I'm going to have to call you back. Someone's just come in. You know how it is. I haven't even been able to take a shit alone in months . . . All right. I'll do that. Buh-bye." He turned to Vita. "I don't know who you think you are barging in here—"

"Shut up and sit down. Do you know what kind of man I hate more than any other?"

He sighed. His complexion was off, and she noticed for the first time that he had lost weight recently. "Vita I don't have time—"

"What kind of man do I hate more than any other?"

"A bully."

"That's right. A bully. What do you mean bringing Julian into your business, huh?"

"You're crazy."

"He knows Vittles, Dana. Your boyfriend Harlan picked me up on the street the other day and threatened me. And now Julian is missing. He's sick, Dana. He doesn't know right from wrong."

"He knows right from wrong, all right. He also knows who he can manipulate. That's you, Vita!"

"You complain that I've changed. That when we lost Alexander I stopped being me—I stopped being the woman you married. I became cold, you say. I became distant. That might be true, but at least I didn't turn bad like you have."

Dana pressed his hands to his eyes. "Sit down, Vita."

"I won't sit down."

"We're not going to get anywhere as long as you—"

"So help me God, Dana, I will walk out on you and tell the whole district. I will say what I need to say to end this race. I made you. And I can take you down." When she said the words, she knew they were true, more so than Dana could fathom.

He sat.

"I want it all. From beginning to end. Dominica Padilla, Harlan Vittles, Gretchen Sparks, and her sister."

He sighed. His eyes were set in shadow. He needed a shave. "I just wanted another term, long enough for a significant bill to come into law, so I could run for a seat in D.C. United Hospital Alliance approached me at the start of the session."

"This past year?"

"No. The year before."

"Who?"

"Harlan. He wanted to talk to me about the district, about the health of the district. I hadn't thought then that I would run for

Washington. I hadn't thought I'd stand a chance. My father—"

"Your father had something to do with this?"

"No. Except the usual glaring disappointment in me."

"I'm not interested in justifications. I need to know what kind of trouble we're in."

"Harlan's made some significant contributions to the campaign."

"How significant?"

"He has connections. He's formed some PACs."

"But PACs aren't illegal."

"They're not. But they're limited in what they can contribute. Everyone's limited. So he pulled some strings to get a few donations under board."

Something tightened inside of her. She wondered what the penalty would be and if Gretchen Sparks was on top of this. "And Dominica Padilla?"

"There's nothing to her."

"Who is she?"

"She was a woman who died in the hospital. People die in hospitals every day. But her daughter didn't like the way it was handled, and Vittles thought she'd kick up dust just before his precious cardiac center opened." He rolled his eyes. "A buddy of his was involved somehow in whatever decisions were made."

"What's that to you? Why did you have her name?"

"Vittles threatened to expose the contributions if I didn't keep her quiet."

Her face was hot. "And you employed Julian to do this."

"Just a visit. I said, 'wear a suit, say you're from immigration.' I practically gave him a script. And I paid him! For once he earned some of the money I put in his pocket."

"Are you crazy?"

"He wasn't alone. Harlan's brother went with him."

"Harlan's brother? The ex-con?" She shook her head in disbelief. "Then what?"

"And then nothing. The daughter stopped complaining."

"What about Gretchen Sparks?"

"The reporter. She started snooping around. Vittles saw her down at the Padillas'—with you, I might add. And he started making threats. About the contributions, about you."

"He wasn't ever down there."

"He's connected, Vita. Don't you see?" Dana's neck was strained and his voice sounded high and lonesome. "He's got us all under his control. He could be listening right now."

"Where's Julian, Dana?"

"I don't know." He put his hands up. "I have no fucking idea."

"You're lying."

"I'm not. You have to believe me, Vita. I thought I was doing right."

"Accepting illegal contributions is hardly right. What else has Vittles done?"

"The reporter wasn't the first to start snooping around. There was another one—an older guy. I felt sick about what I made Julian do, going to the daughter like that. I couldn't bear it. So when Vittles wanted me to deal with the reporter, I said no. I said absolutely not. He didn't like that. He said again he'd expose me. And now he had the Padilla thing to pin on me. That's what he does. He gets you tangled up in his long string of lies and then begins to pull."

"I have suffered through how many dinners and brunches and lunches with him? And that wife?"

"I know. I had to. Don't you get it, Vita?"

She did. She got it too well. She cleared her throat. "Did Vittles have anything to do with that other reporter? His heart attack?"

"I don't know."

"I don't believe you."

"You don't want to—"

His phone vibrated as several texts shot in.

"Leave it," she said.

"I think Harlan's brother may have . . . done something to the guy."

245

She sucked in her breath. Every part of her wanted to flee, but this was it. It was the moment she had felt herself hurtled toward since she'd found the name in his planner.

"And Julian," he said, "found some girl . . . the reporter's sister. But I had nothing to do with that!"

"Where is she?"

She looked out the window at the city. How many other girls were somewhere they weren't supposed to be? How many women were trapped somewhere, unable to move, unable to call out to anyone?

THIRTY-FIVE

Nicola Sparks turned the bath water off with her foot. She loved a good soak that left her whole body pruny, and in the suite's oversized tub, she could stretch out from fingers to toes. It was a tub for two. Or three. Nico wasn't particular.

Luxury! She wore it like a cashmere-lined glove. How could she go back to the single-stall shower with its moldy curtain and hair-clumped walls in her dorm suite? Gabby's snoring? Marcie and Jason's endless humping on the other side of the wall? Especially after sleeping in the big round bed that rotated—for God's sake—so she could lie on her side and gaze at the city through floor-to-ceiling windows or rotate more to see the Hudson River and its little purposeful boats. Italian sheets. Huge flat-screen TV with HBO and Showtime *and* Netflix. She had re-watched *Pretty in Pink*, *Sixteen Candles*, *Heathers*, and *The Breakfast Club* (the eighties were *so* in!). Plus she'd binged season four of *Teen Mom*.

Nico put her head underwater and looked up at the vaulted ceiling, the contemporary bathroom chandelier. Just on the other side of the half-wall were those big windows. How strange to be so exposed up on the twelfth floor, yet so anonymous. Nobody, in all of the city, in all of the world, knew where she was. Except her Julian, she assumed. Still, the freedom from responsibility soothed her, along with the minibar that refilled itself whenever she went down to the hotel spa.

She opened the drain and reached for a bath sheet. She had never used one until she'd arrived Tuesday night. Early Wednesday morning, really. Or rather, Wednesday afternoon when she'd woken up and tried to locate her phone. How long had she been asleep? What time was it? And where in the hell was she? Nico had gotten out of the fantastic cloud of a bed and wrapped a sheet around her superb naked body and walked to the window. The water of the river glittered, and she saw, with a shock, a whale shoot up from the surface, turn, and flop back down on its back. She pinched her arm.

"Nope, not sleeping," she said. The room had a modern-looking dresser and a plush dove-colored carpet. "Hello?" She tiptoed into the next room. It was a suite! With a sofa and a glass coffee table! Had she died and gone to heaven?

She was still getting her bearings straight, when a knock came at the door.

"Hang on!" She scurried into the bedroom. Not a scrap of clothing lay anywhere. She found a robe in the bathroom closet and tied it around her waist.

A waiter brought the cart right into the room. A pile of scrambled eggs, crispy bacon, pancakes, toast, a carafe of coffee and cup of half-and-half, and a bowl of fresh fruit. Nico salivated.

"There must be some mistake," she admitted. "I didn't order anything."

"Your patron placed the order not an hour ago."

"My patron?"

"That's how he described himself. Please sign."

What had happened last night? She added a ten dollar tip and scratched her name on the receipt. "What day is it?"

The waiter raised his eyebrows. "It's Wednesday. October fourteenth."

"Oh, fuck me!"

"Miss?"

"I should be someplace."

"Your patron has left instructions to give you an open tab. There's a binder in the desk with everything you need to know about our amenities." He'd retreated, leaving the cart in the living room.

He had come out of nowhere, it seemed, when she'd been studying in the park on Monday. "Excuse me," he had said, "this will sound strange, but I'm a photographer and think you're quite stunning." He held a small digital camera that seemed more like what a dad would take on a family road trip than what a photographer would carry around. But what did she know?

After he snapped a couple of shots, he asked her out.

She had been feeling lonesome ever since she'd left Gretchen's. She had squirmed out of her sister's arms and left without waking her. Her birthday should start the best week of the year. But since Dominic had died, it was a bleak reminder of a life she felt she might not deserve. Most days, she could bat those thoughts away, remind herself that her brother would want her to live fully, to have everything she wanted. He had said that and more before he'd left. They had gone for a long walk, all the way from Union Square to Bryant Park, on a sunny Sunday just as the last days of summer made their escape. She had told him all of her doubts about school, friends, and her abilities. She had told him how trivial she knew she was, all junk food and junk TV, eighties dance parties, and sleeping through exams. He had been kind and generous, put his arm around her and kissed her on the head. "I'll see you for Christmas, Muffin," he'd said. On the subway ride back to the dorm, the pressure had built in her chest, the crushing weight of her love for Nicky, and for Gretchen, too.

She had agreed to the date with the photographer.

The evening had started in Chelsea at a bar too fancy and quiet for Nico, who tried to make conversation with her date. He was sexy in a way unlike any guys whom she had dated before. Older, graying hair, deep, dark eyes and a big mouth with very straight, very large teeth. He asked her questions: about what she was studying, what she liked to read, her friends and family. She had felt self-conscious at first, like she was talking too much, but a few drinks calmed her nerves.

And after the fancy Chelsea bar—he paid with one of those black credit cards for super-rich people—she asked him where he really hung out, and before she knew it, they were in a cab going west, and all the liquor caught up with her. She remembered the flashing lights of the dance floor, kissing a girl with a nose ring, the black-and-white-tiled bathroom at the club.

She checked the time. One o'clock. The family would be back at Ma's now, scarfing down something or other. Ma would be livid. Nico had ruined everything. Again.

But by the time she had licked all of the plates and poured a second cup of coffee, she'd decided to stay. Julian must be a fancy photographer to afford such luxury. But where was he?

Now that it was Monday, she was still wondering. But the hotel staff had assured her that the room was taken care of, that her meals were taken care of, and that, no, they hadn't seen her clothes but she was welcome to sashay to the spa in her robe.

One more day, she promised herself again. Every day that passed would multiply her mother's rage by a thousand. She'd call her tomorrow. Definitely tomorrow.

She wrapped her hair in a towel, grabbed a wine cooler from the minibar, and climbed into the bed to order some porn.

There was a knock at the door.

THIRTY-SIX

The drink was sweet and fruity and nothing she would have ordered herself, but it slid down her throat just the same. Gretchen didn't know what it was, nor did she know the man with his hands on her ass and his lips on her neck. She dropped the empty cup on the floor as he hiked her up against the wall of the handicapped stall. She heard him unbuckling his pants.

"We'll get thrown out," she said.

"Honey, you know what bar this is?"

She didn't. She had started at the El Dorado on Mercer where she'd been snubbed by a suit. Then she moved to Stardust on Mulberry where the bartender was silently reading *Pride and Prejudice*, and then she had gone somewhere else . . . where was it? He tugged her boots off. She looked down at him: young, muscular, black hair parted on the side, a square face. He pulled her pants off one leg at a time, and she closed her eyes, thinking she was glad she was wearing socks.

Then she was alone. Her underpants were hanging off the toilet. The jacket was slung over the stall wall. She pulled it down and fumbled with it. What had happened? She felt between her legs. It didn't feel like she had just had sex. But how could she be sure? The thought of it made her gag, and she stooped to vomit in the toilet.

She had been at the hospital, then back working on Misty's list of names. Then Conway called her into her office. Then what?

251

She had stormed out before Conway could complete her sentence. Gretchen was off the story.

Is that what happened? Or had Conway said they wouldn't pursue the story at all?

She had screamed, "He's dying over there! Do you know that? They killed him! Have you *even* visited him, any of you? He's fucking dying!"

Zaiden and Brooklyn, the interns, looked up from their phones. Zaiden said, "Fucking psycho."

And Gretchen had smacked him across the face.

She had gone to her desk, sat down, and regarded her notes. Her colleagues gawked from their cubicles when a security guard and Janet from HR escorted her downstairs. She went quietly, feeling the ground slip out from under her with every step, and when she got outside, she crossed the street and sat on the steps of the park.

Her phone had then buzzed with a text. From Roberta. Who never texts.

Gretchen, it said, *he's gone.*

The bathroom was cold and bright. She wanted her bed, her apartment, her life back to what it was before she followed a fucking seagull down the block.

With a start, she remembered Nico, and the memory made her quake with fear. She searched the pockets of the jacket for her phone.

"Hey," a woman's voice said. Someone knocked on the door. "Hey!" She thought it must be the bartender and stood very still.

"Is this your shoe?" The voice sounded helpful. Gretchen looked around. She smelled something sweet, familiar.

"Unlock the door, Gretchen."

The door swung in, and she jumped out of the way.

Vita Quinn stood with her hands on her hips. "Well, you're a bit of a mess, aren't you."

Gretchen tried to cover herself with the jacket.

"Don't worry about it. I was a pageant girl, remember? I've seen it all. Here." She took the jeans and began to turn a leg right side out. "Fucking cops. Always after it. Lemme guess. That young one with shoulders?"

"Cops?"

She held out the jeans. "You're wasted. Right foot in, come on."

"What do you mean *cops*?" Gretchen said.

"Left foot. You're in a cop bar, sweetheart."

A cop bar?

She needed a drink.

Vita pulled the jeans up over Gretchen's hips and buttoned and zipped them. "Can you manage with your bra?"

"Nico, my sister, she's been gone now . . ." She tried to remember what day it was, what day she had been to the cemetery. She thought of her ma slapping her in the face, her neck strained with rage.

"We're getting it all sorted out, *capisce*? Come here, turn around." She hooked Gretchen's bra and pulled up the straps. "Did you come in wearing a shirt?"

"What time is it?" she asked.

"No shirt needed. Let's get that crazy jacket on."

Gretchen reached up and petted Vita's hair. It felt warm and soft; the woman radiated heat. Gretchen slid her hands along Vita's lovely face and wrapped her in a hug. "Vita," she said. "Beautiful Vita. How did you find me?"

"So you're that kind of a drunk, huh?" Vita said. "You've been texting me all night." She gently pulled away and began to close up Gretchen's jacket. "You're missing a few buttons." She tied the belt. "But I think it'll do. Now. Boots."

"But you don't understand. My sister. She's one of the girls. We have to find her."

"Let me get you out of here first, OK, kiddo?"

"I got fired."

"Well, worse things could happen." She tied the boots. "OK, come on. I got a surprise for you."

When they came out of the bathroom, a roar of laughter greeted them. The young guy with the square jaw waved a flag pole, but instead of a flag, someone had attached Gretchen's blouse, the word WHORE written in big black letters.

"Jesus." Vita draped Gretchen's arm across her shoulders. "Come on."

They started chanting something Gretchen couldn't make out. The room spun. "I just need to sit down."

"Not here you don't."

A cold flash of air. A mist of rain. The black Mercedes. Maurice looking out of the driver's seat in disgust. Vita opened the backseat door.

"Gretch-EN! I am so happy to see you!"

THIRTY–SEVEN

They came banging on my door, all of them, after ten o'clock. Nico, in a white bathrobe and slippers, nearly knocked me over with a hug. The chestnut-haired Bay Ridge Beauty followed, and then Gretchen. Gretchen, in jeans and a trench coat and a bra, smelled ripe with booze.

"Can you watch them?" Vita Quinn said.

"Watch them?"

"I've done everything I can, but these two . . ." She made the sign of the cross.

"I think Nico needs to get to her mother's house."

"Where's that?" Vita said.

"Kew Gardens."

"Where?"

"It's Queens!" Nico finally let me free of her hug. "But please don't take me there. Ma is gonna kill me." She pranced over to the sofa and sat beside her sister. "Gretch-EN, please don't make me go home. Please!"

Vita looked at her watch. She put her hands on her hips. She regarded the two of them. "Fine. But don't say I never gave you nothing."

"Wait!" I said. "You can't just leave them here. They have to go home."

"What's your name?"

"Raj."

"Raj. I may be paranoid. But I'd feel better if your girlfriend weren't alone tonight."

"She's not my girlfriend."

"Good for you. I wouldn't wish her on my worst enemy. Goodbye, Raj. Goodbye, Gretchen." Vita Quinn turned and walked out the door.

I tried to get them out myself, but Gretchen Sparks, in her jeans and bra, had already passed out, a string of drool stretching from lip to sofa cushion, her little sister petting her hair and looking on adoringly.

Once I heard the whole story, I insisted she stay. Just while she worked on the piece. I kept her hydrated and eating and away from liquor while she made phone calls and printed documents on reams of paper and crisscrossed the boroughs in my Volvo.

She went through United Commercial Codes files with a microscope, cross-referencing Quinn's campaign contributions with any debtor or filer associated with South Brooklyn Hospital or Harlan Vittles. She spent days on the City Register website, scrutinizing every property surrounding the hospital, seeking out those that had recently been sold. She kept at it with Philosophy Gurrrl and eventually found herself on the phone with Diane Lupinacci of District 23.

She called the Corporate Information Office in Albany and got the names and addresses and affiliations of all of South Brooklyn Hospital's stockholders.

Gretchen found a lawyer representing another patient in a suit against the hospital who was willing to meet with Gloria Padilla. And then Gloria agreed to meet with Gretchen too.

She spent her mornings at the Department of Health, poking around, learning everything she could about the rules that govern hospitals. I set her up with a RAC I found through some old nursing home contacts, a jolly, heavyset older man with frameless glasses who insisted we call him Old Crow. He called everyone else Boo. He extrapolated enough data to show the hospital's cuts in staff and equipment, all at the expense of the cardiac wing. They were severe. Oh, and he identified that the holdup on the hospital's accreditation was due to a clerical error on the part of Harlan Vittles.

Between lawyers and Cora Carter, Gretchen talked to more families who'd lost loved ones, went without care, or found that care negligent. And Cora even brought her a couple more nurses to corroborate these stories.

She slept on the couch, and I lay in bed weighing it all in my mind. Vidya had given me two weeks to come to a decision. Gretchen had made no promises, asked for much, needed much. Needed me.

As her investigation broadened and deepened, she asked me to help poke holes in it. I brought over a couple other *Crier* folks to listen and read and poke. She seemed to enjoy this part the most—the ongoing questions, the possibility for error, the challenge of leaving no stone unturned.

That, I knew, was something she'd learned from Marty.

Marty. We attended his funeral together, Gretchen in a black dress with a lace collar, her hair brushed to a shine. Roberta Krom was so strong and so magnificent a host, even under the circumstances, and it seemed to me like half the city turned out to honor Marty.

"He gave me so much," Gretchen said. Her eyes grew to saucers, and she cried.

But the more she discovered, the closer she got to the whole damn capital-T truth, the more obsessed she became with Harlan Vittles. His name makes bile rise in my throat. She attempted to make contact, leaving messages at his 5th Avenue office, at the Heart Institute, and eventually on his cell phone once she found that number. Could he explain some of the documentation from Medicare to her? Would he chat about the hospital's allocation of resources? About the morale among nurses and orderlies? Among doctors? No? When could she call back?

She brooded. She talked until late at night to Avery Lane, listening to all manner of conspiracies about Jessup Landry, with whom Lane was obsessed. She had Avery Lane going to the court house, to the Department of Labor, to the Secretary of State.

"You're scratching a very sore blister," Avery Lane said. "Not my blister. For me, it's more of an erogenous zone. But Tennessee doesn't want to deal with UHA again anytime soon."

She couldn't link the South Brooklyn property being bought up to UHA. I didn't think there was a link. I told her so—again and again I told her. "You have enough. Write the damn story!"

Stubborn. Gretchen Sparks is stubborn.

One Sunday, I made the decision as I brewed the coffee and listened to her fingers fly across her keyboard. She was wearing a pair of gray leggings and a red thermal shirt. It was November 1st and chilly. The following day was V-Day: Vidya would be waiting to hear from me. I convinced Gretchen to take a shower and brush her hair and go work at a coffee shop that afternoon. I said I needed some time to myself. She relented, and I scrambled to the grocery and back to whip up a meal of ossobuco and Milanese risotto.

Before I lit the candles, I texted her to come home. And she did. She came in saying, "You wouldn't believe the attitude at that place—" and stopped. Put down her bag. Smiled. "You never give up, do you?"

I looked down, convinced I had gone overboard and blown the whole thing. But, I thought, better to know now than to keep up this foolishness any longer. I said, "I learned it from you."

She took off her boots, walked across the room, and took my hands. I kissed her then. *I* kissed *her.*

And then, my dear Gretchen sat down at my table—our table—unfolded her napkin, and put it on her lap.

Gretchen Sparks isn't the type of girl you take anywhere. She takes you.

The next day, I came home from work with a pizza to find a wooden doubloon and a small gold key on the counter, and beneath them, a note.

Raajen. Gone to Nashville. Be back in a week. Love, G.

I haven't heard from her since.

EPILOGUE

Avery Lane had circled the airport for an hour and left voice messages. Then she parked and went in. Gretchen had been on the flight from LaGuardia to Nashville, but her suitcase hadn't been claimed.

It is three months now since the arrest of Dana Quinn. Dana has been indicted for fraud but not for conspiracy. Julian wasn't so lucky. They found him around Elizabeth, New Jersey, sleeping outdoors, and they charged him with abducting Nicola. They thought at first that he was responsible for all the missing women, but as he was in custody, more went missing and the hysteria continued. A few weeks later, all seven were discovered held captive in a garden shed in Long Island. They arrested the guys soon after—a man and his adult son—and miraculously, everyone survived. Julian awaits trial in Riker's. Dana didn't maneuver for a safer placement for his brother-in-law.

Vita, feeling finally like she was getting things right, waited in the Kings County prosecutor's office one morning until the D.A. came back from court. Vita was able to make a deal as a cooperating witness. She lives in Jersey now, by the ocean in Bayhead. When I visited her there, she made a fire on the beach, and we sat for a long time talking into the night and early morning, moving inside to her enclosed porch when the chill picked up. "I like the cold," she had said, looking off into the ocean. "It makes me feel awake."

Gretchen's old friends at the *Crier* beat *Metro* to the story. Marty would have been thrilled. Afterward, UHA settled out of court with Gloria Padilla. She ended up with $350,000, enough to pay some medical bills and put some away for the boy, Jaime, and for her retirement. Not much, considering. And Cora Carter, her friend Osha, and two other nurses who came forward, got hired at United Methodist on 7th Avenue in Brooklyn. Gloria and Cora were suspicious of me at first, but after I told them about Gretchen and me—about our years together, about Gretchen's brother's death and how it turned the light off inside of her until this story came along—they spent long hours with me rehashing the details.

"This mess," Cora Carter said. "It's greed. That's all it is. I can't believe they did her like that."

"My mother is at peace now," said Gloria Padilla. "But where is the peace for Gretchen's mother?"

"Something about her was different," Roberta told me as we sat at her kitchen table. "She had that look in her eye. I could tell she was in trouble, but I knew from Marty that when they get in that place, there's no yanking them out."

Misty Phelps echoed that sentiment. "I didn't like it. But what was I to do? Let her face it alone?"

"Look," Conway said, "of course I feel shitty about it. I didn't want any harm to come to her. I could tell she was too emotionally involved, so I took her off the story. She assaulted an intern."

"I can't talk to you without my lawyer present," said Dana Quinn from his house in Bay Ridge, sitting on the couch with his legs crossed, his ankle bracelet flickering its green light. "But I never wanted harm to come to anybody. I swear."

"If she woulda just focused on Leonard and ignored this other shit, she'd be fine," said Darlene Dabrowski, ashing a cigarette into an empty tuna can. "Borough Features blog. Ha. Can't hang that on the bulletin board."

"I shouldn't have listened to her," Danny Russo said in my office at the *Crier*, hands shaking, pants rumpled. "I should have gone to the police after they tossed her apartment. I should have followed my gut. She was so damn stubborn." Then, "Is. She *is* so damn stubborn."

The hospital is back under state supervision, and Howard Quinn with New York District 23 Senator Diane Lupinacci drafted the Dominica Padilla Patient Accountability Bill, which puts new, stricter limits on for-profit medical facilities in the tri-states. It's likely to pass in May.

And Vittles? United Hospitals of America had its army of lawyers sweep it all up under their multibillion dollar rug. Vittles returned to Nashville with his wife to direct a hospital there.

"I don't know what I've done to deserve so much grief," said Carla. "I pray to God to bring her home, just like He brought home Nicola. Ungrateful child that she is."

"Gretchen?" said Otto Sparks in the Brooklyn nursing home that Nico picked out. "She died. Crossing the Atlantic." His condition has worsened, but they take good care of him there. And he never asks anyone about Dominic. Or Gretchen for that matter. But Nicola has stepped up to the plate marvelously. She sits beside him in the evenings. He watches television while she studies. She's to graduate in December.

"I know that it's not my fault," she said. "But I'm alone now. There's no . . . crushing weight of goodbye. There's just . . ." She searched for words. "There's just me."

"I'm taking kickboxing classes," Vita said. "I read a lot. I've started keeping a journal. I think"—she traced the tabletop—"I think that day at Green-Wood Cemetery she was trying to tell me something else. Something I couldn't hear."

"But what?" I asked.

"I think she was asking me how to go on, how to move through grief and live again. I think she was telling me that she couldn't. She was wrong about that."

"How so?"

"Well, she's doing it right now." She put her hand to her chest. Her eyes looked ancient and wise. "I can feel her, Raj. I can feel that she's still alive."

And maybe she is. A month ago, Nico called me in the early hours of the morning. She had started scouring Craigslist for any scent of her sister—and she thought she found something in the Missing Connections section. It said: "Nico. I am underground like Oma. Take care of Ma." That could be anything, couldn't it? A whisper in the wind. But something to cling to.

I moved into the bungalow my parents bought as a gift to themselves when I graduated college. They hardly ever use it. The busy season will start soon, and vacationers will drag their chairs and umbrellas through the sand past me, and there will be no quiet.

But for now, it is early March. The water is frigid. Only the sternest, or stupidest, seagulls remain.

I told Avery Lane where she could find me, and I made friends with the lighthouse keeper, should Gretchen be summoned by the old language she shared with her brother.

    .... . .-.. .-.. ---
    H-E-L-L-O
    ...- . -. ..- ...
    V-E-N-U-S
    .- -. --- -- --- .-.. -.--
    A-N-O-M-A-L-Y

As I've mentioned, the news doesn't tell the whole story. And I don't claim to either. But I knew Gretchen once—what made her tick, what pissed her off, what brought her joy. I've taken some liberties in order to get to the capital-T truth, knowing Gretchen, loving Gretchen, losing Gretchen twice now—twice.

It should be obvious where I've improvised, where I've imagined her in private, pacing her tiny apartment, walking the streets. I retraced her every move as best I could.

It is still not enough.

It will never be enough.

The night, dear Neruda, is shattered and she is not with me. Oh, Gretchen. Are you out there? Do you still draw breath?

—Raajen Patel
Cape May, New Jersey
March 3, 2016

ACKNOWLEDGMENTS

I wrote most of *Borough Features* in an old, immobile Airstream among the goats at Yellow Bird Art Farm in Woodbury, Tennessee, as well as at Penuel Ridge Retreat Center in Ashland City, Tennessee, and at Rivendell Writers Colony in Sewanee, Tennessee. All of these folks provided very cheap or free lodging to me so I could unplug and work on my book. The Nashville Public Library selected me to use the private Writer's Room across the hall from the *Nashville Banner* archive. I was inspired by the storied newspaper during my time there. To these folks and institutions, I will always be grateful.

Thanks also goes to my editor Jen Chesak of Wandering in the Words Press, whose sharp eye and big heart saw this book through to the finish; my teachers Suzanne Heyd, Tom Piazza, Chris Chambers, and David Gates; my friends, especially Julia Sorrentino, Mishka Shubaly, Christy Carew, and Laura Huston; my family; and the staff of the *Nashville Scene*.

This book is dedicated in memory of Tama McCoy, who hired me to help children write novels in 2016. I wrote my first pages seated beside them.

And I thank my one love, Tony Youngblood, always my port in the storm.

ABOUT THE AUTHOR

Photo by Daniel Meigs

Erica Ciccarone has worked as a waitress, grocery-store teller, high school teacher, college professor, dog walker, journalist, editor, and feral cat wrangler. She holds an M.F.A. from The New School Creative Writing Program and a B.A. from Loyola University New Orleans. She is an associate editor at BookPage. In 2022, she was recognized by the Association of Alternative Newsmedia with the David Carr Award in Investigative Journalism for her work at the *Nashville Scene*. She lives in Nashville.

9 798989 328536